Strangled in the Stacks

A Booker Falls Mystery

by

Kenn Grimes

Kenn Grimes

This book is fiction. All characters, events, and organizations portrayed in this novel are the product of the author's imagination or are used fictitiously. Any resemblance to actual persons—living or dead—is entirely coincidental.

For information, email **Cozy Cat Press**, cozycatpress@aol.com or visit our website at: www.cozycatpress.com

ISBN: 978-1-939816-98-6

Printed in the United States of America

Cover design by Paula Ellenberger
www.paulaellenberger.com

1 2 3 4 5 6 7 8 9 10

This book is dedicated to my friend,
colleague, and fellow author
of many years,

Madge Walls

whose unsparing critique of my work
helped make me a better writer

Acknowledgements

My thanks to the following individuals who helped make this book a reality: the two members of my Louisville writing group, Becky Fahy and Teaberry Smith (who was also one of my readers); my other readers, Madge Walls, Linda Miller, Judy Grimes and Randy Evans; and my writing instructor whose class inspired the book, John Risner.

CHAPTER ONE

Myrtle stopped the car in the middle of the road, leaned back and took a deep breath. The hand-painted sign perched precariously against a large oak tree off to one side told her she had at last reached the end of her journey.

WELCOME TO BOOKER FALLS

⚜

HOME OF ADELAIDE COLLEGE

It had been fifteen days and over thirteen hundred miles since she'd departed New Orleans. The used automobile she'd purchased there—a 1907 Model N Ford previously owned by a now deceased Presbyterian minister—was as tired as she was.

It had cost two hundred dollars—almost all of Myrtle's savings—but it was a purchase she hadn't been able to resist.

Maroon-colored, with black leather seats and brass trim, the vehicle sported some added items not found on the basic model, among them front headlights, a horn, and running boards. A convertible top, down at the moment, allowed Myrtle to enjoy the splinters of sunlight dancing their way through the overhanging tree branches that formed a green canopy above her.

She had no problem with the steering wheel being on the right, as she'd learned to drive while in France, where many cars were of a similar design.

The Goyard steamer trunk she'd brought back with her from Europe that held the total extent of her worldly possessions was safely secured on a small platform at the back of the vehicle, next to a nearly empty two-gallon gasoline can.

Holding up traffic was not a concern: The year was 1919, and she hadn't seen another vehicle aside from a few farm wagons since she'd left Menominee.

It was pleasant for September, but the crispness in the air had already begun to herald the pending arrival of winter. The pastoral scene spread out before her—trees in full bloom, a panorama of wild flowers: goldenrod, blazing star, fireweed, and countless others, none of which Myrtle had ever seen before; fields of sweet corn and squash she glimpsed through the gaps in the woods on either side—reminded her she was no longer in New Orleans.

In the valley below, the town itself beckoned to her.

Another deep breath; time to move on and discover what her new life as assistant librarian at the Adelaide College Library would bring.

She squeezed the ratchet handle and moved the hand control all the way forward. Then she pulled the throttle lever down and gently depressed the left pedal with her foot. The Model N inched forward.

That's when she saw it.

Ambling out from a stand of trees, the moose sauntered to the middle of the road, stopped, turned its head and looked directly at Myrtle's car, quietly assessing this strange new apparition.

Startled, Myrtle's eyes opened wide, as did her mouth in a silent, "Wow." Even Penrod, normally quiet, let out an almost inaudible, "Woof."

Realizing the animal wasn't about to move, Myrtle quickly closed the throttle with the tip of her finger and depressed the brake pedal. The car glided to a stop, barely two feet from the moose, which still stood in the road, his attention focused on the Model N.

As tall as the car itself, and weighing nearly thirteen hundred pounds, it was the biggest creature Myrtle had ever seen. She'd seen deer in Louisiana, where she'd been born and grew up, as well as in Europe, where she'd served the last year and a half with the Allied Expeditionary Forces.

But those all paled in comparison to this behemoth which now blocked her path.

What should she do? Wait? Blow the horn? She realized she didn't know what that would sound like: She'd never had occasion to use it.

A minute passed. Then another. Still the moose wouldn't budge.

Myrtle decided she'd have to take matters into her own hands.

Rooting through the rucksack she'd brought back with her from Europe, she found what she was looking for: the two Jersey Mac apples she'd purchased from a roadside stand on a farm in Wisconsin. She had no idea what moose ate, but supposed it might be the same type of food as deer.

She opened the door and stepped down onto the road. Holding one apple out before her, she cautiously approached the moose, who watched intently as Myrtle drew near, and when her hand was directly in front of his nose, gently took the fruit from her and began to chew.

As he did so, Myrtle tossed the other apple into the woods. The moose watched, then headed off in that direction.

Slowly, Myrtle inched her way back to the car and slid in. With trembling hands, she shifted the gear lever.

Minutes later she was on her way again.

*****

Entering the town, Myrtle passed through a neighborhood almost devoid of trees. Along each side of the dirt road stood identical, modest, two-story, frame structures, each with attic dormer windows and a small porch in front.

Myrtle wondered if the trees she assumed had once grown here had provided the material for the houses which now stood in their place.

At one time, the buildings had all been painted the same gray color, with trim of a darker shade. It was obvious that many of them had not seen a paint brush in some time, if ever, since that initial coating.

On the side streets, off to the left and right, were more houses, identical to those on either side of them, their backyards—such as they were—butting up against those of the homes behind them.

Tendrils of smoke that matched the color of the houses from which they emerged, drifted lazily upward from every chimney.

Overhead, electric lines ran from street poles to each home, their numbers so prolific it looked as though a gigantic fishnet had been tossed over the whole neighborhood.

Myriad children frolicked everywhere, while women, hanging clothes on lines that filled every back yard, or gossiping with their neighbors, kept a careful watch over them, making sure they wouldn't be done in by the horseless carriage chugging down the street.

Every one stopped to watch Myrtle—to watch Myrtle's car, to be more exact.

There were no men to be seen, except one older fellow sitting on the steps of one house, smoking a pipe. He waved and Myrtle waved back.

At the end of the row of houses was a set of railroad tracks. Though she hadn't heard the sound of any train,

Myrtle decided the better part of caution was to stop and make sure none was coming.

As she looked to her right, she saw that the tracks extended to the horizon. To the left, about a hundred yards away, they ran past a building Myrtle assumed was the depot.

A ribbon of grass separated the tracks from the first of the business buildings.

As she entered the downtown, Myrtle was surprised to discover the street was macadam, a significant improvement over the dusty stretch of road upon which she'd just come.

As she continued on, she was equally taken aback by the size of the structures, some as tall as four stories, all finely constructed of wood or brick or concrete.

She had envisioned a town where the people lived in tents or shacks or lean-tos, where animals—not only dogs and cats and pigs, but wild animals—raccoons, possums, maybe wolves—ran loose in the streets.

Her short trip through the residential neighborhood had changed her mind about the living conditions, and now the only animals in sight were a few dogs and a multitude of horses: horses carrying riders; horses drawing wagons and carriages and buggies; horses tethered to hitching rails placed at strategic intervals.

What she didn't see were automobiles. Not a single one.

Since it was apparent horsepower—real horses, not automobiles—provided the main means of transportation, Myrtle wondered at the absence of an excess of manure. The question was answered when she spotted an old man who appeared to be well into his eighties, head covered by a broad-brimmed hat and sporting a white beard that reached to his belt, pulling a wheeled-barrel. Every few feet the man stopped and, with a small broom he carried, brushed the horse droppings into an oversized dustpan, which he then emptied into the barrel.

As Myrtle drove past, the old man tipped his hat to her. She smiled and waved to him.

A multitude of people made their way over wooden sidewalks that stretched along both sides of the street, entering and leaving the various establishments: J. P. Finnegan's Fancy Groceries and Fresh Meats; de Première Qualité Women's Wear; L. L. Reynolds Funeral Parlor; and the Salle de Spectacle Theater. In the next block, across from the courthouse, stood the Booker Falls Bank & Trust; Paige Turner's New, Used, and Rare Books; and Miss Madeline's Eatery, next to which Myrtle was especially delighted to spot The Polar Bear Ice Cream Parlor.

Myrtle dearly loved ice cream!

Almost every passerby stopped to stare at the Model N as it motored past.

Further down, two churches stood facing one another across the street. The larger and more imposing of the two, St. Barbara Catholic Church, was constructed of Jacobsville Sandstone, pink, with light-colored streaks and spots. Opposite it stood St. James Lutheran Church, a plain building made of the white pine that once blanketed the area, the same material used in all the homes Myrtle had passed on her way into the main business area.

At this time in the afternoon, St. James, the considerably shorter of the two structures, stood completely in the shadow that St. Barbara threw across the street.

Myrtle was so intent on examining the two-story, double-bay fire station with its imposing corner tower that she didn't see the horse or hear the distressed cry of its owner until the animal was right in front of her.

"Whoa! Whoa, Jessie!"

The horse reared, tipping the carriage behind it, nearly depositing the driver into the street.

Moving quickly, Myrtle was able to bring her car to a stop before it hit the poor beast. Two close calls with large creatures in one day!

"Whoa!" called the man once again, as he managed to get the mare under control.

Before Myrtle knew what was happening, the man had jumped down from his seat, dashed to the driver's door of the car and stood pointing his finger at her.

"Madame," he said, icily, "if you cannot properly operate your vehicle, perhaps it would be best to refrain from driving it in town, on the city streets. In fact, perhaps it would be best to do so even if you *could* operate it properly."

Shaken, Myrtle's words poured out in a torrent. "I am so sorry, sir. I was distracted and did not see your carriage or your horse."

"My point exactly," said the man, his face contorted in rage. "There simply is no place on our streets for contrivances of this sort, eh?"

"Again, I am sorry, sir, I—"

"Madame, sorry is not sufficient! You very nearly ran over my horse and knocked me to the ground in the process."

By this time, Myrtle had regained her composure. She had apologized to the man twice—she had no intention of doing so a third time.

Looking at him now, for the first time really, she realized he was colored—a mulatto, judging by the lightness of his skin. She was well acquainted with people of such ancestry from growing up in New Orleans. About her age, somewhere in his late twenties or early thirties, she surmised.

A small crowd had gathered, but Myrtle was unconcerned about what they might be thinking. She was irritated by the man's rude behavior.

"Sir, I have apologized to you, twice in fact. Now I would appreciate you moving your horse and carriage so that I may pass."

The man stared at her, stunned by her impertinence.

When he didn't move right away, Myrtle said, "I can use my horn to move your horse, if that is what you would prefer."

The man scowled, then said, "I will move the carriage myself, madam."

The man returned to his carriage, climbed back up onto the seat and urged his horse forward. As he passed in front of Myrtle's car, he glared at her.

"As I presume you are merely passing through town on your way to somewhere else," he said, "I look forward to not encountering you again."

"Then you may be unpleasantly surprised, as would I," Myrtle retorted, "because I have come to Booker Falls to work and settle here. And these are public streets, sir, available for all conveyances, including motorized."

Myrtle shifted the appropriate levers and pedals, and the Model N continued on its way.

Despite the man's impudence and her aversion to Negroes—the result of growing up in a segregated South, the child of openly racist parents whose own parents had been slave owners—Myrtle had to admit, the fellow wasn't half-bad looking: not exactly handsome, but not altogether unattractive either.

"Miss! Miss?"

Myrtle turned her head to see a man, again about her age, nattily dressed in a pin-striped, blue suit, a panama straw boater perched on his head. He wielded a black wooden cane with a silver handle and was doing his best to catch up to her.

While she was in no mood for another confrontation, she didn't want to appear insensitive to someone possibly disabled. She slowed the Model N down, allowing the man to overtake her.

"Yes, what is it?" she asked in a not too friendly tone.

"Madame, my apologies," said the man, struggling to keep up, even at the car's slow pace. "Might I have a moment?"

"What do you want?" she asked again, more testily this time.

"My name is George Salmon. You said you were going to be working here in town. Might I inquire where?"

"Why do you ask?"

"I admired your spunk back there. I thought if you did not already have a placement I might offer you employment."

Myrtle smiled. She imagined the man might have some agenda beyond that of employment—something of a more romantic nature. But he seemed sincere.

"At the college," she said. "At the library."

"Yah, I see," said the man, clearly disappointed. "Good luck, then. Might I ask where you will be staying?"

Perhaps this fellow might be of some use, thought Myrtle, since she didn't know the exact location of the boarding house where she had arranged to reside.

"Mrs. Darling's boarding house," said Myrtle. "Can you tell me how to get there?"

"The next street up, the first one past the park, is Joshua Road. It goes off to the left. Mrs. Darling's is about two miles out that road. You'll pass Amyx Road on the right—that takes you to the college—and it's just a short distance after that. You can't miss it: There's a sign out front, and a big willow tree in the front yard."

"A Weeping Willow?" asked Myrtle.

"No, it's a Black Willow."

"Is there a difference?"

"Quite a bit—you'll see."

"Thank you," said Myrtle. She lifted her foot from the pedal, shifted the car into its high speed, and left the man standing behind, a confused look on his face.

"But your name . . ." he called out.

Myrtle continued driving and didn't look back.

*****

Henri made his way up Main Street, but his mind was still on the woman—the girl, as he thought of her—whose automobile, moments before, had caused Jessie to rear up, nearly depositing him in the middle of the street.

She'd surprised him with her retort when he'd chastised her. While it angered him, at the same time he had to give her credit that she'd been bold enough to do so.

In spite of his annoyance at almost being run over, he couldn't help but notice she was, not beautiful, but rather, attractive in a simple, wholesome way. A newsboy's cap had covered her head of curly, auburn hair. Her voice had a slight southern drawl to it, not unlike his mother's.

And her figure—what he could see of it as she sat in her car—seemed more that of a teenager than a grown woman.

She wore what appeared to be men's pants, except they were black and green plaid, which matched her cap; not the type of apparel normally seen on women on the streets of Booker Falls.

She must be one of those "free spirits" I've read about, thought Henri.

But that confounded automobile: Henri harbored an intense dislike of the infernal machines. He thought of Lydia, and the misfortune that had befallen her a few years earlier. As far as he was concerned, if God wanted mankind to get around in a motorized conveyance, he wouldn't have invented horses. By association, he felt little amity for those individuals who drove and rode in them.

Nevertheless, he couldn't get the woman out of his mind. Had Jessie not automatically turned at Blanchard Street, he would have driven right on by the courthouse, where his office was located.

CHAPTER TWO

Mrs. Darling's Boarding House was a three-story Victorian, with a porch running across the front and along one side that displayed an assortment of spindle work. Three dormer windows peeked out onto the road from the third floor attic.

Dating from 1859, the house was originally the home of the Overmyer family, who farmed the surrounding four hundred acres. By 1885, the last of the family's five children had left home. Unable to continue operating the farm on their own, the couple sold the land to one buyer, and the house and barn and five acres to Rebecca Darling, whose husband had passed away earlier in the year, leaving her a tidy sum. After adding a second upstairs bathroom, she turned the home into a boarding house and began taking in lodgers.

Though the house wasn't new, to Myrtle it looked warm and inviting; it would be her home now for who knew how long.

As she walked up the path from the road to the house, a woman in her late sixties, no taller than she was wide, head covered in a floppy-brimmed straw hat, came bounding towards her from the porch with a sprightliness belying her age. Grinning broadly, she hurriedly wiped her hands on the starched, cotton apron that covered her from her neck almost to her shoes.

Myrtle glanced at the ruffles at the bottom, a fashion more suited to a decade earlier.

But what she found most intriguing were the oval-drop earrings swinging from the older woman's ears—black onyx stones outlined in gold filigree.

Myrtle would discover her new landlady had a fancy for dangly earrings, and was almost never seen without one of the many pairs she had accumulated over the years.

"Miss Tully, you finally made it," gushed Mrs. Darling. "Welcome to Booker Falls." She thrust out her hand.

It was a surprisingly strong hand for such a short, and not-so-young woman, thought Myrtle.

"Mrs. Darling, I am very happy to be here."

"You're a cute one, you are," said Mrs. Darling, looking Myrtle up and down. "But no more than a wisp of a thing, eh? How much do you weigh, dearie?"

"I guess . . . maybe a hundred and ten," said Myrtle, feeling a blush come to her face. "I don't know—I haven't weighed myself lately."

"Well, never you mind. We'll put some meat on your bones while you're here. Which I hope will be a long time. Come now, let me show you to your room. You must be exhausted, you poor dear."

Mrs. Darling wrapped her arm around Myrtle and started to march her to the house.

"My steamer . . ." said Myrtle.

"Yah, it'll do dere for now. We'll have Mr. de la Cruz go fetch it later."

"Mr. de la Cruz?"

"One of my other boarders. He's da county constable, a nice young man, yah? You'll like him."

Myrtle looked back at the Ford. "My dog . . ."

This brought Mrs. Darling to a stop.

"Eh? A dog? You got a dog?"

Myrtle frowned. She hadn't said anything to Mrs. Darling about Penrod. Then, again, he hadn't been in the picture last month when she'd made arrangements to stay here. He was a recent addition to the few worldly possessions she'd brought with her to Michigan.

He'd been walking—staggering was more like it—along the road outside Mendota, Illinois, when Myrtle had passed by him. Though she'd been pushing to make Rockford before nightfall, there was no way she could leave the poor animal there.

Stopping the car, she'd hurried back, gathered the emaciated creature up in her arms and deposited him gently on the seat next to her. She'd guessed him to weigh no more than ten or twelve pounds.

He became her traveling companion, quickly putting on weight from the generous portions of food she'd fed him.

Now, here they were. What would Mrs. Darling say?

"Well, den, don't just stand dere—go get da poor ting and let's get him in da house so's he can have a drink of water."

"Right," said Myrtle, more than a little relieved. Hurrying back to the car, she scooped up Penrod and rejoined Mrs. Darling.

"Oh, you sweetheart," said Mrs. Darling, looking into Penrod's eyes and stroking his head. "I bet you could use a drink." Wrinkling her nose, she added, "And a bath, too, I warrant, eh?"

"We didn't—" Myrtle started to say.

"Shoosh, shoosh. I know ya been traveling. Come now and bring your friend. What's his name, anyhow?"

"Penrod."

"Penrod? Dat's a strange name."

"I named him after a character from books by Booth Tarkington."

"Never heard of him," said Mrs. Darling, leading Myrtle around to the back of the house.

"The books have been out a couple of years."

"I see. Don't read much, myself. Okay, den, see dat big tub a' leanin' up against da back of da house, dere? Dat's what we're going to wash Mr. Penrod here in."

*****

Twenty minutes later Penrod, much to his disgust, was one wet, but very clean dog, tied up to a post in the yard and left to dry, but content with the hambone Mrs. Darling had procured for him.

Myrtle sat at the kitchen table, keeping an eye on her dog through the window, as she sipped tea that included orange and spice, from a rose-colored cup, and munched on an almond cookie. Mrs. Darling sat across from her, a matching cup in front of her.

"I hadn't thought about how you might feel about a dog," said Myrtle, setting the cup down. "I'm sorry I just sprung him on you."

"Dearie, don't you worry yourself none about dat," said the old lady. "See dat box over dere?"

Mrs. Darling pointed to a wooden box sitting on its side next to the stove. An old rug lay in the bottom of it. Myrtle hadn't noticed it before.

"Dat was Alfred's. He passed away a couple weeks back—old age. I warn't sure I was going to want to get another dog. It's hard when you lose one. I guess God must have made da decision for me by bringing me you and Penrod. You tink your dog would mind taking over a second-hand bed?"

"I don't imagine he'd mind at all," said Myrtle, smiling.

She liked Mrs. Darling. The old woman reminded her of Madame Léger, the landlady at the boarding house in Chaumont in France where Myrtle had spent a year and a half with seven other women, all of them telephone operators for the army.

She'd been like a mother hen, watching over her flock of young chicks, doing her best to make sure they stayed out of trouble—and not always succeeding.

Myrtle had the impression that Mrs. Darling was cut from the same bolt of cloth, a feeling that gave her a sense of reassurance, knowing someone in this new, strange town would care about her.

She had just raised her cup to her mouth when a loud clanging sound came from somewhere in the house, nearly causing her to spill the tea. The noise was quickly followed by three more booms.

"What *is* that?" she asked, her eyes almost as large as the saucer on which she had hurriedly placed the cup.

"Oh, my," said Mrs. Darling, jumping up from her chair. "I didn't realize da time. I must start dinner at once. Mr. Pfrommer insists on eating precisely at five o'clock."

"Mr. Pfrommer?" said Myrtle, more composed now since it appeared no major calamity had occurred. She realized what had rattled her was a clock striking the hour.

"One of my other tenants."

"How many boarders are there?" asked Myrtle.

"Three others plus you," said Mrs. Darling.

"I see. Mrs. Darling, may I help with dinner?"

"Oh, no, no help needed, though I tank you for da offer. Why don't you see if your dog is dry? If he is, bring him on in so's he can get used to da place."

*****

Penrod was, indeed, dry, and weary of chewing on the hambone. He could hardly restrain himself as the rope was loosened from the collar Mrs. Darling had placed around his neck, a collar which, until recently had belonged to Alfred. Dashing to the back door, he stood, quivering, until Myrtle opened it, then raced in as though he'd lived there forever.

Instead of following him, Myrtle walked back around to the front of the house. She was anxious to get her trunk inside, get unpacked and relax. She had no idea when Mr. de la Cruz might show up. Although she'd managed to grapple with the trunk on her own several times over the past two weeks, she didn't feel she had the energy to do so today.

"Some automobile you got there."

Myrtle looked around to see a woman walking towards her. Tall, close to six feet, she appeared to be somewhere in her mid-forties. Attractive, but not beautiful. More of an athletic build. Pleasant face.

"Thanks," said Myrtle. "I like it."

"You must be Myrtle," the woman said, sticking out her hand. "I'm Daisy."

Myrtle looked confused, but took Daisy's hand. "I'm sorry, am I supposed to know you?"

"Not yet," said Daisy, pushing her glasses up on her nose. "But you will. I'm one of Mrs. Darling's other boarders. She's been regaling us for the last month about this 'Southern Belle' who's coming to dwell among us."

"Southern Belle, huh?" Myrtle chuckled. "I don't know about that."

"You just get here?" asked Daisy.

"About an hour ago. I'm waiting for Mr. de la Cruz to show up to bring my steamer trunk in."

"Oh, shoot," said Daisy, eyeing the trunk. "It's got handles on each end; you grab one and I'll grab the other and we'll get it in lickety-split."

Without waiting for Myrtle's response, Daisy loosened the straps securing the trunk to the platform and grabbed one end. "Come on, now, ain't got all day—almost dinner time."

Myrtle grabbed the other end and together they hauled the box to the porch, where they set it down to rest for a minute.

"Good lord, that's heavy," said Daisy, wiping her forehead with a handkerchief. "How many gold bars you got in there?"

"No gold bars. But a number of books—that's what makes it so heavy."

"Did you bring enough to restock the shelves at the library?"

"Nope. These are all for my own personal use."

"Okay, then," said Daisy, once again grabbing a trunk handle. "Let's get this monster in the house." She opened the door and led the way.

"I don't know where my room is," said Myrtle, as they stood in the foyer.

"I do," said Daisy. "Up these stairs. Come on—you lead, I'll bring up the rear."

Moments later, both women, breathing hard from their efforts, stood on the second floor landing.

"Right down here," said Daisy, moving so quickly Myrtle almost lost her grip on the handle.

Once inside the room, they set the trunk down. Daisy collapsed onto a chair, while Myrtle stood and surveyed her new surroundings.

In addition to the ladder back on which Daisy now rested, the room held a cast iron and brass French Empire-style bed, a washstand, a small desk and a double-door armoire that reached two-thirds of the way to the twelve-foot high ceiling. Originally made of white oak, the years had faded the color almost to gray.

Myrtle didn't care. It was a place to store the few articles of clothing she'd brought with her, including the uniform she'd worn in France.

She walked over to the room's only window. It looked out onto the back yard, beyond which stood a large, two-story barn. Myrtle wondered if she'd be able to keep the Model N in it.

"All righty," said Daisy, jumping up. "Dinner's in thirty minutes. You and I share the bathroom at the end of the hall here. I imagine you want to freshen up before you go down. I know I need to. You want to go first, or me?"

"Why don't you," answered Myrtle. "I won't take long, and that will give me an opportunity to unpack a few things."

"Okay, then." Daisy stopped at the door. "Don't be late. Mr. Pfrommer likes to eat promptly at five."

"So I've heard," said Myrtle. "Hey, by the way—what about Mr. de la Cruz?"

"What about him?"

"What's he like?"

"Young—about your age—and kind of cute."

"So—"

But Daisy was gone.

*****

George stood gazing out the window of his office, his mind fixed on the young girl he'd just encountered on the street. There was something about her he found intriguing.

He thought about what it might be: that she was driving an automobile, or the fact she was dressed like a man or that, in her own unique way, there was a comeliness that couldn't be hidden even under the clothes she wore: the plaid pants, the newsboy cap?

And then there was her voice; soft, lilting–she was somewhere from the deep south, that much he could tell.

She said she would be working at the library. Must be the assistant librarian. *Unless Frank left town since our last poker game and didn't tell me.*

Think I'll pay Henri a visit tomorrow. See what he thinks.

*****

When Myrtle reached the dining room, Mrs. Darling and Daisy were already there, along with a man Myrtle assumed was Mr. Pfrommer. In his late seventies, Adolph Pfrommer stood over six feet tall with a rail-thin physique. A plum cravat, matching the color of his brocade waistcoat, sat at the neck of a white shirt with sleeves that peeked out below the arms of a black dress suit, shiny with twenty years or more of wear.

Completely bald, he sported copious snow-white muttonchops which reminded Myrtle of a photograph she'd seen once of Ambrose Burnside with her grandfather, when the former was Chairman of the Foreign Relations Committee, and the latter a candidate for a position in the Department of State.

"Ah, there you are, dearie, looking all bright and fresh," chirped Mrs. Darling. "Miss Tully, dis distinguished-looking gentleman here is one of your fellow boarders, Mr. Adolph Pfrommer."

Mr. Pfrommer stood, gave a slight bow, waited while Myrtle and Daisy took their seats, then sat back down.

Mrs. Darling glanced nervously at the grandfather clock which stood against one wall, the source of the horrible clanging earlier: two minutes until five o'clock.

The minute hand had moved one degree closer to the hour when they heard the front door opening and closing. Moments later, Henri de la Cruz entered the room.

"Sorry, I'm—"

Henri's jaw dropped, as did Myrtle's.

"You!" they both said in unison as the clock struck its first clang.

Mrs. Darling looked from one to the other. "You've met?"

"We ran into each other downtown," said Henri, frowning.

The clock clanged again.

Mr. Pfrommer started to fidget.

"Literally, had I not exercised my excellent driving skills," snapped Myrtle.

"Which so-called skills almost caused us to collide in the first place," retorted Henri.

The clock clanged for the third time.

Mr. Pfrommer was becoming more restless.

"I assume you're the much anticipated Miss Tully," said Henri.

"And you are boarder number four, Mr. de la Cruz," said Myrtle. She had almost called him the "cute" Mr. de la Cruz, following Daisy's description, but caught herself in time.

"And I am da very hungry Mr. Pfrommer," said Mr. Pfrommer, speaking for the first time with an unmistakable German accent. He looked at Henri, and then at Myrtle.

"Everyone, sit," said Mrs. Darling, hoping to restore some order to what suddenly had become a prickly situation. "Dinner is coming now."

The clock struck five.

Henri took his seat.

For the remainder of the meal the only conversation was that between Daisy and Myrtle.

Neither Henri nor Mr. Pfrommer was the keenest of conversationalists.

CHAPTER THREE

Following dinner, Myrtle retired to her room for a short rest, shorter even than she had anticipated, as she was awakened by the now vexatious tolling of the dining room clock as it struck seven.

Wearily, she got up, slipped her feet into her shoes and made her way down the stairs. She glanced out the window and spotted Daisy on the front porch, wrapped in a bulky, forest green cardigan, sitting in one of a half dozen oversized rocking chairs. She was smoking a cigarette and Penrod was snuggled in her lap.

"Looks like you've made a friend," said Myrtle, settling into the rocker next to Daisy.

"He's adorable. Has he been with you long?"

"Long? About a week. Picked him up on the side of the road."

"Mrs. Darling said his name's Penrod? From one of Tarkington's books?"

"You're familiar with Tarkington?" asked Myrtle.

Daisy pushed her glasses up. "I am. I read a lot. I suppose not as much as you, though, seeing as how you're literary and all, being a librarian."

"I'm not sure I'd classify myself as a librarian—or literary, for that matter."

"But you work in a library. You've come here to work in the college library. At least, that's what I've heard."

"This will be my first time," said Myrtle.

"You've never worked in a library before?"

Myrtle shook her head. "Nope—first time."

"What *have* you been doing?"

Before Myrtle could answer, Mrs. Darling came bouncing out of the house, carrying a serving tray holding two cups of something very hot, judging from the steam swirling up from them.

"Thought you two girls could use a cup of tea," she said, cheerfully.

Placing the cups on a small table, she returned to the house as quickly as she had appeared.

"That was nice of her," said Myrtle.

"She does that every evening whenever I'm out here," said Daisy, removing a small silver flask from one of the cardigan's pockets. "And every evening I add a little something."

She poured a shot into her tea cup and extended the container towards Myrtle.

"Care for a nip?"

Myrtle waved her hand. "I thought Michigan was alcohol-free."

"Sometimes it is and sometimes it isn't," Daisy answered. "And some places it is, and some places it isn't. All depends on which law's been passed recently and where you are."

Myrtle sipped her tea, then looked into the cup. "This isn't the same flavor I had earlier."

"No, this is Mrs. Darling's after dinner tea—dandelion."

"Dandelion?"

"Oh, yes," said Daisy. "Mrs. Darling is very big into everything dandelion. You stick around here long enough you'll have dandelion jelly, dandelion salad, dandelion fritters, dandelion soup. And in the spring we get dandelion pancakes."

"Dandelion wine?" asked Myrtle.

Daisy shook her head. "Sorry to say, that's the one thing Mrs. Darling doesn't make. She's a teetotaler."

"What does she think about your drinking?"

Daisy smiled. "What she doesn't know won't hurt her—or me."

"Perhaps I should try a bit of your 'additive'," said Myrtle, reaching out her hand.

As she poured a bit of whiskey into her cup she noticed engraving on the side of the flask.

"Who's GF?" she asked, handing the flacon back to Daisy.

"Why, it's . . . uh, it's . . ." Daisy stammered.

"An old boyfriend?" asked Myrtle.

"That's right—an old boyfriend. Somebody I used to know."

"I won't embarrass you any further by asking for details."

"Thank you," said Daisy.

"So, where do you get your whiskey?"

"From my current boyfriend, Leonard."

"And where does Leonard get it—Canada?"

"You might say, Leonard's connected," answered Daisy.

"Connected?"

"He's an officer on the state police force. They confiscate a lot of illegal alcohol coming into the state. Let's just say not all of it gets dumped, eh?"

"You have a police officer as a boyfriend who supplies you with confiscated illegal liquor? Sounds like a sweet deal."

"But don't say anything to anybody," said Daisy, her brows furrowing. "He could get in a lot of trouble."

"I bet he could," said Myrtle. She stood and stretched. "Think I'll call it a day. I'm going to take a bath, then hit the hay."

"You start at the library on Tuesday?"

"Uh-huh."

"What are you doing this weekend?"

Myrtle shrugged. "Hadn't thought about it."

"Why don't you let me show you around—in your car. I could drive."

"You know how to drive?" asked Myrtle.

"You could teach me."

"I think I'll drive," said Myrtle.

*****

As tired as she felt, Myrtle still found it hard to fall asleep.

Her mind kept going back to the moment she'd decided to come to the Upper Peninsula of Michigan, a place she'd never been to, never even heard of.

The war had ended, and she knew her stint in Europe was drawing to a close. She had enjoyed her time operating a switchboard for the Army, and the opportunities—few as they were—she'd had to see France, including several trips to Paris.

As wonderful as the whole experience had been, she was ready to return home to America—though not to New Orleans.

With both of her parents deceased and no other relatives there any closer than second or third cousins, she'd decided she wanted to see a new part of the country.

A chance conversation with Gladys Zimmerman, another Hello Girl—a name affectionately bequeathed on the women operators by the U. S. servicemen—had given her the idea.

"What do you like to do in your spare time?" Gladys had asked her.

"I guess read, mostly. I very much enjoy reading."

"Why don't you become a librarian?" asked Gladys.

Myrtle stopped to think for a moment. She'd never considered being a librarian. "That doesn't sound very exciting," she said.

"Eh, I don't know about that," said Gladys. "But I do know the college I went to is looking for an assistant librarian. They sent me a letter seeing if I was interested, but I'm not."

Gladys went on to describe Adelaide College, gushing over how charming the area was, wild, with thousands of acres of virgin forests, and lakes with water so blue they made the sky pale in comparison.

By the time she finished, Myrtle knew that was where she wanted to go. Spend the rest of her life there? That she wasn't sure of. But she definitely wanted to see Michigan.

Lengthy correspondence followed with Frank Mitchell, the head librarian at the college and, finally, here she was.

It might not be exciting, she thought, but she knew this was what she should be doing at this point in her life.

*****

If the sunlight pouring in through the window hadn't awakened her, the aroma of bacon frying surely would have.

Myrtle rolled over to better see the little oval alarm clock with a bell on top that sat on the nightstand. Like the furniture in her room, it was fifty years old, if a day. But it worked. And had a much more pleasant sound than the downstairs grandfather clock.

Only eleven minutes remained until breakfast was to be served precisely at seven o'clock. As with dinner the previous evening, Mr. Pfrommer expected the meal at a certain time. And since he was the boarder who had been with Mrs. Darling the longest, what Mr. Pfrommer wanted, he got.

Springing from the bed, Myrtle threw on the same clothes she had worn the night before and hurried to the bathroom to wash her face and run a quick comb through her hair.

Minutes later, she burst into the hallway in time to see Henri emerging from his room.

Each of them hesitated for the briefest moment, then continued.

"Mr. de la Cruz," said Myrtle, coolly, as they met at the landing.

"Miss Tully," replied Henri, extending his arm in an invitation to precede him down the stairs.

When they reached the dining room, Mr. Pfrommer and Daisy were already seated. Mrs. Darling was pouring coffee into their mugs.

Mr. Pfrommer stood up.

"Good morning," chirped Mrs. Darling. "Miss Tully, I trust you had a good night's sleep?"

"I did," replied Myrtle, surprised when Henri pulled the chair out for her. "Thank you, Mr. de la Cruz," she added.

Henri merely nodded, then took his place, as did Mr. Pfrommer.

"So," said Daisy, when everyone was seated, "are we still on for a tour today?"

"That sounds good to me," said Myrtle, sipping her coffee.

"Nine o'clock, then?" asked Daisy.

"Perfect."

"Mrs. Darling said you were in Europe," said Daisy. "Did you enjoy it? Did you get to go anywhere, see anything, do anything?"

"A few times we received leave, and some of us went into Paris."

Mr. Pfrommer stopped eating and turned toward Myrtle.

"I bet that was fun," said Daisy.

"It was—especially one night in particular."

"I lived in Paris vunce," said Mr. Pfrommer.

The other three at the table looked at the old man.

"It vas a long time ago," he said, returning to his breakfast.

*****

After a quick change of clothes, Myrtle was ready to head out with Daisy for her first real look at the town of Booker Falls.

"Do you know what happened this morning?" asked Daisy, as they settled into their car seats.

"What?" asked Myrtle.

"Mr. Pfrommer spoke. Like in real conversation, I mean. In the three years I've been taking meals with him, I've never heard him say anything more than 'Please pass das salt,' or 'It's time ve vas eating.'"

Daisy spoke the words in a guttural voice, imitating Mr. Pfrommer's speech. "I really think he's taken a shine to you."

Myrtle laughed and shifted the gears. "I think it was just because I mentioned Paris. So, Daisy, have you ever ridden in an automobile?"

"Please," replied Daisy, faking an air of indignation. "I didn't grow up in this burg. I've lived in real cities, you know. And just because I can't drive doesn't mean I've never ridden in an automobile. So, what about that one night in particular in Paris?"

"What about it?"

"Tell me about it."

"Maybe sometime—not now. Okay, here we go. First I want to see the library; then you can give me the five cent tour."

CHAPTER FOUR

Erected in 1874 and surrounded by a stand of white pine trees hundreds of years old, Adelaide College Library, the third oldest building on campus, was a two-story structure constructed of Jacobsville Sandstone, the same as St. Barbara's Catholic Church and many of the finer buildings in town.

On the southwest side of the building, protected somewhat from the fierce north winds that blew down from Canada in the winter, sat a garden ablaze with a cornucopia of wild flowers, some of which, like blazing star and goldenrod, Myrtle had seen on her way to town, plus others that were new to her: red baneberry, smooth aster, and tickseed.

Three benches and a picnic table afforded places for people to sit and read, or think, or dream—or sleep. At the far end a small, rocky grotto completed the picture.

An eight-foot high oak door that gave evidence of having weathered almost a half century of Upper Peninsula winters graced the north face of the building, flanked on either side by three large, stained glass windows, each seven feet high. The second floor held seven more windows of the same size. The middle window above the door displayed a rendering of the crucifixion. The other twelve windows portrayed each of the disciples, including late-comer Matthias.

Daisy swung open the door and they entered a cavernous hall, fifteen feet high.

A check-out desk stood in the middle of the room, facing the front door. A portly, balding man stood behind it.

He must be my new boss, thought Myrtle.

Never married, Frank Mitchell had been head librarian at Adelaide College for over thirty years.

A member of the initial graduating class of Adelaide in 1876, he had immediately filled the newly-created position as assistant librarian at the college. In 1888, when the head librarian passed away unexpectedly, Frank was promoted to that position.

His pride and joy, aside from the bright red horseshoe mustache he scrupulously groomed, was the gold incisor on the right side of his mouth, which he was happy to share with the rest of the world via a perpetual smile.

"Mr. Mitchell?" said Myrtle, approaching the desk.

Frank looked up. "Yes, how may I assist you?"

"I'm Myrtle Tully, your new assistant librarian."

"Miss Tully!" exclaimed Frank, smiling. "You're early. You're not supposed to be here until Tuesday."

"Oh, I know. I arrived in town yesterday and my friend, Daisy—" Myrtle turned back but Daisy was nowhere to be seen "—anyway, I just stopped by to introduce myself."

"Well, I'm glad you're here. It's been rather hectic trying to take care of all this by myself." Frank made a sweeping gesture with his hand at the nearly deserted floor. "Anyway, welcome. Would you care to look around?"

"No, Daisy's showing me the town, so we'd best be off. But it's nice meeting you, and I'm looking forward to working with you."

Five minutes later Daisy joined her out front.

"Where now?" asked Myrtle.

"Let's walk around campus. There aren't any streets, so you can leave the car here."

For the next hour and a half, the two of them walked the tree-lined paths of the college, past the two original buildings: Amyx Hall, where all the classes were held originally, and which now housed the administrative offices; and Recamier Logement, the living quarters for female students. Male students were expected to find their own lodging in town.

Next came the Booker Center, which contained the gym and auditorium; Centre de Musique; Pétain Hall, named for the first President of Adelaide College, François Pétain, and home to all the curricula of the college; and the Osborn House, named in honor of Chase Osborne, a resident of the Upper Peninsula and Governor of Michigan at the time the home was renovated eight years before to serve as a residence for the college's President.

By eleven o'clock they found themselves back at the car.

"You ready to take in the downtown now?" asked Daisy.

"But we haven't seen the chapel."

"There is no chapel."

"No chapel?" said Myrtle. "For goodness sakes, why not?"

"I don't know. I guess Mr. Amyx was more interested in minds, rather than souls."

"How sad," said Myrtle. "But the library has all those stained glass windows."

"Ah, yes," said Daisy. "But the library was built two years after the college was founded, and Monsieur Amyx had no involvement with it. Shall we go?"

"Lead on, Macduff!" Myrtle cried out.

*****

As they motored into town, Daisy turned to Myrtle.

"Are you going to find it a little creepy working there—at the library?"

"Creepy?" said Myrtle. "Why would you say that?"

"You know what happened there almost thirty years ago, don't you?"

Myrtle shrugged. "I guess not. What?"

"March 8th, 1891. A young woman was strangled to death: Yvette Sinclair. She was a student at the college. And she held the same job you have now—assistant librarian."

"No kidding!"

"No kidding. And they never found out who killed her. I'm writing a novel about it."

"A novel?" said Myrtle. "I'm impressed. How's it coming?"

Daisy scrunched up her face. "Not so good, I'm afraid. In fact, I haven't written a single word yet. I've been researching ever since I moved here, but all I've been able to find are the original newspaper articles, and there wasn't much there, except there were two suspects: Paul Momet and Claude Amyx. But they could never pin the crime on either of them, and after a while the whole matter just went away."

"Sounds like it would make an interesting book," said Myrtle.

"So—no creepy?"

"I imagine whoever killed that girl is long gone by now. But I'll keep my eyes open."

"What brought you to Booker Falls?" asked Daisy. "To the college?"

Myrtle gave Daisy the same story she'd been rolling over in her mind last night before she fell asleep.

"I've never been to France," said Daisy, when Myrtle finished. "Never been anywhere, really, not to speak of, anyway. What was it like over there? What was your job like?"

"It was wonderful. I guess when our army first arrived in France, all the telephone operators were French girls. Needless to say, there was a definite language gap between them and our men, since hardly any of our boys spoke French, and what little English the French girls could speak was barely understandable. So General Pershing recruited American girls who were bilingual and could speak French, like me, to join the army and come to Europe to operate the switchboards for our troops. I was one of the lucky ones. I'd worked as a telephone operator in New Orleans for six years, so I met all the qualifications. The men called us the 'Hello Girls.'"

"The Hello Girls?"

"That's because when the French girls answered the phone, they'd always say '*Bonjour*.' When we answered with 'Hello,' the men knew an American was on the line."

"How many of you were there?"

"Close to three hundred, I think," replied Myrtle. "At least, that's what I heard."

"Where were you stationed?"

"I was at the General Headquarters in Chaumont. I was paid sixty dollars a month."

"That's pretty good," said Daisy.

"Yes, you'd think so," said Myrtle. "Except we had to buy our own uniforms."

"Uniforms?"

"A dark blue wool Norfolk jacket with a long matching skirt; a white blouse; black, high top shoes and brown army boots; a hat, an overcoat, a rubber raincoat and woolen underwear. What we really resented though, was that we had to wear black sateen bloomers under our skirts."

"What in the world for?"

"We think it was because the brass was afraid the wind might blow our dresses up."

Daisy laughed out loud.

"And that all cost me three hundred and ninety dollars," added Myrtle.

Daisy let out a long whistle. "Eh, that's a lot!"

"Six and a half months' worth of salary," said Myrtle, disgustedly. "But I brought everything with me up here—all except those blasted bloomers!

"One girl I worked with was from Michigan, from Marine City. She was younger than me, about nineteen, I think. I thought I might look her up now that I live here. Do you know where Marine City is?"

"Somewhere around Detroit, I think."

Myrtle frowned. "That's a long way from here, isn't it?"

"Kiddo, *everywhere's* a long way from here," said Daisy. "We're closer to Minnesota than we are to Detroit."

"You mean Wisconsin, don't you? I know I drove through there on my way here."

Daisy shook her head. "No, I mean Minnesota. You'll find out once you've been here for a while: We are at the edge of civilization as we know it."

CHAPTER FIVE

Henri stared at the paperwork spread out on the desk before him.

He was supposed to be working on the budget to be submitted to the town council in five days.

Instead, his mind was on the young woman who'd just arrived in town and whom, he discovered, much to his surprise, would be living at the same boarding house where he resided.

She lacked certain lady-like characteristics—that much he knew. And, while she wasn't beautiful, she wasn't unattractive either. She was unlike any woman he'd met before. But then, he, himself, was different than most of the townsfolk of Booker Falls, being one of only a handful of non-white people who lived there.

Born in 1891 in French Guiana, the illegitimate child of a mulatto mother, Henri had moved with her to Booker Falls in 1908, where he'd attended the college, graduating in 1911 with a teaching degree.

Over the next five years he'd taught history and science at the high school, at the same time working part time for Constable Richard Barnoble. Upon Barnoble's death in 1916, Henri reluctantly gave up teaching when he was elected as the new constable. Oftentimes he wished he could go back to his old job.

He shook his head and tried to concentrate once again on the figures before him.

He heard a tap on his office window. He looked up and saw George Salmon waving at him. Henri gestured for him to come in.

"Mr. Mayor," said Henri, when George was seated across the desk from him. "To what do I owe the honor of your visit?"

"I dropped by to see how you're doing," said George.

Henri looked perplexed. "What do you mean?"

"After your exchange with that young woman yesterday and her horseless carriage."

Henri grunted. "Infernal machines. George, I want you to issue a proclamation banning all automobiles from the city limits."

George laughed. "Yah, you know I can't do that. Nor would I. Those 'infernal machines' as you call them are the face of the future."

"Not as far as I'm concerned," Henri snarled.

"Nevertheless," said George, "they are. But here's what I really want to know: the young woman—she asked for directions to Mrs. Darling's. Is she staying there?"

"Unfortunately, she is."

"And how do you find her?"

"Find her?"

"What do you think of her?" asked George.

"She's rude, she's impertinent, she dresses in men's clothes—"

"Men's clothes?"

"You saw what she had on yesterday: trousers, what looked like a man's shirt, a newsboy's cap. She should dress like a woman. And did I mention she's impertinent, has no respect for those in authority?"

"Yah, you did, and I assume you mean someone such as yourself?"

"I mean men in general," roared Henri. "And, yes, someone like myself."

"Henri, I think you were born in the wrong century."

"No, I was born in the right century; I'm just living in the wrong one."

George cleared his throat. "So, you don't like her?"

Henri looked at him quizzically. "Like her? What do you mean, *like* her?"

George straightened his shoulders. "You wouldn't mind if I asked her out?"

Henri sat back in his chair. "Ask her out? Why would you want to do that? And why should I mind?"

"Have you looked at her—closely, I mean?" asked George. "Despite the way she dresses, she's a very attractive woman."

Henri shook his head. He couldn't believe what he was hearing. George wanted to ask this woman—this *girl*—out?

"Out to where?" he asked.

George smiled. "I don't think that's any of your business."

Henri stiffened. "Well, I don't think it's any of my business whether or not you ask her out, so I don't know why you're asking me if it's all right."

"Fine," said George, rising. "Just wanted to make sure I wasn't stepping on anyone's toes. Have a good day."

George stopped at the door. "By the way, what's her name?"

Henri chuckled. "You're going to ask her out and you don't even know her name? Tully—Myrtle Tully."

George thought for a moment. "Myrtle. I like that—Myrtle."

Then he turned and left.

Henri watched as George walked past his window. So George was going to ask Miss Tully out. Henri was surprised to find that he wasn't completely at ease with that news.

*****

Not wanting to chance running into Henri again, or anybody for that matter either riding a horse or in a carriage, Myrtle parked her car at the train station, a block away from Main Street.

From there, she and Daisy walked to where the shops and businesses were, most of which Myrtle had seen the day before as she'd passed through. They spent a good hour and a half in de Première Qualité, where Daisy ended up buying a warm pair of gloves for the coming winter. Though she tried her best to persuade Myrtle to do likewise—"You have no idea how cold it gets up here"—Myrtle insisted the pair she'd worn for a year and a half in France would do nicely. She couldn't believe Michigan could be any colder than France had been.

Cater-cornered across the street from de Première Qualité, stood the two-story courthouse. Unlike the handsomer buildings in town, this one was made of concrete—gray and singularly undistinguished. There was no question it had been built with the goal of utilitarianism in mind, rather than aesthetics.

"That is perhaps the ugliest building I've ever seen," said Myrtle, when she and Daisy were once again out on the sidewalk.

"The courthouse?" said Daisy. "You're right—it's hideous. That's where Henri's office is—right up that street." She pointed up Blanchard Street. "And the mayor's too, on the other side. Come on, I want you to meet Paige."

In the middle of the block across from the courthouse, nestled between the bank and Miss Madeline's Eatery, was the book store. Myrtle had made a mental note yesterday to stop in at her earliest opportunity. Through the window, she saw a pleasant looking woman about Daisy's age standing behind the counter.

"Daisy!" the woman said, looking up at the sound of the bell above the door which heralded their entry.

"Hi, Paige," said Daisy, as the two women embraced. "Paige, I want you to meet my friend, Myrtle Tully. She's just arrived in town and she's staying at Mrs. Darling's."

Myrtle smiled at the fact that Daisy was already referring to the two of them as 'friends.'"

Paige wrapped her arms around Myrtle and hugged her as vigorously as she had Daisy.

"Well, welcome to Booker Falls. I'm Paige Turner. This is my shop."

"I like the name of your shop," said Myrtle.

Paige grinned. "Paige Turner's New, Used and Rare Books? It is rather catchy, isn't it?"

"And your name really is Paige Turner?" said Myrtle.

Paige nodded. "It is now. It was Paige LaSalle before I married Mr. Turner."

"And who is this?" asked Myrtle, spotting a large yellow cat curled up on the counter.

Paige picked the cat up. "This? This is the obligatory book store cat, Ginger."

"And where is Pickles?" asked Myrtle.

Paige raised her eyebrows. "I see you know your literature."

"What?" said Daisy, puzzled at what was going on.

"Ginger and Pickles are the main characters in a book by Beatrix Potter," said Myrtle. "Ginger was a yellow tomcat and Pickles was a terrier. Together they owned a shop that sold all sorts of things."

"The same Beatrix Potter who wrote *Peter Rabbit*?" asked Daisy.

"One and the same," said Paige. "My, Myrtle, I'm impressed."

"Myrtle's the new assistant librarian at the college," said Daisy.

"Really?" said Paige. "Well, that explains it. So, you're into books. I'll look forward to seeing you in here often."

Thirty minutes later, Paige finished showing Myrtle through the store. "So, remember, if you're looking for something and I don't have it, I can order it."

Breakfast had been good—corned beef hash, two poached eggs, toast, and coffee—but that had been hours ago.

"I'm hungry," said Myrtle.

"I've got just the place," said Daisy. "Right next door."

Miss Madeline's Eatery was exactly what Myrtle had envisioned: warm and snug, with a fire blazing in the fireplace, giving the room a cozy feeling. Photographs of people and town buildings over the past thirty years covered the walls. Above the front door hung a stuffed moose head, one almost as large as that encountered by Myrtle the day before.

Miss Madeline, in her eighties, going on forty, was the cook, while her granddaughter, Mona, served as the waitress and a grandson, Danny, cleared the tables and washed the dishes.

Daisy insisted Myrtle try a pasty.

"What's a pasty?"

"It's kind of like a sandwich, but not really. It's meat and usually potatoes, maybe onions, wrapped in a pastry and baked. They're delicious."

Having eaten her share of food of unknown origin while in France, Myrtle had developed an openness for trying anything different. "Okay, I'll give it a try."

"And tea," said Daisy. "You'll enjoy the tea."

"Not dandelion tea, I trust," said Myrtle.

Daisy laughed. "No, not dandelion tea."

While Myrtle enjoyed the pasty—she had chosen the special with elk meat; Daisy played it safe with beef—what she found most interesting was the tea.

"What kind is this?" she asked.

"Thimbleberry," answered Daisy.

"It's delicious."

"I wouldn't recommend drinking more than one or two cups at a time, though."

Myrtle looked perplexed. "Why not?"

"Thimbleberry has what you might call, uh, purgative qualities."

Now Myrtle looked confused.

"You wouldn't want to get too far away from a privy," said Daisy.

Myrtle's face lit up. "Oh, now I see what you mean."

She finished the last of her pasty and wiped her mouth with her napkin. "You know what I'm thinking about now?"

"I have no idea," answered Daisy.

"Dessert."

"Dessert?"

"Didn't I see The Polar Bear right next door?"

Daisy nodded. "Ah, yes, The Polar Bear."

Five minutes later, they found themselves shoveling down huge scoops of ice cream, bananas, and toppings of strawberries and peaches.

"I'm anxious to see the rest of the town," said Myrtle, between spoonfuls.

"But remember," said Daisy, "we still have to be home by five for dinner."

Myrtle groaned.

CHAPTER SIX

It had taken all Myrtle could muster to finish off dinner: two pork chops, fried potatoes, kale, beets, and cherry pie. Not that everything wasn't delicious—it was some of the best food she'd ever eaten, especially the kale. But she hadn't wanted to hurt Mrs. Darling's feelings by leaving anything.

She noticed, with some resentment, that Daisy hadn't seemed to have suffered any distress at all in cleaning her plate.

Later, as the two women sat on the front porch watching Penrod scamper around the front yard, while enjoying the tea Mrs. Darling had brought them—its taste enhanced considerably by the contents of Daisy's flask—Myrtle was startled by the first clang of the grandfather clock striking six o'clock.

"I don't think I'll ever get used to that," she said.

"Oh, you will," said Daisy. "It took me two months, though."

When the clock struck its final bong, the sound of violin music came wafting through the air.

"Do you hear that?" asked Myrtle.

"That's Mr. Pfrommer," said Daisy. "He plays each evening at six for an hour. Beautiful, isn't it?"

Myrtle agreed that it certainly was. Hearing Schubert's *Ave Maria*, she turned to Daisy.

"Daisy, are you a church goer?"

Daisy breathed in the cool evening air before she answered. "Not so much anymore. Used to go."

Myrtle started to ask what had happened, but decided maybe it was too personal a matter.

They sat quietly for a while, each in their own thoughts, enjoying Mr. Pfrommer's playing, until Daisy broke the silence.

"Here comes the mayor."

Myrtle saw a man riding his bicycle up the road to the house, the same man who'd given her directions yesterday to Mrs. Darling's. A cane lay stretched across the handlebars.

"He's the mayor?" she asked.

"You know him?" asked Daisy.

"Met him yesterday on my way into town. He sort of offered me a job."

"What kind of job?"

"I don't think he was really looking for an employee," said Myrtle. "I have a feeling he had something else in mind."

"But . . . oh, I see what you mean. It looks like he's coming up here. Maybe he didn't take no for an answer."

Six feet two, an athletic build and hair the color of wheat, George Salmon was not hard to look at. In contrast to his somewhat conservative attire the day before, he was much more nattily dressed now in a navy blue wool suit with matching waistcoat that served as a perfect complement to his turquoise eyes. A red bow tie along with a dark derby hat perched precariously on his head imparted a devil-may-care appearance.

But today, George was all business. Personal business as it turned out.

"Ladies," said George, tipping his hat as he reached the porch. "I was wondering if I might have a word with Miss Tully."

When neither woman moved, George added, "in private, perhaps?"

"Oh!" said Daisy, jumping up. "Sure. I have to go ...uh, I have to go. See you later, Myrtle."

As soon as Daisy was inside, George removed his hat. Holding it in his hand, he said, "Miss Tully, my name is George Salmon. We met briefly, yesterday."

"Yes, Mr. Salmon, I remember you. Daisy tells me you're the mayor."

George's face turned red. "Uh, yah, yah, that's true—I am."

Myrtle thought she had a pretty good idea what had brought Mr. Salmon around, but decided to tease him a little.

"Are you here on official business?" she asked. "Has someone complained about my automobile?"

"Um, no, ma'am, no complaints. At least none I'm aware of."

I'm certainly not going to mention Henri, thought George.

"What then can I do for you?" asked Myrtle.

George looked down at his black and white saddle shoes, cleared his throat, then looked back up at Myrtle.

"The thing is . . . well, the Lutheran Women's Guild at St. James Church is having an ice cream social tomorrow evening."

Myrtle waited for him to speak, but when he didn't she said, "And?"

George cleared his throat again.

"I thought since you are new in town and all, it might be an ideal opportunity for you to meet some of the local citizens."

"That sounds like a wonderful idea," said Myrtle.

"It does?" said George, wondering if he'd heard correctly.

"It does," said Myrtle.

"And I was hoping I might escort you," said George.

"Why, I thank you so much Mr. Salmon for that most generous offer, but I feel I must decline this time. I'm not in the habit of going out with a man the first time I meet him."

"But we met yesterday," said George. "Downtown."

"We only *spoke* yesterday. We did not really meet until a few moments ago when you appeared on my doorstep. Besides, Miss O'Hearn has offered to show me around the area tomorrow, and I imagine I would be attending the social with her."

George's shoulders slumped. "I see."

"Another time?" said Myrtle.

George brightened up. "Yah, by all means, perhaps another time." He replaced his hat on his head. "Then I bid you good day, Miss Tully."

"Good day, Mr. Salmon."

As George walked his bicycle back down the path to the road, he thought, *she did say another time*. His gait quickened, and he began to softly whistle.

As soon as George was out of sight, Daisy came bounding out from the house. "So, what did he want? Did he ask you out?"

Myrtle still wasn't sure what had just taken place. She couldn't remember the last time a man had asked her for a date.

"He did," she said. "To the ice cream social tomorrow night at the Lutheran Church."

"And what did you say?" asked Daisy.

"I said no."

"No? You said no? You did hear me when I said George Salmon is the mayor of Booker Falls, didn't you?"

"Yes."

Daisy rolled her eyes. "Then I don't understand you."

"I did tell him perhaps some other time," offered Myrtle.

Daisy flopped back down in the rocking chair. "Well, that's something. Maybe there's hope for you after all."

"By the way," said Myrtle. "You're my date to the ice cream social tomorrow night."

CHAPTER SEVEN

Adolph Pfrommer removed his cravat and carefully placed it into a drawer in the dresser, then loosened the top button of his shirt. Moving to the armoire that occupied one corner of his room, he took off his suit coat, hung it on a rod and slipped on a smoking jacket.

He walked back to the dresser, looked in the mirror, rubbed a hand over his bald head, and pulled out the pocket watch his father had given him on his twenty-first birthday, a Junghans und Tobler model. Adolph's watch was one of the first ever manufactured.

He checked it against the clock on his dresser, an E. N. Welch model he'd salvaged from the trash. While it originally featured an hour strike on gong, he had removed that in order not to compete with the grandfather clock in the dining room.

Content that both timepieces showed the same time, he returned the watch to his waistcoat pocket, picked up his violin—and waited.

Minutes later the grandfather clock downstairs began to strike. Adolph nodded, continuing to do so with each strike of the hammer.

When the last chime struck at six he drew the bow over the strings and commenced playing. For the next hour he was lost in the music of his homeland, as the works of Mendelssohn, Beethoven, Bach and Mozart sprang from his instrument.

When the grandfather clock struck again, announcing seven o'clock, he laid aside the bow and violin and walked to the chest at the foot of his bed.

From it, he removed a nine-year-old bottle of Absinthe La Constantine and poured its contents into the Pontarlier glass that sat on his dresser until they reached the etched line at the bottom.

Laying an absinthe spoon across the rim of the glass, he placed a cube of sugar in it, allowing the ice cold well water from the glass he'd brought with him from downstairs to slowly drip onto it.

When the absinthe turned from green to opaque, Adolph deposited what remained of the cube into the glass and stirred the whole concoction with the spoon.

When he'd first taken up his habit shortly after moving to Quebec, he had drunk the absinthe straight. But after several unfortunate incidents in which the spirit produced disastrous results, he'd decided it would be prudent to dilute its potency.

Absinthe had been banned in the United States for the past four years, but Adolph continued to obtain it from a source in Canada, where it was still legal.

He settled into his easy chair, slipped on his eyeglasses and picked up the book he'd borrowed from the Adelaide College Library: *On the Genealogy of Morality: A Polemic,* by Friedrich Nietzsche. A devotee of the author, Adolph had read all of his works, some more than once. He was on the third reading of this book.

Leaving Germany in 1879 at the age of thirty-nine, he had made his home in Quebec for ten years before moving to Booker Falls, where he was employed as a watchmaker in the shop of Ernst Becker. When Ernst died in 1912, his son had decided to close the business and Adolph found himself unemployed at the age of seventy-one.

But he'd been prudent with his money, almost to the extreme of frugality: other than one pair of underwear purchased two years ago when Oosterman's Men's

Wear had a sale—practically giving away their merchandise in Adolph's opinion—he had not purchased any new clothes in over two decades.

He still paid Mrs. Darling the same monthly rent he first paid when he moved in in 1891: thirty-five dollars, which included all meals.

In addition to reading and playing the violin, Adolph also had an obsession with watches, of which he had accumulated a rather impressive collection over time—in earlier years, pocket watches, and more recently, wristwatches, all of them kept in six black leather cases on top of the armoire.

Life in Booker Falls had been good for Adolph—until 1917, when it became apparent that America was about to join the Allies in their fight against Germany and Austria-Hungary. For almost two years, from that fateful day on April 6, when the United States declared war, until the end of hostilities in November of the following year, he had kept a low profile, rarely venturing out into public, not even to the library to check out books or read the *Quebec Chronicle* and the *Quebec Gazette*, newspapers received at the library by mail three times each week.

By nine o'clock, the absinthe was gone. The book fell open on Adolph's lap.

He was asleep, glasses resting precariously on his nose, his nightly ritual complete.

In a few hours, he would awaken and go to bed.

CHAPTER EIGHT

"Good Lord," said Myrtle, "if I eat like this every day I'll turn into a fat pig."

Monday morning's usual fare for breakfast at Mrs. Darling's was pancakes served with real Michigan maple syrup, sausage links, fried potatoes, apple sauce, orange juice and unending cups of coffee.

"Thanks," said Daisy.

Myrtle looked at Daisy. "I didn't mean . . ."

"I'm kidding," said Daisy. "If it weren't for walking into work every day and traipsing up and down these steps, I'd be even heavier than I am."

"I don't think—"

Daisy put her hands up. "Be quiet, skinny. So, did you enjoy the social last night?"

"I did," said Myrtle. "Met a few people, ate a lot of ice cream and pie. Just warming up for breakfast this morning."

"Listen," said Daisy, "you don't start work 'til tomorrow. What are you doing today?"

"Hadn't thought about it."

"Let's go over to Red Jacket."

"Red Jacket? Why would I want to go to Red Jacket?" asked Myrtle.

"Because I *need* to go, and you're my transportation there," said Daisy.

Myrtle chuckled. "So it's not my scintillating personality you're after, is it? It's my automobile."

Daisy grinned. "You do have a 'scintillating' personality, as you put it, but, yes, you also have an automobile."

"And what's so important that we—you—have to go there?"

"To pick up my new Underwood," said Daisy.

Myrtle looked confused. "And what, may I ask, is an underwood?"

"A typewriter. An Underwood typewriter. It's a humdinger."

Now Myrtle was more confused than ever. "A typewriter that's a humdinger?"

"That means it's really good. How long were you gone from America, anyway? Come on, let's go and I'll buy you lunch at the Michigan House."

*****

"First," said Myrtle, as she and Daisy settled into the Ford, "I need to know where I can get some gasoline."

Long before reaching Booker Falls, Myrtle had been fortunate enough to come across a farm that employed a gasoline-powered tractor. The farmer had sold her enough—at a highly-inflated price, she thought—to fill her engine and her two-gallon can.

But that had been a long time ago.

"Gasoline?" said Daisy. "That would be Red Jacket."

"Red Jacket Street?"

"No, Red Jacket—the town where we're going."

"No, I mean here in town—gasoline for my automobile."

"I know you've only been in town three days, but how many automobiles have you seen since you got here?"

Myrtle shrugged. "Why, none, now that you mention it."

"That's because there are no cars in Booker Falls—except yours."

Myrtle's eyebrows went up. "No cars? Why not?"

"Guess nobody ever felt the need to have one—not when horses and bicycles will get you where you want to go."

"So, no cars . . ."

". . . no gasoline stations," said Daisy.

"How far is Red Jacket?" asked Myrtle.

"About thirty miles, give or take a few."

Myrtle's eyes grew large. "Thirty miles? I'm not sure we can get that far before we run out."

"Let's find out," said Daisy, a mischievous tone to her voice.

"But what if we *do* run out before we get there?" asked Myrtle.

"I took two apples from the kitchen. If we run out of gas, we'll pull over to the side of the road and park, find a shady place to spread our blanket, sit down and eat our apples and enjoy the scenery until some farmer comes by with his team to pull us into town."

"Are you kidding?" Myrtle couldn't imagine such a thing.

"Nope. Come on, let's get going."

Following Daisy's directions, Myrtle headed out of town toward Red Jacket, certain they would never make it there.

"I told you what brought me to Booker Falls," said Myrtle. "How about you? Why are you here? What do you do for a living? And where did you come from?"

Daisy squirmed. "Lots of questions there."

"Just answer one for now. How'd you end up here?"

"First of all," said Daisy, "I hope I haven't, as you put it, *ended up* here. I can't see spending the rest of my life in Booker Falls. But, like I told you, I'm planning on writing a novel about Yvette's murder. That's why I want this new typewriter. Also, I'll use it at the newspaper—*The Rapids*. I work there as a reporter."

"You knew about the murder before you moved here?"

"Uh, yes. I was in . . . in Detroit, working for a newspaper—"

"Oh? Which one?"

"The . . . uh, *The Chronicle*, I worked for *The Chronicle*, and I ran across an old clipping about the murder. Plus, one of the old guys who'd been there for a long time had a photograph of the crime scene. It sounded intriguing, and I'd always wanted to try my hand at fiction, so I thought—why not?"

"And three years later here you are."

"And haven't written a word yet."

Both women laughed.

"Okay, I lied," said Myrtle. "One more question: Since you work in town and don't have any transportation, why are you living way out in the country at Mrs. Darling's?"

"Oh, that's an easy question to answer: money. Everything in Booker Falls was more than I could afford. Now I have a question for you—what do you think of Henri?"

"Henri? Why, I think he's rude and obnoxious."

"Because of your run-in with him on Friday."

"I haven't seen anything to change my mind since then," said Myrtle.

"Okay, but that aside, what do you think of him?"

Myrtle shook her head. "I don't know what you mean."

"Do you think he's *attractive*? My God, woman, do I have to spell it out?"

"Do I think he's attractive?" said Myrtle. "I hadn't thought about it. No reason to."

"Why not?"

"I mean, if he were to ask me out—and I think that's what you're getting at—and I don't think he would—but if he were—there's no way I would accept."

"Why not?"

"Because I don't believe in the races mixing. Not that way, anyway."

"You mean because he's part Negro?" asked Daisy, staring at her, not sure what she was hearing.

"Yes, because he's colored," said Myrtle, keeping her eyes on the road.

"I can't believe you," said Daisy. "You're prejudiced!"

Myrtle turned and looked defiantly at Daisy. "No, I just know the way things are, that's all."

Daisy slumped back in her seat. "Unbelievable," she said.

Neither spoke again until they reached Red Jacket.

*****

Myrtle gave a sigh of relief when she saw the Shell Oil sign as they approached the edge of town. After filling the tank and her two-gallon can, she and Daisy were off. They soon found themselves on Sixth Street. Myrtle was surprised to see what looked like a railroad car bearing down on them.

"What is that?" she asked.

"The streetcar system," said Daisy. "It runs from Hancock up to Mohawk, and has a couple of spurs, too. Some day when we have more time, we'll take a trip on it. For now, let's drive around and I'll show you the town. Then we can pick up my typewriter."

If Myrtle had been surprised when she'd first arrived in Booker Falls, she was astonished at Red Jacket.

With a population of almost four thousand, the town boasted twice as many businesses as Booker Falls, with wider streets, taller buildings, and a glut both of people and automobiles jamming the downtown area.

The seat of Houghton County, which had a population of some seventy thousand people, Red Jacket was the hub of industry and commerce for miles around.

"There's the theatre," said Daisy, pointing to a large, yellowish-brown building. "It's absolutely gorgeous inside. Some time we'll come over for a play. I was here in June to see Rita Romilly in *The Bird of Paradise*. You'll love it."

Daisy instructed Myrtle to turn right onto Elm Street. Two blocks later, they passed a large, red brick building.

"See that sign at the top of the building?" said Daisy.

Myrtle looked up. The sign read, "Società Mutua Beneficenza Italiana."

"That's the Italian Hall," said Daisy. "Six years ago over seventy people died there."

"My goodness," exclaimed Myrtle. "How?"

"There was a dance and someone yelled *fire*. There wasn't any fire, but people stampeded and some were crushed to death."

"How awful."

A left, and then a block further, the towering spires of St. Paul's Catholic Church came into view. Built of the same Jacobsville Sandstone as St. Barbara's, the church had been constructed eleven years earlier. Myrtle marveled at the glorious stained glass windows.

Minutes later, they parked on Fifth Street, in front of P. Ruppe & Son's.

While Daisy picked up her new Underwood, Myrtle strolled around the store, impressed by the variety of merchandise displayed on every shelf, particularly the latest women's fashions—tubular dresses, cami-knickers—even *pants*!

"You should see Vertin's," said Daisy, when she met back up with Myrtle. "In fact, you will. It's right across the street from the Michigan House, and as soon as I put this in your car, we'll walk around the corner to get something to eat. I'm famished."

*****

Myrtle loved the Michigan House.

Just ten years old, it occupied the spot where a previous structure, a hotel and saloon, had been torn down.

Though it was only September, and not yet as cold as it would get later in the year, a roaring fire blazed in the fireplace. While they waited for their food, Myrtle studied the large ceiling mural above the enormous wooden bar, portraying a picnic where brew readily flowed.

*****

Myrtle finished the last bite of her Wild Mushroom Ravioli and picked up her napkin.

"That was utterly delicious," she said, dabbing at her mouth.

"Have you ever tasted wild mushrooms before?" asked Daisy.

"I had truffles once in France, but this was every bit as good. What was it you had again?"

"Chicken Dumpling soup."

"Yum. I'll try that next time."

*****

As they crossed the street to Vertin's Department Store, Myrtle's eyes were drawn to a coat on display in the front window.

"Look at that—it's beautiful!" she exclaimed. "I want that coat!"

"You know what kind of fur that is?" asked Daisy.

"No—I just know I want it."

"It's skunk. You know, the smelly little creature?"

"I'm sure the coat wouldn't smell," said Myrtle. "Otherwise they couldn't sell it. Let's go in."

"Besides, it's a really cheap fur," said Daisy. "You should get something like beaver, or fox."

"Nope," said Myrtle, enthusiastically. "This is the one I want."

Sewn entirely of skunk skins, the black and white striped coat hung slightly below the top of Myrtle's shoes. It was the perfect length to go with her boots. The attached hood would do an admirable job of warding off the bad weather just around the corner.

As they were getting into the car, they heard someone shout out, "Gwen! Gwen!"

Myrtle looked up to see a man, his head stuck out of a third-story window, staring at them. Daisy started to turn, then said, "Come on, let's go."

"But—do you know him?" asked Myrtle.

"No. Let's go," said Daisy. "I don't know him and, besides—my name's not Gwen."

Minutes later they were on their way out of Red Jacket.

*****

Daisy poured herself a stiff drink. No tea this time.

Was that really Billy who called to her earlier today? But why would he be in Red Jacket? How could he know she was up here in the U.P.? Mom? It's possible she could have slipped and given him the information.

She took a drink, then walked to the window and looked out onto the road that ran in front of the house.

At least it had been in Red Jacket—it would have been worse if she'd run into him here in Booker Falls. But she'd have to be careful. If it was him, it could only mean one thing: He was looking for her and he had revenge on his mind.

She gulped the rest of the drink down, walked back to the dresser and refilled the glass.

CHAPTER NINE

Giving in to Daisy's insistence, Myrtle reluctantly agreed to wear her skirt, rather than her trousers, for her first day of work, along with the white, long-sleeved blouse she'd worn as a telephone operator in France.

"Why do I have to dress up?" Myrtle had asked.

"Because you're going to be meeting the public," Daisy answered. "You're not going to be sitting in a room somewhere staring at a machine along with a dozen other women. You have to look presentable."

"But I don't have to wear the jacket, do I?" implored Myrtle.

"No, you don't have to wear the jacket. Not until winter sets in and it gets colder. Then you'll be glad you have it, believe me."

Myrtle grimaced.

*****

The first stop on Myrtle's tour of the library had been the check-out desk, where she would spend most of her day. She would soon discover that its location, facing directly toward the front door, no more than twenty feet away and located on the north side of the building, was not the ideal spot in the middle of winter.

"This is my office," said Frank, opening the door to a small room, no more than nine by nine. It was barely large enough to hold a desk and a four-drawer file cabinet. But it was Frank Mitchell's refuge to which he retreated every day—more so now that he had someone else to take care of the day to day duties of the library.

With its glass windows and sitting to the left of the check-out desk, against the west wall, the office afforded Frank a vantage point from which he could keep an eye on that side of the main room, as well as the tables in the front section.

Other than the check-out desk and the office, the only other things on the main floor were the stacks, the reading tables, the catalog desk and the restroom situated at the far back end of the room. Myrtle said a silent prayer, grateful that it was indoors.

Before starting up the metal spiral staircase that led to the second floor, they stopped at the desk that held the catalog information.

"You're familiar with the Dewey Decimal System, I presume?" asked Frank.

"I am," said Myrtle, thankful her father had introduced her to it on her sixteenth birthday, when he had taken her to the newly-opened public library in New Orleans.

At the top of the stairs, a large display case, some nine feet in length and four feet deep, greeted them.

"This is a display about the founding of Booker Falls and Adelaide College," said Frank. "Artifacts, ledgers, models of the first buildings. We're quite proud of it."

It was impressive—Myrtle had to give him that. What impressed her more was the imposing portrait of a woman that hung on the wall above the case.

"She's beautiful," said Myrtle. "Who is she?"

"That's Betsy Hutchinson Amyx," said Frank. "She was the wife of Louis Amyx, who founded Adelaide College. It was a real tragedy."

Myrtle looked at Frank. "What was?"

"She killed herself. Hung herself from their balcony. She was only twenty-three. She'd just had a baby like the week before."

"My goodness!" said Myrtle. "Why in the world would she have done that?"

"You haven't met Claude yet, have you?"

"Claude?"

"Claude Amyx, the Amyx's son. He's the custodian here at the college."

"Their son is the custodian?"

Frank nodded. "Almost thirty years, now. Claude's a dwarf, and not too bright, eh? Word is that's why Mrs. Amyx took her life—out of shame for having given birth to a dwarf."

"How horrible," said Myrtle. "So Mr. Amyx had this portrait of her put here? But Daisy told me he didn't have anything to do with the building of the library."

"He didn't," said Frank. "It was Mrs. Amyx's brother, Barnard P. Hutchinson. He had the library built as a memorial to Mrs. Amyx and had her portrait placed here. In fact, not only did he pay for the library, he supervised its construction. Let's continue on."

Along the back wall behind the display case, Myrtle saw four doors, and to the right and left, doors to two more rooms.

"What's in those rooms?" she asked.

"Mostly storage," said Frank. "We won't bother with those right now. You'll have plenty of time to see them."

Similar to the main floor, stacks and tables took up the rest of the second floor.

"Now for the vault," said Frank.

"The vault?"

"It's really a basement, but it's always been called the vault."

The vault was, hands down, Myrtle's least favorite part of the library. Cold, dank, musty, it felt like the catacombs she'd toured on one of her trips to Paris, the final resting place for some six million souls.

Here could be found papers, books, letters, documents and other material no longer considered worthy of display upstairs, but for some reason never disposed of. A string of naked bulbs ran down between each row of shelving, and along with a single small window high on each of three of the walls, provided what little light was available.

Myrtle was to discover that once winter arrived and snow began to pile up outside, the windows were no longer of any use.

One corner of the room was partitioned off to hold the boiler that heated the entire building.

A concrete floor guaranteed a stay here of any length would produce chilled feet. Oddly enough, in one corner a wooden floor approximately four hundred square feet in size had been placed over the concrete. When Myrtle asked Frank about it, he said he didn't know what its purpose was, that it was there when he first began working at the library shortly after it opened.

Once back on the main floor, Frank asked Myrtle if there was anything else she'd like to see.

"Yes," said Myrtle. "I'd like to know where Yvette Sinclair's body was found."

Frank looked at her as though she'd just assaulted him with indecent language.

"That incident is not something we speak of," said Frank.

"You were here at the time?" asked Myrtle.

"Was there anything else?" asked Frank, clearly intent on directing the conversation away from the incident that had happened some three decades earlier.

"I noticed the paintings along the walls," said Myrtle. "I'd like to take some time to see them."

When Myrtle had stopped by the library on Saturday she'd noticed the art work, twelve pieces altogether, six positioned along each of the side walls. They were all large, at least five by five, and even from a distance Myrtle could tell they were of a fine quality.

Frank's face broke into a wide smile. This was a subject he *did* enjoy talking about.

"Ah, yes, our art collection," he said. "Allow me to accompany you—I can give you some background on the artists and the works."

As they walked to the first painting, Frank said, "All the paintings were bequeathed to the library by Mr. Amyx when he passed away in 1888. I had become head librarian shortly before that, and he and I had developed a close relationship over the years."

"You knew Mr. Amyx—the man who started the college?" asked Myrtle.

"Yes, I'd met him when I became the assistant librarian twelve years earlier. That was in 1876."

"My," said Myrtle, duly impressed.

"I had just graduated from Adelaide with a degree in art history," said Frank. "Unfortunately, I soon discovered there was little demand for my expertise as far as making a living was concerned."

"I would suppose not," said Myrtle.

"Except for teaching," said Frank. "But I knew I was not cut out to be a teacher. I liked it here in Booker Falls, and at Adelaide, and when the assistant librarian position came open I jumped at the chance. I've been here ever since. And just so you know—I have no plans to retire any time in the near future."

Myrtle smiled. "And just so *you* know—I have no desire to be a librarian the rest of my life."

"There, then, that's settled. Now, let me show you what we have."

As they moved from piece to piece, Frank gave Myrtle a brief biography of each artist, none of whom she had ever heard of.

Until they came to the last two.

The first was a French landscape by Cézanne.

"Wow," exclaimed Myrtle. "He's a very famous artist. This painting must be worth a fortune."

"I don't know," said Frank. "We've never had it appraised. But I suppose you're right. Cézanne is my favorite artist."

"Why are the green areas so dark?"

"Cézanne liked to mix arsenic in with his green paint. Over time, the shade gets darker and darker."

Myrtle's mouth fell open when she saw the name of the artist of the final painting: Pierre Renoir.

"Goodness gracious," said Myrtle. "You have a Renoir here, too?"

Frank beamed. "I know. Impressive, isn't it?"

"I met him," said Myrtle, studying the painting.

"What do you mean, 'you met him'?" asked Frank.

"Last month. As I was leaving to come back home. I'd gone to Paris on my way to Cherbourg. I decided on my last day there, I'd see the Louvre. I was standing in front of a painting by Renoir when this old man came and stood next to me. He asked me what I thought of the painting. I told him I loved it. I loved all of Renoir's work.

"He bowed and introduced himself. 'I am Pierre Renoir,' he said. Of course, I didn't believe him, but I pretended like I did. We chatted for a few minutes, then went our separate ways. I walked over to a guard and asked him if he knew who the man was. 'Why, that's Monsieur Renoir,' he said. 'He's a famous artist. In fact, that's one of his pieces you were looking at with him.'

"I was flabbergasted. And now, here I am, standing and looking at another one of his works."

Frank's mouth hung open.

"You met Renoir," he managed to get out. "I thought he was dead."

"Yes, I met him," said Myrtle. "And I'll never forget it."

"What was the painting—the one you saw at the Louvre?"

"Mrs. . . . Carpenter?" said Myrtle, uncertainty in her voice.

"Mrs. Charpentier and Her Children."

"That's the one. Now, I think it's time I earned my keep. Where would you like me to begin?"

Frank gave Myrtle a list of chores, then retired to his office.

*****

In his mid-sixties, Frank Mitchell was a nice, if somewhat peculiar, man. He was more than happy to turn over the day to day running of the library to his new assistant, content to sit in his office, drink Southern Comfort and read dime novels, especially detective ones such as *The New York Detective Library* and *Old Sleuth Library.*

What he didn't like was to revive the memory of Yvette Sinclair's death.

It had been an unsettling time in his life.

*****

Over the next week, Myrtle settled into her job, becoming more familiar with where everything was and how the library operated. Almost every student who came in introduced himself or herself, as did the few townspeople.

Working five days a week, Tuesday through Saturday, ten hours a day, from eight-thirty to six-thirty, with a half hour for lunch, it wasn't possible for Myrtle to make the dinner hour at the boarding house except on the two days she was off. Mrs. Darling had promised she'd keep her meal warm for her and let her eat it in the kitchen.

She was able to have breakfast at the regular time at seven, though that meant scurrying off afterwards in order to be at work on time.

Myrtle was surprised on Thursday by Mr. Pfrommer's appearance at the library. He'd gone straight to the section where out of town newspapers were kept. She watched from the corner of her eye as he read the current issues of all the papers from Quebec.

When he left over an hour later, he glanced over at Myrtle, but gave no sign he recognized her.

Myrtle was happy when six-thirty on Saturday arrived. It had been a long time since she'd put in a full day's work, let alone five days in a row. She looked forward to dinner and a warm bath before going to bed.

Daisy had other plans.

"No, no, no," said Daisy, emphatically, shaking her head. "The band is playing tonight in the park. And we are going to be there."

"Why?"

"Because that's where the men are."

"Men? What men?"

"Eligible men," said Daisy. "You're no spring chicken, you know. You need to start thinking about your future."

"You trying to set me up?" asked Myrtle, bemused at the thought.

"No, just making you show your wares," answered Daisy.

Myrtle laughed. "My *wares*? Like I'm on the auction block?"

"Something like that. Now, change your clothes. Wear something . . . well, I was going to say *flirtatious*, but I doubt you have anything like that. Just wear whatever. Come on, it'll be fun."

*****

Daisy was right about two things: It was fun, and there were a lot of men there.

Giovanni's Italian Band, twelve members in all, had come in by way of three automobiles from Houghton to provide dance music that lasted until eleven o'clock.

Myrtle made the most of the occasion, dancing almost every dance, pausing only for refreshments. All in all, she had swung, boogied, swayed, and twirled with at least a dozen and a half men. The one who secured the most turns was George Salmon. While Myrtle spotted Henri standing off by himself, he made no effort to approach her.

Daisy herself counted nine partners during the evening.

At eleven o'clock, the band played the last number—"At The Jazz Band Ball"—and commenced packing up.

"Ready to head home?" asked Daisy. "Or did you get a better offer?"

"Actually, I received several offers—but none better than yours. Yes, let's go. I'm exhausted."

*****

After her first full week of work and an exhausting—but enjoyable—evening at the dance, Myrtle had spent most of the day Sunday on the front porch, reading and cuddling with Penrod.

By the time Monday morning came, she felt refreshed and invigorated as she went downstairs for breakfast.

Neither Henri nor Daisy had yet made an appearance. Mr. Pfrommer, as usual, was at his place, patiently waiting. He stood as Myrtle approached.

"Good morning," said Myrtle, cheerily, as she took her place at the table.

Mr. Pfrommer nodded, then sat back down. He stood again quickly, as Daisy and Henri entered the room, then waited for Daisy to be seated before taking his seat.

True to form, most of the conversation during the meal was between the two women.

Then Myrtle turned to Mr. Pfrommer.

"Mr. Pfrommer, I very much enjoyed listening to your music last night. I especially delighted in hearing the *Kreutzer Sonata*."

Mr. Pfrommer sat back in his chair, a quizzical look on his face.

"You are familiar with Herr Beethoven's verk?" he asked.

"Somewhat," answered Myrtle. "I'm not that familiar with all of his works, but that particular piece was a favorite of my mother's. She was one of the first violinists hired by the New Orleans Symphony Orchestra when it first started."

"You are from New Orleans?" asked Mr. Pfrommer.

"Yes," said Myrtle. "Born and raised there."

"A city I vould like to visit someday," said Mr. Pfrommer. "Perhaps sometime you could tell me about it."

"I would love to," said Myrtle.

Mr. Pfrommer nodded, and turned back to his pancakes.

CHAPTER TEN

By the time December arrived, Booker Falls, like the surrounding countryside, had transformed into the spectacle Myrtle envisioned when she first decided to move north: blanketed by snow.

Lots of snow.

Over four feet of snow.

The Model N was stored in Mrs. Darling's barn, and Myrtle had no expectation of seeing her car again until long after spring arrived. Fortunately, Daisy had the foresight of convincing her to have it winterized before putting it away.

Myrtle and Henri had maintained a distant, but not unfriendly, attitude towards one another.

All in all, Myrtle's life had fallen into a regular routine of work at the library five days a week, with her two days off given to reading or palling around with Daisy.

George Salmon continued to drop by from time to time to ask Myrtle out, and she continued to decline his invitations.

She'd gone with Daisy to the Red Robin Outdoor Supply store where Daisy helped her purchase a pair of snow shoes, for which Myrtle was extremely grateful. Otherwise, the two mile walk from the boarding house to the library would have proven even more exhausting than it was.

Daisy had been right about Myrtle's jacket—it was a welcome addition to her work dress.

The location of the check-out desk was such that whenever someone opened the front door a surge of cold air accompanied them, and headed straight for Myrtle. She had suggested to Frank that perhaps the desk might be relocated.

The desk had been there since the library had first opened, Frank informed her, and he saw no need to move it now.

So when Professor Corrigan, head of the English Department, bundled up against the weather, entered, his presence was preceded by an icy blast.

"Miss Tully," he said, approaching the check-out desk, "I wonder if I might impose upon you to do a favor for me."

"Of course, Mr. Corrigan," said Myrtle.

"I'm looking for a paper you might have here, possibly in the vault downstairs. Do you suppose you would be able to find it for me?"

"It would be my pleasure. Do you need it today?"

"Oh, no. Next week would be fine."

Myrtle slid a notepad and a pencil across the desk. "If you'll write down the title, I should have a chance to look for it later."

*****

Promptly at twenty-five minutes after six, Frank Mitchell emerged from his office, as he did every day.

"I'm off now. Be a good girl and lock up, will you?"

Without waiting for an answer, Frank bolted out the door, a wave of cold air rushing in behind him.

"Of course," said Myrtle, to the empty room.

She locked the door and walked back to the check-out desk, picked up the note on which Professor Corrigan had written the title of the paper he needed, grabbed her coat from the hook on the wall, put it on, and headed for the steps leading downstairs.

The string of lights provided the only illumination, as the three windows were now completely blocked by the snow outside.

Frank was claustrophobic, and so spent as little time as possible there. In fact, since the day when he'd first shown Myrtle where everything was, it had been her duty to procure whatever was required from its depths.

She hadn't minded much, except that as the weather turned colder, the room had followed suit, although it never got as cold as outside.

While she had a fair idea where the box might be that held the paper for which she was looking, it was a good thirty minutes before she laid her hands on it. Another carton stood on top of the one she wanted, and as she maneuvered hers out, the top box came crashing down, littering the floor with sheets of paper.

Myrtle jumped back, startled for a moment, then uttered a silent curse word as she knelt down to gather up the contents. Picking up the first sheet, she saw it was a letter. She returned it to the box, then scooped up a handful. As she was about to reunite those with the first one, she noticed the name of the recipient: Yvette.

The second thing she noticed was the date: February 25, 1891.

Myrtle remembered the conversation she'd had with Daisy about the young girl who'd been murdered in this very building: March 8th, 1891, Daisy had said. And her name was Yvette.

Could this be the Yvette she'd talked about? The one who was killed only a few weeks after this letter was written?

Myrtle gathered up the rest of the papers, which she could now see were also letters, returned them to the box, and replaced the lid. Laying the material she'd secured for Professor Corrigan on top, she picked up the box and proceeded up the steps, pausing to switch off the lights.

Once upstairs, she glanced at the large Ansonia clock on the wall next to Frank's office: twenty minutes after seven. She shrugged and set the box on one of the reading tables: might as well be even later than usual.

She laid her coat on the table next to the box and removed the letters. Altogether there were eighteen of them, written by a number of different people, all in English except for one that was in French.

Sorting the letters by the different handwriting, and then by date, she found they had been written by five different individuals. The one in French was signed 'Cee-cee'. Six were signed 'Mother,' another six, 'Paul', three contained only the initial 'W,' and two were unsigned.

Glancing quickly through the ones from 'Mother,' Myrtle saw they were what one would expect: news of happenings back home; who had died; who had gotten married.

Of the three missives signed merely 'W,' two were gushy love letters. The third, dated two days before the murder, was a warning of serious consequences if Yvette were to tell 'W's wife about the affair.

The two unsigned letters, written by the same hand in a flowery, decorative style—and, oddly enough, in red ink—were declarations of love, apparently from an anonymous suitor.

This girl sure got around, thought Myrtle.

The letters from 'Paul' were love letters, except for the last one, dated three weeks before Yvette's death, in which he professed his undying love for her, accused her of seeing someone else, and threatened that if he couldn't have her, no one else would.

Myrtle's eyes grew wide as she read. "Wow," she muttered. *If that wouldn't have made him a suspect, I don't know what would.*

It was the last letter, though, the one written in French, that brought Myrtle up short.

My Dear Yvette

After all we've been through, I cannot believe you would tell the administration of my condition, for if they knew, they would never allow me to graduate. As it is, my child will not be born until after commencement day, and as I do not show, they would never know of my condition. We have been through much, you and I, lovers these past two years. However, the time has now come for us to go our separate ways. You have many admirers to choose from. I know one of them will make you happy. As much as I love you, I must warn you that if you betray my confidence, I will kill you. And you know I mean it. I trust you will do the right thing, for both our sakes.

Yours

Cee-cee

Myrtle sat back and took a deep breath. *I will kill you*. Pretty strong words. Did Yvette tell? And, if so, did Cee-cee, whoever she was, follow through with her threat?

Myrtle bundled up the letters and slipped them into her rucksack. She couldn't wait to show them to Daisy.

CHAPTER ELEVEN

"Where did you find these?" asked Daisy, laying aside the last letter.

Myrtle explained how she had accidentally found the letters in the library vault.

"What are you going to do with them?"

"I suppose I should show them to Henri," said Myrtle. "After all, he is the constable. But I don't know."

"What's the problem?"

"I don't think he likes me very much."

"I wouldn't blame him," said Daisy.

"What do you mean?"

"You don't think he senses how you feel about him?"

"You mean because he's colored?" asked Myrtle.

Daisy nodded. "You go out of your way to avoid him. I don't think he can help but feel it's because of his race; because he's really a very nice fellow."

Myrtle's head drooped. "I suppose you're right. I'm not very nice, am I?"

"Regardless, as you said—he *is* the constable. And he's a good one, too."

Myrtle nodded. "Okay, but I want you there when I do."

"I wouldn't miss it," said Daisy.

*****

Henri asked the same question of Myrtle and received the same answer as Daisy as to where she'd found the letters.

"These might have been important evidence when that girl's death was being investigated," he said.

"Do you know any of the senders?" asked Daisy.

"Aside from her mother, the rest that were signed were the ones from Paul, and this Cee-cee, whoever that might be. And the initial 'W'? That could be a lot of people. I imagine this Paul is Paul Momet, who was Miss Sinclair's boyfriend at the time she was murdered. I remember reading in the file that he had an alibi for when she was killed."

"Does he still live around here?" asked Daisy.

"Yah, he owns the hardware store in town—married to Charlotte Lindsey."

"Perhaps we should go interview him," said Myrtle.

Henri looked at her quizzically. "We?"

"I *am* the one who found the letters."

"That doesn't make you a police officer—or a detective," said Henri.

"But I have military experience. That should count for something."

"Yes, that should count for something," Daisy chimed in.

Henri looked at Daisy. "What are *you* doing here anyway?"

"Daisy's writing a novel about Yvette's murder," said Myrtle. "So she has to be included in the investigation."

"Investigation?" said Henri, raising his eyebrows. "*What* investigation?"

"Now that you have this new information, you can't just ignore it," said Myrtle. "This definitely calls for a new investigation."

Henri shook his head. "Tell you what I'll do. I'll ask Jake McIntyre what he thinks."

"Who's Jake McIntyre?" asked Myrtle.

"Jake's the Prosecuting Attorney for the county. If there were an investigation, and anybody was charged, he'd be the one to prosecute."

"You'll let us know what he says?" asked Myrtle.

Henri didn't answer as he walked out of the room.

*****

Daisy was startled by the knock at her door. No one ever knocked on her door, except two or three times over the past three years when Mrs. Darling needed her.

"Who is it?"

"Daisy, it's me, Myrtle. I have something exciting to tell you."

"Oh, okay, come on in. It's not locked."

Myrtle turned the handle and gingerly went in. In the three months they'd been living in the same boardinghouse, this was the first time she'd been in Daisy's room.

A quick glance around told her Daisy was not the neatest of housekeepers. Although it was four o'clock in the afternoon, the bed had still not been made: a pile of clothes cluttered one corner of the room; and books, magazines and papers lay scattered around.

"Don't mind the mess," said Daisy, as she hurriedly removed a box from the only other chair in the room. "It's only like this . . ." she shrugged her shoulders ". . . okay, then, it's always like this."

Myrtle laughed. "Never mind. I've heard writers are notoriously messy. Listen, I have good news—Henri says he'll start an investigation. This Mr. McIntyre seems to think there's enough in the letters to at least talk with Paul Momet. Henri says he thinks McIntyre hopes it might develop into something with which he can make a name for himself. Anyway, I don't care, but the investigation is on."

"When do we go talk with Paul?"

Myrtle scrunched up her face. "That's the bad news. Henri says he's willing to let me tag along, but three's a crowd. And I had to beg him to let me go."

"I can't go?" said Daisy, slumping down in her chair.

"But I'll keep you up to date. I'll report everything we find out—promise."

"Okay, I guess that will have to do. When are you seeing him?"

"Tomorrow. Henri's picking me up at the library when I get off."

CHAPTER TWELVE

Myrtle was surprised when she walked out the front door of the library to see Henri waiting for her in a horse-drawn sleigh.

Snow had fallen all day, and while the street cleaners worked diligently to keep the downtown streets cleared, county roads received little, if any, attention. A wheeled-carriage would have gotten bogged down in the snow that blanketed everything.

In New Orleans, where Myrtle grew up, snow was a rarity. She remembered that when she was three years old, in 1895, the city had received over eight inches in forty-eight hours. She'd helped her father build a snowman in the courtyard that lasted only a few days before it had dissolved into a watery pool.

Although she'd spent a winter in France, which had received its share of snow, Myrtle had never had the occasion to ride in a sleigh. This would be her first time. But she had no intention of letting Henri know that.

She pulled the hood of her coat up over her head, both to ward off the snow and to protect against the biting wind that swirled around the building, making the air feel colder than the twelve degrees it actually was.

Henri watched as she started down the path towards the road. In spite of his dislike of her automobile, something about the woman herself intrigued him. She wasn't beautiful in the classic sense; nevertheless, he felt a strange attraction towards her. But he had a feeling she didn't like him at all.

When she drew near, Henri jumped down and ran around to her side. It was obvious he intended to help her up into the sleigh.

Myrtle frowned. She was a grown woman—she didn't need a man to help her into a sleigh. She thought she'd made that obvious months earlier, with the carriage. Still, a tiny spark in her told her maybe she didn't really mind Henri helping her.

"Cold out here tonight," said Henri, offering Myrtle his hand and helping her up.

"Here's a lap robe," he said, after taking his place beside her on the seat. "Drape it over your legs. Although with your coat, I don't know that you'll need it. What is that—skunk?"

"Yes, yes, it is," answered Myrtle, smiling and making no effort to hide the pride she felt in wearing such an unusual article of clothing.

She rubbed her hand down the lapel of the coat and pulled the lap robe further up over her. She decided that, even with her coat, the woolen robe, which sported a dark background with a cornucopia of brightly colored flowers spilling forth—red, yellow, white, purple—was a welcome addition.

"I would have expected one with more of a manly theme," said Myrtle, a teasing note to her voice.

"It's my mother's," said Henri, dryly. "I borrowed it for this evening."

"I'm sorry, I didn't—"

"Forget it," Henri interrupted her. "You can put your feet up on the foot warmer. It helps."

Myrtle looked down at her feet and saw a black metal box. "What is it?" she asked.

"A foot warmer. We put hot coals inside and it helps keep your feet warm."

Myrtle lifted her feet and placed them on the box.

"My, that does feel good," she said, thankful Henri had thought of this along with the lap robe.

Maybe he wasn't such a bad sort after all.

*****

Paul Momet's home was one of those non-descript, gray houses that Myrtle had passed coming into Booker Falls a little over three months ago.

The small porch allowed scant protection from the wind that had now picked up. The loud barking of a dog somewhere inside announced their presence, and before Henri could knock, the door opened to show a man in his late forties, hair disheveled, shoeless, dressed in jeans and an undershirt.

"Yah?" he said. "What do you want?"

"Mr. Momet?" asked Henri.

"Dat's right—who are you?"

"Constable de la Cruz," said Henri, showing Momet his badge.

Momet's demeanor changed noticeably, becoming much more agreeable.

"Constable! Come in, come on in out of da weather."

"How can I help you?" asked Paul, when they were comfortably inside, a large fire in the fireplace providing comfort from the weather raging outside. "I'm sorry—where are my manners? Please, have a seat. Something warm to drink? Hot cider? Coffee?"

"Not for me, thanks," said Henri.

"I would love some hot cider," said Myrtle, wishing their host had offered something a bit stronger.

Minutes later, Paul appeared with Myrtle's drink.

"Now, den," he said, "what can I do for you?"

"We have some questions about the death of Yvette Sinclair," said Myrtle.

Henri looked at her, a scowl on his face.

"I'm sorry," said Paul, "I din't catch your name."

Myrtle started to answer, but Henri interrupted her. “This is Miss Myrtle Tully. She’s the new assistant librarian at the college; she’s assisting me.”

“You mentioned Yvette?” said Paul.

“Yes, we’ve opened an investigation into her death,” said Henri.

Paul sat back, surprised. “Wow. Dat happened like—what? Turty years ago? I’d almost forgotten all about it.”

“Almost twenty-nine,” said Henri. “I believe you were a suspect at the time.”

Paul shrugged. “Don’t know exactly I was a suspect. Da constable, he had some questions for me.”

“And you didn’t have an alibi,” said Henri.

“Nope, not one I could prove, anyways. I was out fishing on da Kennekuk Lake da night Yvette got murdered. I wasn’t even in town.”

“And no one could confirm that,” said Henri.

“Nope. Din’t make no difference, though. Constable Barnoble din’t have no evidence dat I’d done da crime, ’cause I din’t.”

“Except you threatened her,” Myrtle jumped in.

“Threatened her? Shoot, no, I never threatened her. Where’d you get dat idea, eh?”

Henri pulled the letter from his inside jacket pocket and handed it to Paul.

“This letter, dated three weeks before Miss Sinclair’s death—you said if you couldn’t have her, no one could.”

“Oh, heck, year, I remember dis now,” said Paul, when he finished reading. “I was really ticked off at her. But I din’t mean I’d do anything to her.”

“Yet three weeks later, she was murdered,” said Henri.

“Not by me! By den I din’t have no reason to kill her, even if I did in da first place—which I din’t. And as far as being threatened, she was da one who threatened me."

"Oh?" said Myrtle.

"Yeah, 'cause a week after I sent her dat letter, I met Charlotte."

"Charlotte, your wife?" asked Henri.

"Yeah, dat Charlotte. I met Charlotte and it was love at first sight. When I went to tell Yvette about it, she got all mad, said she'd cut my heart out if I din't stop seeing her. I told Yvette get her knife ready, 'cause Charlotte and I was getting hitched."

"And I guess you did," said Henri.

"Yep—da next week. We run off to Marquette and got married by a JP. Den da next week I took off fishing, 'cause I din't have no job. And dat's when Yvette went and got killed."

"I don't suppose anyone can confirm you met with Yvette," said Myrtle.

"No, but you can see Charlotte and me is married. And look here—on da wall. Here's our marriage license with da date on it. Charlotte put it up dere as a reminder to me not to do no funny stuff."

Henri stood and walked over to the framed certificate. The date was February 28, 1891, eight days before Yvette's death.

"I don't understand why da constable never questioned Yvette's roommate," said Paul.

"She had a room—" Myrtle started to speak but Henri interrupted her.

"She had a roommate?" he said. "What was her name?"

Myrtle gave Henri a dirty look, but he didn't seem to notice.

"I don't know—I never met her. But I know she had one. Da night I went over to tell Yvette it was over between me and her, her roommate was dere, and dey was having an argument. I heard it from da hallway, so I waited 'til da roommate left before I went in. I guess it wasn't da best time to break da news to Yvette right after she'd just had dat row, but I din't want to wait no longer."

"What were they arguing about?" asked Henri.

Paul shook his head. "I don't know for sure, but I think it was about someone Yvette was seeing. I wasn't no fool, eh? As you can see from my letter, I knowed she was seeing other men. At this point, though, me being with Charlotte, I din't much care.

"Anyway, when da other girl left da room, I turned my back so she wouldn't see who I was."

"Is your wife available that we might ask her some questions?" asked Henri.

"Right now she's upstairs with one of our grand-kids. Oh, wait, here she comes."

Henri and Myrtle turned to see a woman coming down the stairs cradling a baby in one arm. A good-looking woman when she was younger, Charlotte Momet, after bearing and raising five children, now looked merely old and tired.

"Who are these people, Paul?" she asked when she reached the bottom of the stairs.

Paul explained who Myrtle and Henri were and why they were there.

"I have one question, Mrs. Momet," said Henri. "Can you verify that your husband was fishing at Kennekuk Lake the night Miss Sinclair was murdered?"

"Well, as I'm sure you know, I weren't there. And I couldn't swear Paul was, neither. But he said he was, and when he come home Tuesday night, he brung about thirty pounds of walleye and perch . . ." Charlotte cast a disapproving eye at her husband. ". . . that *I* had to clean, as I recall. I reckon he must have been there, eh, else I don't know where else he'da gotten those fish."

"Okay, then," said Henri. "I guess that's all the questions I have for now."

"Anytime, Constable," said Paul. "And I hope you do catch da son-of-a-bitch who killed her. No matter how things ended between us, Yvette and I were real close dere for a while."

A harrumph from his wife caused Paul to turn to her. She had a scowl on her face.

"Well, *kinda* close," he said.

*****

"Where do we go from here?" asked Myrtle, when she and Henri were seated back in the sleigh.

"Unless we can discover the identity of the other letter writers, I'm not sure there's much more we can do."

"That's it? We just give up?"

"Unless you have another suggestion."

Myrtle thought for a minute. She didn't have any other suggestion.

"I guess not. I have a question, though."

"Shoot."

"Even though Mr. Momet owns the hardware store, it's pretty obvious from his house and how it's furnished he doesn't have a lot of money. Yet I noticed the floor in his front room was really nice wood—hardwood?"

"Yes, that was hardwood, probably cherry. But did you notice the large rug that covered most of the floor?"

Myrtle nodded.

"Underneath that rug was undoubtedly cheap pine. A lot of people do that up here. Make most of the floor out of pine, except for the area around the walls, then get a rug to cover the cheap wood. Makes them feel a little richer."

"That's a new one on me."

"It's too late to get dinner at Mrs. Darling's," said Henri. "Are you hungry?"

Myrtle looked at Henri. Was he asking her out on a date?

"I am," he said, without waiting for her answer. "I've hardly eaten all day. We could stop at Miss Madeline's. I'm sure she's still open."

"Okay," said Myrtle, reluctantly. "But only if we go Dutch."

"Of course," said Henri. "I wouldn't have it any other way. And one other thing."

"Yes?" said Myrtle.

"Let me ask the questions from now on. I *am* the constable, you know."

Myrtle smiled. "Of course you are."

CHAPTER THIRTEEN

Myrtle did not consider herself to be a very good Catholic.

Since the untimely death of both of her parents some five years earlier, her attendance at Mass had been sporadic, to say the least, mostly Easter and Christmas and sometimes not then. Her visits to the cathedrals in France had been strictly as a tourist.

She was no longer a virgin, sometimes ate meat on Friday, and could not remember the last time she'd taken communion, choosing to abstain even when she had been at church, because she didn't feel worthy.

As for her rosary: she didn't know where it was, or if she still had one.

Her worst transgression, though, at least in her opinion, was that it had been seven years since her last confession.

But since this was her first Christmas since arriving in Booker Falls, she decided to attend the Christmas Eve Mass. Besides, she was burning with curiosity as to what the inside of St. Barbara's looked like.

She thought of asking Daisy to accompany her, but remembered from their conversation months ago that Daisy was not a church-goer.

Though Wednesday was a normal day for the library to be open, Frank had closed the doors at noon and sent Myrtle home. She'd spent the rest of the day doing laundry, using Mrs. Darling's new Happy Days washing machine, of which the old lady was exceedingly proud.

Up to now, Mrs. Darling had washed Myrtle's clothes as the need arose, but Myrtle wanted the experience herself.

After two loads, she decided she'd be content to let Mrs. Darling handle that chore for her in the future, a task the old lady was happy to do.

Hanging the last garment up on the line that stretched the length of the closed-in back porch, Myrtle glanced at her watch and saw she had but thirty minutes until dinner.

Taking the steps two at a time, she bounded upstairs to the bathroom, washed her face, brushed her teeth and her hair, and at three minutes before five was in her chair at the table, for a change, not the last one to arrive, beating both Daisy and Henri.

But not Mr. Pfrommer.

As with the previous meals, the only conversation was mostly between Myrtle and Daisy. But when Myrtle mentioned going to church, Henri looked up.

"Which one?" he asked.

"St. Barbara's," said Myrtle.

"I attend St. Barbara's," said Henri. "I'd be happy to give you a lift."

Daisy looked down at her plate, a knowing grin on her face.

Myrtle stared at Henri, too startled to speak. Finally she said, "That would be nice."

"I have to go over to my office afterwards," said Henri, "to finish up some paperwork."

"That's no problem," said Myrtle. "I'll enjoy the walk back."

Minutes later, upstairs, Daisy came bouncing into Myrtle's room. "Ooh la la," she said, batting her eyelids.

"What's ooh la la?" asked Myrtle, a rosy glow coming to her cheeks.

“You’ve got a date with Henri,” said Daisy, flopping down on the bed.

“I’d hardly call it a date,” huffed Myrtle. “He’s giving me a ride to church. I don’t intend to sit with him.”

“Of course not, because he’s too ugly for you to be seen with.”

“Oh, that’s not it and you know it,” said Myrtle. “Besides, he’s—he’s . . .”

“He’s what?” said Daisy.

“Nothing,” said Myrtle. “Now, get out of here—I have to get dressed.”

“I thought you *were* dressed,” said Daisy, running her eyes up and down Myrtle’s plaid shirt and khaki colored trousers.

“I’m dressing for church,” said Myrtle.

“I know what you’re dressing for,” said Daisy, as she made a hasty flight out the door to avoid the brush flying across the room. “And it sure ain’t the church.”

*****

Myrtle walked out the front door and saw Henri’s sleigh out front—but no Henri. Quickly, she strode down the path and climbed up into the passenger seat. Minutes later, Henri emerged from the house.

“I would have helped you up,” he said, obviously perturbed.

“I’m sure you would have,” said Myrtle, “but I’m quite capable of getting into a sleigh by myself, thank you.”

That was the extent of the conversation on the trip to the church.

*****

Myrtle found the interior of St. Barbara’s to be as impressive as the exterior.

While the church did not compare in size or opulence with St. Louis Cathedral in New Orleans or

Paris's Sainte Chapelle, or any of the other grand cathedrals in those two cities—many of which Myrtle had visited— nor with any of the local churches she would see over the coming years, namely St. Anne's and St. Paul the Apostle, both in Red Jacket, and St. Joseph's in Lake Linden, she would always believe St. Barbara's to be the best.

Completed in 1892 at a cost of fifty thousand dollars, the church featured a curved cathedral ceiling that rose forty feet above the main floor. Niches flanking the circular chancel held statues of Joseph and Mary on one side and St. Barbara on the other. A fifteen-foot-long crucifix hung suspended above an altar made of the same material as the exterior of the church, while an elevated pulpit some eight feet on one side allowed the priest a commanding view of the congregation.

A balcony at the rear held a choir loft along with a four-hundred-pipe organ with ten ranks.

What intrigued Myrtle most were the eight stained glass windows, four on either side of the nave, depicting the life of St. Barbara.

Almost every seat was filled. Myrtle squeezed in next to a young mother trying, with limited success, to control two young boys. Henri had left as soon as he'd secured Jessie, to join a group of men.

The Mass was long—as Catholic services were wont to be—but Myrtle felt a sense of peace being there, hearing the Word of God preached, participating in the liturgy. Still, she did not take communion. Maybe after she made confession—if she ever did—she'd be ready, she thought.

Following the service, she lit two votive candles, one for each of her parents.

As she prepared to leave, the priest, a middle-aged man with a pleasant face, stopped her.

"I haven't seen you here before," said the priest. "I'm Father Fabien."

Myrtle stuck out her hand. "Myrtle Tully," she said. "I'm relatively new in town."

Myrtle went on to tell the priest about her new job and her lodging with Mrs. Darling.

"A fine woman," said Father Fabien. "But not a very committed church-goer, I fear."

"The story of my life, too, I'm afraid, Father. But maybe I'll do better now. St. Barbara's is a beautiful church."

"As was St. Barbara," said Father Fabien. "She's the patron saint of miners, you know."

"I did not," said Myrtle.

"Well, Miss Tully, it's been a pleasure meeting you. Have a very nice day."

"I have a question," said Myrtle.

"Oh, what is that?"

"Where can I buy a rosary? I think I've misplaced mine."

"I know Mrs. Turner has them at her book store. But come with me."

Father Fabien led Myrtle back to the vestry where he removed a rosary from a small drawer.

"I think this one will serve you," he said, handing it to Myrtle. "It's a St. Barbara rosary. See her figure in the medallion?"

The rosary was made of white wooden beads that had specks of red on them. The medallion showed the standing figure of a woman, St. Barbara, in a gown, a halo around her head.

"Yes, thank you," said Myrtle. "What kind of beads are these?"

"White pine," said Father Fabien.

"And the red specks?" asked Myrtle.

"Originally the beads were painted red. But over the years they were rubbed so much the paint came off. Mrs. Rumbaugh was a very pious woman."

"This was her rosary?"

Father Fabien nodded. "Yes. She passed away a few months ago. She had no family, so she asked me to pass this along to someone who could use it."

"Well, I will certainly cherish it," said Myrtle.

"*And* use it," said Father Fabien, smiling.

Myrtle returned his smile. "Yes, Father—*and* use it."

CHAPTER FOURTEEN

Myrtle was pleasantly surprised when she walked out of the church to find George Salmon sitting on a bench across the street in front of St. James, snow swirling down around him. As soon as he spotted her, he jumped up.

"Mr. Salmon," said Myrtle.

"Miss Tully," said George, tipping his hat.

"You look lonely out here. Were you waiting for me?"

"I was," said George. "I mean, I am. I was hoping I might walk you home."

"What makes you think I don't already have transportation?" asked Myrtle.

George looked around at the empty street. "The street appears to be deserted," he said. "Perhaps your 'transportation' tired of waiting."

Myrtle laughed. "No, I'm kidding. I was planning on walking. Certainly, I would be happy to have your company."

As they walked, George asked Myrtle how she'd enjoyed both the service and the church.

"I felt very moved by the service," she said. "It's been a while since I've been at Mass. Father Fabien is an excellent speaker. And the church is beautiful."

They continued talking about the service, then George asked, "How are you getting along with the other boarders at Mrs. Darling's?"

Myrtle smiled. She was pretty sure George's interest lay primarily in how she was 'getting along' with Henri.

"Daisy and I have become best friends," she said. "I enjoy listening to Mr. Pfrommer's violin playing. He's quite accomplished. And Mrs. Darling—well, she *is* a darling. She's like a mother to me."

"And Henri?" said George. "How do you get along with Henri?"

"For the most part, we manage to stay out of each other's way," said Myrtle.

"I see," said George.

They walked for a while without speaking before George broke the silence.

"I was in Mr. Pfrommer's room once."

Myrtle stopped and looked at George. "You were?" she said, a hint of disbelief in her voice.

"Oh, yah. You probably know he was a watchmaker. He worked for my Uncle Becker, my mother's brother, until the shop closed up some years back. He has an extensive collection of watches, and he had recently obtained a rather fine specimen, a large Swiss silver pivoted detent pocket chronometer by Mathile he wanted me to see. He keeps them in six black cases on the top of his armoire."

Myrtle was impressed. "You seem very knowledgeable about watches."

"I'm not just a pretty face, you know, eh?" replied George, smiling.

*****

Christmas Day breakfast at Mrs. Darling's boarding house was always a special occasion: baked apples with sweet cream; broiled smelts with tartar sauce; creamed potatoes; ham omelets; cinnamon rolls; buttered toast; and pancakes with maple syrup, all washed down with good, strong coffee.

Afterwards, Henri departed for the service at St. Barbara's with Mrs. Darling. As a gesture of appreciation for the sumptuous repast their landlady had prepared, Daisy and Myrtle volunteered to wash and dry the dishes and clean up the kitchen.

Mr. Pfrommer, as usual, retired to his room.

"Okay," said Daisy, when she and Myrtle were finally alone in the kitchen. "Let's hear it. I've been dying to know."

Myrtle's brow furrowed. She had no idea what Daisy was talking about.

"That particular night in Paris," said Daisy. "You said you'd tell me. So tell me."

Myrtle grinned. "You really want to hear it?"

"You know I do!" said Daisy. "Now, come on."

"Okay—but only if you wash. I'll dry."

Daisy's head bobbed up and down. "Okay, okay, I will."

"I'd gone to this cabaret on Boulevard de Clichy, the Le Chat Noir, with three of the girls I worked with. We spent the evening drinking cheap wine, listening to musicians and poets, most of whom, to be perfectly honest, weren't very good.

"Somewhere in the evening we were joined by three men. Two of them were French—I have no idea what their names were—and the third was an Englishman: Thomas. He'd come to Paris before the war to study at the École des Beaux-Arts. Anyway, Thomas and I—well, we hit it off—and we ended up going back to his place. I knew I'd had too much to drink and I'd never make it back to the house where we were staying.

"He lived just down the street from the cabaret: number eleven, Boulevard de Clichy. I'll never forget that address."

Suddenly Myrtle was silent. She had stopped drying the dishes, and Daisy had stopped washing them as well.

"Well?" said Daisy, after a few moments went by. "What happened? Did you—you know—did you . . .?"

Myrtle grinned—and nodded. "Twice, in fact."

"You devil, you!" exclaimed Daisy. "So what happened then?"

"Morning came, I got dressed, and took a taxi back to the boarding house."

Daisy frowned. "That's it? Whatever happened to Thomas?"

Myrtle shrugged. "I don't know. Never saw or heard from him again."

"But he must have made quite an impression if you remember the address of his apartment."

Myrtle laughed. "Oh, I remember it well; but not because we made love there or that he lived there."

"What then?"

"It was the drawing on the wall."

"The drawing on the wall?"

"As I was leaving in the morning, I noticed this strange painting on the wall, just shapes and figures—nothing real. I asked Thomas if it was his. He said no, it was done by someone who had lived in the apartment about ten years earlier: Pablo Picasso."

"Pablo Picasso? *The* Pablo Picasso?"

"One and the same."

"Wow!" said Daisy. "So do you ever wonder what happened to him?"

"Picasso? No, I—"

"No, not Picasso!" said Daisy. "Thomas. Do you ever wonder what happened to Thomas?"

Myrtle shook her head. "No idea. Maybe he's still in Paris. I don't know."

*****

Once all the dishes had been washed, dried, and put away, Daisy and Myrtle moved into the parlor and spent the next hour playing Rook.

They had just finished their game and set up the Monopoly board when Henri and Mrs. Darling returned.

"Oh, good," said Daisy. "You're just in time. Come join us in a game."

"Sorry, dearie, but I can't," said Mrs. Darling. "I've got to fix lunch and den get da dinner started.

Both Myrtle and Daisy groaned—more food!

"I'm not sure I can eat anything ever again," said Myrtle.

"But, Henri, you'll join us, won't you?" implored Daisy.

Henri shrugged and sat down at the table.

"I must warn you," he said. "I'm ruthless."

True to his word, in less than ninety minutes, Henri had bankrupted both women.

"All finished?" asked Mrs. Darling, entering the room. "Wonderful. Lunch in five minutes."

*****

Myrtle and Daisy were both grateful the noon meal was a light one: tomato soup and grilled cheese sandwiches. But they knew fortune would not be as kind to them for dinner, as they had peeked into the kitchen to see all the preparations Mrs. Darling was undertaking.

*****

That evening, Mr. Pfrommer took seconds of everything—turkey, cranberry sauce, mashed potatoes, green beans, creamed corn, and a slice of each of the pies—pecan and apple—while it was all Daisy and Myrtle—even Henri—could do to finish one serving.

Afterwards, Mrs. Darling invited everyone into the parlor to decorate the tree Henri had cut down earlier that day, not tall but very full. She hauled out box after box of brightly colored balls, spheres, crosses, angels, a miniature harp, and cotton-pressed and spun ornaments: fruits and vegetables, elves and snowmen, donkeys, cows, and sheep.

Once all the decorations were carefully placed, the tree was strewn with tinsel or, as Mr. Pfrommer called it, *lametta*.

Then it was time for hot egg nog and stollen and the gifts Mrs. Darling had for each of them, scarves she'd knitted herself. She was moved to tears when Myrtle gave her the present she and Daisy and Henri, even Mr. Pfrommer, had gone together to buy her: dangly earrings, each with a cluster of sixteen natural blue moonstones in gold settings.

"Oh, my," she said through her tears. "You shouldn't have."

"Oh, yes, we should have," said Myrtle.

"You're like a mother to us," said Daisy.

"Well, perhaps not to Mr. Pfrommer," said Myrtle. "But I know he thinks very highly of you." She looked at Mr. Pfrommer, who nodded, but said nothing.

"Now it's time to sing," said Mrs. Darling, wiping the last of the tears from her face.

For the next hour, they joined together, singing carols while Mr. Pfrommer accompanied them on his violin following a minimum of urging from Mrs. Darling.

CHAPTER FIFTEEN

Daisy stood on the porch, cigarette in hand, watching the light flurry of snowflakes as they fluttered to earth. The ground was already covered with a foot and a half of snow, but there'd been no significant additional accumulation in the past three days. Today, however, the sky looked angry, as though it was in a foul mood.

We're going to get a lot more of this stuff, thought Daisy, as she flicked the butt out into the yard. Then she remembered Mrs. Darling's dislike of her habit. She sighed, pulled the shawl around her shoulders and scurried down the steps. She waded through the calf-high snow to where the butt had landed, picked it up, retreated back into the warmth of the house and headed upstairs for a nap.

When she awoke an hour later, she got up and looked out the window. The snow had picked up in intensity.

Minutes later, she knocked on Myrtle's door, but there was no answer. *She should be home by now,* thought Daisy. Maybe she was downstairs.

"Mrs. Darling, have you seen Myrtle?" asked Daisy, finding her landlady in the kitchen, cleaning the stove. "She's not in her room, not in the parlor, either."

"Nah, I haven't," replied Mrs. Darling. "She's late today."

Daisy returned to the parlor and plopped down in the wingback chair that faced the window and waited. Mrs. Darling soon joined her.

*****

Daisy glanced nervously at the mantle clock, for the tenth time in the past fifteen minutes. Finally, she could no longer contain her concern.

"Something's wrong, I know it," she blurted out. "Something's seriously wrong."

She looked at Mrs. Darling, who was sitting by the fireplace, wringing her hands.

"I fear you're right, dear," said Mrs. Darling.

"I'm going to get Henri," said Daisy.

Moments later, Daisy was knocking furiously on Henri's door.

When he finally opened it, he looked irritated.

"What do you want?" he asked, gruffly.

"It's Myrtle. She's not home yet."

"What time is it?" asked Henri.

"After nine. She should have been home well over an hour ago. We're worried something's happened to her. The wind's whipping the snow around out there—it's like a blizzard."

Henri walked to his window and looked out to a world of whiteness.

"It *is* a blizzard," he said. "Let me get my coat and I'll be right down."

A few minutes later, he stood in the parlor, wearing a heavy raccoon coat that hung down below his knees. Mr. Pfrommer, hearing the commotion, had appeared as well.

"She's usually never this late, is she?" asked Henri of no one in particular.

"Never," said Mrs. Darling. "Unless she lets me know she'll be late."

"I'll go look for her," said Henri.

"I'll go with you," said Daisy.

Henri started to protest but decided that four eyes were better than two, and two voices better than one.

"Alright, Daisy, you come."

"I, as vell," said Mr. Pfrommer.

"You should stay here," said Henri, "and keep Mrs. Darling company, so that she doesn't get too upset." He wasn't sure that a man almost eighty might not be more of a hindrance than a help.

Mr. Pfrommer nodded.

Henri pulled the hood of his coat up over his head.

"Take da toboggan from da barn," said Mrs. Darling. "Just in case."

"I'll get my coat," said Daisy.

"And don't forget your chook," said Mrs. Darling.

Henri and Daisy headed off towards the library, Henri pulling the toboggan behind them, each holding a lighted lantern.

Daisy had been right about the weather. The wind swirled around them, causing the snow that was lifted from the ground to clash with that coming down, producing a white-out effect. It was impossible to see more than five feet in front of them. In addition, the actual temperature of ten seemed more like ten below—or worse.

As they walked along, no easy matter in over two feet of snow, even with snowshoes, they called out Myrtle's name.

*****

Myrtle huddled against the base of the maple tree, her hood pulled up over her head, her scarf covering her face in a vain attempt to ward off the biting snow that felt like pin pricks stinging her.

She had no idea where she was.

It had been difficult enough, slogging her way through the drifts that were piling up, even before the strap on her snowshoe broke. Unable to keep it on, she had removed the other one and, carrying them both, attempted to make her way on foot, hoping she was going in the direction of the boarding house.

Then she stepped off a hillock, lost her balance and tumbled into the snowbank. She'd tried to stand up, but had fallen again. She'd sprained her ankle and couldn't put any weight on it.

To make matters worse, she now had no idea in which direction she should be heading.

Spotting the maple some twenty feet away, she'd dragged herself to its base and hunkered down, trusting that either someone would come by to help or the wind and snow would abate. But even if the latter were to happen, she realized, there was no way she could get back on her own.

She'd have to wait and hope.

*****

"Myrtle!" Daisy called out.

"Myrtle!" Henri echoed her.

They'd been searching for over thirty minutes without any success. The only living creature they'd seen had been a rabbit.

"Henri, I'm really worried," said Daisy, as she pulled the collar of her coat further up around her neck.

"We'll find her, don't worry."

"What if we get all the way to the library and we haven't found her?"

"Then we'll start back. I won't give up until we find her."

Twenty minutes later, they reached the library and found it locked.

"All right," said Henri. "She's somewhere between here and the house. How are you doing?"

Daisy was near collapse herself, but she wasn't about to admit it.

"Fine," she said. "Let's go find her."

Shouting out Myrtle's name, they began retracing their steps.

*****

Myrtle shook her head. She would not allow herself to fall asleep. If anyone was looking for her, she needed to be able to hear if they called out her name.

But it was so cold. And sleep was so inviting.

Myrtle took hold of her rosary, which she'd worn as a necklace since receiving it from Father Fabien, and said a silent prayer.

Then she heard it: a faint voice, somewhere in the distance. Had someone called her name?

Myrtle.

Myrtle forced herself to sit up. She pulled the hood back from her head.

Myrtle.

There it was again. Someone was definitely calling her name.

"Over here!" she cried out. "I'm over here!"

Henri stopped short. "Did you hear something?"

Daisy stopped as well and listened. "I don't hear anything."

They stood still, ears straining to hear against the wind, whistling and swirling around them.

Then they heard it. A faint cry: "Over here!"

"That's her!" Daisy cried out. "That's her!"

Henri started off towards the sound, Daisy struggling to keep up with him.

"Over here!" cried Myrtle, hoping her voice could be heard over the wind which had picked up in intensity.

Suddenly two figures appeared in front of her, like apparitions out of a fog.

"Myrtle!" Daisy cried out. "Are you all right?"

Myrtle began to cry, the tears forming rivulets of ice as soon as they left her eyes.

"Now," she mumbled. "I am now."

With Daisy's help, Henri lifted Myrtle onto the toboggan.

"Let's go home," he said.

*****

"Da doctor says she'll be okay," said Mrs. Darling, coming down the stairs. "He wants her to stay home for a few days."

"I was so worried," said Daisy. Her eyes filled with tears.

"We found her and she'll be fine," said Henri.

"Thank you," sobbed Daisy, wrapping her arms around Henri. "Thank you."

CHAPTER SIXTEEN

By the time Claude Amyx had turned three, it was apparent that, in addition to his dwarfism, he was "slow-witted," as it was referred to in those days.

Louis, knowing that when he passed away, his son would require the assistance of others, created a trust to provide funds for the hiring of a caretaker until the boy turned eighteen. He also specified that the trust he set up for the college required that Claude be allowed to live out his life in the carriage house, and that he have a job at the institution for as long as he lived.

For over thirty years, Claude had served as the campus janitor, taking care of cleaning the buildings and grounds and occasionally making simple repairs.

Because of his two conditions, many students—and not a few of the faculty—had, over the years, referred to him as "Creepy" Claude, though never in his presence.

At four foot four and weighing one hundred and fifty pounds, Claude was unusually strong for his size. He once carried an injured six-month-old calf that weighed about the same as he did, half a mile from where he'd found it in a creek bed, back to its barn.

Myrtle had seen Claude numerous times in the three months that she'd been at Adelaide, but had never had an occasion to interact with him. She remembered Daisy had mentioned him as one of the two suspects in Yvette's murder. She decided to make it a point to have a conversation with him.

She watched as Claude ran his broom over the floor of the library—the room at the moment devoid of any other people. She looked around for the heaviest object she could find: a table.

"Claude!" Myrtle called out to him. "Could you help me here for a moment?"

Claude stopped what he was doing and looked at Myrtle. He carefully propped his broom against one wall and wobbled over to her in the curious gait he had.

"Missus?" he said, when he reached her.

"Claude, I'm Miss Tully. I'm the assistant librarian."

"Yah, missus, I know who you are."

"Although I've seen you around, we've never been formally introduced."

Myrtle held out her hand. Claude hesitated, then gently took it, but quickly let go.

"Claude, I need some help moving this table."

Claude looked at the table, sizing it up.

"I'll take one end," said Myrtle, "if you'll take the other. We need to move it a few feet to the right."

Claude nodded, then picked up one end and together they moved the table.

"Claude, how long have you been here at Adelaide?"

Claude thought for a moment. "All my life," he said. "My papa started da college, you know."

Myrtle nodded. "I know. That was a long time ago. So you were here when Miss Sinclair was murdered."

Claude looked confused. He scratched his chin.

"In 1891. The young girl who was strangled to death right over there in that corner," said Myrtle, pointing.

Claude looked, and an expression of realization came to his face.

"Oh, yah," he said. "I remember now—long time ago."

"Yes, it was. As I understand it, you're the one who found her."

Claude nodded. “She was dead.”

“I also understand the authorities thought you might have done it.”

A panicked look came over Claude’s face.

“No, no—I didn’t do it! She already dead when I find her. Not me, not me!”

“No, it’s all right,” said Myrtle, realizing she’d upset him. “I know you didn’t do it. The authorities know it, too. Tell me this—when you found Miss Sinclair, was she lying on her back or was she face down?”

“On her back. I shook her to see if she was asleep, but she didn’t move. I stuffed da scarf in my shirt and went to Mr. Wilfred’s home to tell him.”

Myrtle stiffened. “Scarf? What scarf?”

“She had a scarf ’round her neck,” said Claude. “It pretty. She didn’t need it no more—she was dead.” He looked down at the floor. “I guess maybe I shouldn’t of took it.”

“What did the scarf look like?”

“Black, with white circles—big white circles.”

“Like polka dots?” asked Myrtle.

Claude shrugged. “I don’t know polka dots.”

“What did you do with the scarf, Claude?”

“Still have it. In my house.”

A tingle of excitement ran through Myrtle. No mention had been made of any scarf!

“Can I see the scarf, Claude?”

Claude thought for a moment. “I guess.”

When Claude didn’t move, Myrtle said, “Can I see it now?”

Claude nodded, then turned and left.

A scarf, thought Myrtle, excited at this new development. *That’s something new!*

Fifteen minutes later, Claude reappeared and laid the scarf on Myrtle’s desk.

"Claude, may I keep this for a little while?" asked Myrtle.

Claude frowned and for a few moments didn't say anything. Then he said, "I guess so. But I'll need it back."

"Of course," said Myrtle, though she thought it unlikely that would ever happen.

*****

Myrtle thought Daisy might be in her usual place on the porch when she returned to the boarding house, but she wasn't. Nor was she in her room.

She found her in the kitchen, drinking a glass of milk and eating an oatmeal cookie.

"Didn't you have dinner?" Myrtle asked, teasingly. She knew Daisy harbored a voracious appetite.

Daisy grimaced. "Yes, but I was still hungry."

"I have something," said Myrtle.

"What?"

Myrtle held out the scarf.

"What's this? A gift?" asked Daisy.

"Better," said Myrtle. "Evidence."

"Evidence? Evidence of what?"

"This is the scarf Yvette Sinclair was wearing when she was murdered," said Myrtle, jumping up and down in excitement.

"What! What are you talking about?" asked Daisy. "There was no mention of a scarf in the official police report."

"That's because Claude took it before the constable showed up," said Myrtle, smugly, dropping the scarf onto the kitchen table.

"Claude? Creepy Claude, who works at the college?"

"That's the one," said Myrtle, as she ladled out a bowlful of the beef stew Mrs. Darling had kept warming for her on the stove. "Claude Amyx, the guy who found the body. He took the scarf."

"Why would he do that?"

"Because it was pretty."

Daisy picked up the scarf and studied it. "Wow, this is huge. You've got to give it to Henri."

"I suppose so," said Myrtle, taking a spoonful of stew. "You realize, this might be the murder weapon."

Daisy dropped the scarf, a shocked look on her face.

*****

Henri was not as excited about the scarf as Myrtle had been.

"Well, yes, it's new evidence, but I don't see how having it or knowing about it brings us any closer to knowing who committed the crime. But I'll keep it in the file."

Myrtle thought for a moment. "I guess I don't either," she said, finally. "I know Claude is expecting me to return it to him. What shall I tell him, if you're keeping it?"

"Tell him he won't be getting it back. It's evidence. He shouldn't have had it in the first place."

CHAPTER SEVENTEEN

"Is Mr. Mitchell in?"

Myrtle looked up. She'd been so immersed in the weekly newspaper from Quebec that she hadn't heard the front door open.

Before her stood one of the most beautiful women she'd ever seen.

In her mid-forties, Christiane Picot could have passed for thirty: copper-colored skin and long, flowing black hair set off a pair of blazing emerald eyes. Her body, slender but with an ample bosom, sparked a hint of jealousy in Myrtle.

"I'm sorry," said Myrtle. "I didn't hear you come in."

Christiane smiled: the effect of gleaming white teeth against her dark skin was stunning.

"Mr. Mitchell—is he in?"

"Oh . . . oh yes, I'm sure he is. I'll just—"

"That's all right—I know where his office is."

Before Myrtle could say anything, Christiane turned and headed towards Frank Mitchell's office.

Twenty minutes later, she emerged and swept out the front door. Frank followed her as far as the front desk.

"Mr. Mitchell," said Myrtle, "who was that gorgeous woman?"

"She *is* beautiful, isn't she?" Frank answered. "That, my dear, is Miss Christiane Picot, the Dean of Students here at Adelaide."

*****

When Myrtle got home, she found Daisy in her customary place on the front porch in the rocking chair, enjoying a cup of tea—enhanced, of course, from her flask.

Even though she was hungry—the one pasty she'd taken for lunch had only lasted until eleven o'clock—Myrtle decided to join Daisy. No sooner had she sat down than Mrs. Darling appeared with a cup of tea and a plate of cookies.

"Figured you could use dis," said Mrs. Darling. "Your dinner will still be waiting when you're ready."

"How was your day?" asked Daisy after Mrs. Darling disappeared back inside.

"Daisy, I saw the most amazingly beautiful woman today," said Myrtle, sipping the tea.

"And who might that be?"

"Mr. Mitchell said she was Miss Picot, the Dean of Students at the college."

Daisy whistled. "You're right, I've seen her—she is beautiful. You know who she is, of course."

Myrtle looked at Daisy, perplexedly. "Yes, as I just said—she's the Dean of Students at—"

"She's Henri's mother," said Daisy.

Myrtle's mouth stood open. "Are you serious? *Our* Henri? The one who lives here?"

"As serious as a wolf tracking a doe. How many other Henris do you know?" asked Daisy.

Myrtle shook her head. "I see where he gets his looks from."

"I didn't think you liked him very much."

"I didn't say I liked him or didn't like him," snapped Myrtle. "I said he's not bad-looking."

*****

Myrtle finished brushing her teeth following Sunday breakfast and decided to take Penrod for a walk in the park rather than attending Mass.

She was surprised when she walked out to the front porch to find Mr. Pfrommer in one of the rocking chairs, wearing a greatcoat, black as coal, and a beaver top hat.

"Mr. Pfrommer? Good morning."

"Miss Tully," he said, as he stood up.

"No, please, sit down. I was just taking Penrod out for a walk."

"He is a nice dog," said Mr. Pfrommer. "Vee get along vell. I vas considering a valk myself."

Myrtle was surprised again. She wasn't aware that Mr. Pfrommer even acknowledged Penrod's existence.

Mr. Pfrommer smiled. "You are surprised dat your dog und I are friends. He vill sometimes come up to my room."

"Oh, I'm so sorry. I'll try to make sure he stays downstairs."

"Oh, no, it's fine. I keep biscuits there, and ven he shows up I give him a small piece."

"Well, that is very nice of you. Mr. Pfrommer, would you care to join us on our walk?"

Now it was Mr. Pfrommer's turn to be surprised.

"Vhy, vhy, yes, I vould, tank you."

For a while they walked in silence, enjoying the quiet that March brings in the Upper Peninsula, when snow still covers the ground, the trees stand naked against the sky, stripped of their leaves, and the birds huddle away somewhere safe from the chilling breeze that blows down from Canada.

Finally, Mr. Pfrommer broke the silence.

"So you are from New Orleans. Please, tell me about it. I vould especially like to know about vat is called das French Quarter."

For the next hour Myrtle delighted Mr. Pfrommer, describing in detail what the city of New Orleans was like, going on to share with him how she had come to work at Adelaide College.

When she finished, she said, “So, Mr. Pfrommer, what was it that brought you to Booker Falls?”

Mr. Pfrommer didn’t respond right away; Myrtle was afraid she might have been too inquisitive into a matter that might have been intensely personal.

Then he spoke.

“As you know, I am German, from a small town, Stanberg, near Munich. Ven I was in my thirties, I had visions of becoming an artist, so I moved to Paris. I had a small apartment on da Rue de Clignancourt. It vas dere dat I met Loraine. She vas visiting her aunt. Vee fell in love, and ven she returned home to Quebec I vent vit her. Vee ver very happy together for ten years, but then she died unexpectedly.”

“Oh, I’m so sorry,” said Myrtle.

Mr. Pfrommer nodded.

“I didn’t vant to stay in Quebec any longer; da memories ver too much. Loraine had been a student here at Adelaide and vee had visited once. I thought it vas a nice community, and I vould feel good living here, close to vere she had vunce lived.

“I came and Mr. Becker vas kind enough to hire me on at his vatch shop. I’ve been here ever since.”

“And how long has that been?” asked Myrtle.

“Almost thirty years. I suppose I’ll die here, although I vould like to see my homeland just vun more time.”

Myrtle reached out her free hand and took Mr. Pfrommer’s in it.

“Hopefully, you will,” she said.

Hand in hand, the two of them started back to Mrs. Darling’s, Penrod leading the way.

CHAPTER EIGHTEEN

Myrtle was surprised when she saw George Salmon walk through the door of the library.

In the six months she'd been on the job, it was the first time she'd seen him there. It was also the first time she'd seen him since Christmas Eve, when he'd walked her back to the boarding house from St. Barbara's.

She had thought perhaps he'd decided to give up on courting her—at least, that's what she'd assumed he'd been doing.

"Miss Tully," he said, approaching the desk and tipping his hat.

"Mr. Salmon. This is a surprise. Is there something I can do for you?"

"Indeed there is. Are you familiar with today's date?"

Myrtle thought for a moment. "March 17th—is that supposed to mean something?"

"I don't suppose it does to those of you who are not Irish. But it certainly does to me."

Myrtle brightened. "St. Patrick's Day," she said. "Of course. Although, you are correct—it is not a day people of my heritage make a great deal of. But are you Irish? I thought Salmon might have been English."

"It is both," said George. "My family emigrated from England to Ireland early last century. So, yah, I do indeed consider myself Irish."

"And what is it you need?" asked Myrtle. "Are you looking for a book on Ireland? Something else Irish?"

"I would like to ask you out to dinner—tonight."

For a moment Myrtle stood, stunned. Perhaps he *hadn't* given up on courting her.

"For a traditional Irish meal," said George, noting her lack of response. "Corned beef and cabbage, and all that goes with it."

"And where would they be serving this?" asked Myrtle, now intrigued.

"Ah, now, that's a secret. What say you? Up for an Irish celebration?"

Myrtle thought for a moment before she answered. "Sure," she said, finally. "Will you pick me up or shall I meet you at this secret place?"

George frowned. "Why, I will call for you, of course. A gentleman would never ask a lady to meet him."

Myrtle smiled. "Very well."

*****

Since Myrtle had to work until six thirty, she'd suggested that George pick her up at the library. At five minutes before the half hour, he stopped his carriage outside and moments later escorted Myrtle down the path.

"Are you going to tell me where we're going?" asked Myrtle.

"You'll see," said George.

Twenty minutes later, George stopped the carriage again, this time in front of a lovely Victorian mansion in a section of town where Myrtle had not yet been. Not as old as Mrs. Darling's and considerably grander, still the home paled in significance to the others surrounding it, particularly the one on its right, another Victorian, a two and a half story red brick structure.

"Here we are," said George.

"Here we are where?" asked Myrtle. "Whose home is this?" Although she thought she knew the answer already.

"Why, it's mine," said George, as he hurried around to the other side of the carriage to assist Myrtle out.

Myrtle didn't move. She was aware George's parents were deceased, and that he was a bachelor.

She had a stern look on her face. "This is not appropriate, Mr. Salmon. Not appropriate at all."

"I thought you were more of a modern girl," said George, grinning.

"Please take me home now," said Myrtle, without looking at him.

"Georgie, there you are!"

Myrtle turned to see a woman in her sixties hurrying down the sidewalk.

"Now, then, is this Miss Tully?" she asked when she reached the carriage.

Confused, Myrtle looked at George.

"Myrtle, allow me to introduce my housekeeper, Mrs. Delahanty. This is the woman who takes care of all my needs: prepares my meals, does my laundry, cleans my house, makes sure I look presentable when I leave in the morning."

"Happy to make your acquaintance, lassie," said Mrs. Delahanty, thrusting her hand out towards Myrtle, who reflexively accepted it. "Aye, Georgie, you was right—she's fla."

Myrtle looked at George. "Fla?"

"She says you're attractive."

"It sounded to me like she said that's what *you* said."

George blushed. "Perhaps. But, in any case, Mrs. Delahanty is the finest cuisinier of Irish food in all the Keweenaw Peninsula."

"Oh, pshaw," said Mrs. Delahanty, waving her hand.

"Will you please come in for dinner?" pleaded George. "Otherwise, she would be very disappointed—as would I."

Myrtle sighed and raised one eyebrow. “Very well, then.”

*****

George’s home was filled with furniture clearly chosen more for its utilitarian qualities than any sense of opulence: each piece had been solidly, if rather methodically, constructed.

Other than one landscape painting in the parlor and wall sconces in all the rooms, the only other objects adorning the walls were portraits and photographs—hundreds of them.

“Are these all of your family?” Myrtle asked in amazement.

“They are,” said George. “My family tree has been traced back to a Salamon clericus in Suffolk, England, in 1121. Unfortunately, I am the last in my particular lineage—unless, of course, I should be able to find a woman who would marry me and bear me a son.”

He smiled at Myrtle.

“Well, good luck to you on that,” said Myrtle, returning his smile.

“Dinner is served,” said Mrs. Delahanty, entering the room.

*****

George had not exaggerated his housekeeper’s culinary skill—Myrtle thought it the best corned beef she had ever tasted.

“If I were a cook, I would definitely ask you for this recipe,” she said to Mrs. Delahanty.

“Aye, that’s a secret recipe what’s been passed down in me family for generations,” replied Mrs. Delahanty, wiping her hands on her apron. “Of course,” she added, eliciting laughter from both George and Myrtle, “half da cooks in Ireland have it, too.”

"And now for dessert," said Mrs. Delahanty. "Cherry pie and vanilla ice cream which young Mr. Salmon dere himself churned this very afternoon."

Myrtle looked at George. "Really? You did?"

George blushed, then nodded. "Just for you," he said.

*****

Following the meal—at which time Myrtle offered many "thank-yous" to Mrs. Delahanty—George offered to show her the rest of the house: but only the downstairs, of course.

"As you inferred earlier, it would not be proper for me to take you upstairs," he said.

The last room they came to was what George described as the "game room."

Large, forty feet long and twenty feet wide, at one end it held a Heiron & Smith Billiard Table, nine feet in length with four, hand-carved mahogany legs on two sides. A combination chiffonnier and marking board, imported from Australia, stood in one corner, next to a revolving cue rack.

"What's down there?" Myrtle asked, pointing towards the far end of the room.

"Ah, that's my poker table, where we have our weekly games."

Myrtle's eyes lit up. "Poker games? Do you suppose I might sit in some time?"

"I fear the stakes are somewhat more than what you might be prepared to wager. Other than myself and Frank, the other players are some of the more influential men in town: Mr. Steinmyer, the president of the Booker Falls Bank; Rudy Folger—he's an attorney; Malcolm Middleton, who owns most of the homes over in Greytown; and Judge Hurstbourne."

"Greytown?"

"The area west of downtown. You probably drove through there on your way into town."

"Ah, yes, I remember. It certainly was gray. You said Mr. Mitchell is a regular member?"

"That's right."

"And he has the kind of money you say is required to participate in these games?"

George nodded. "From what he tells me, he was in the right place at the right time. When he became assistant librarian right after he graduated from Adelaide, he somehow became good friends with Louis Amyx."

"Yes, I remember him telling me that."

"It was Frank who influenced Amyx to bequeath the art work to the library. And, I guess, he also made a sizable bequest to Frank, too: a little over eighty thousand dollars, according to Frank."

Myrtle let out a whistle. "That *is* a considerable sum."

"It's allowed Frank to remain in Booker Falls, working at the library—which, as you might imagine, does not pay all that well—instead of leaving and looking for a better position elsewhere."

"Working at the library may be stretching it some," said Myrtle. "I fear Mr. Mitchell does precious little work. So, if it takes money to play in the game, and you play . . ."

"Yah, I'm not hurting for resources. My father was in the lumber industry. My mother died twelve years ago and my father several years after that. He left everything to my sister and me."

"Sister?"

"Lydia. She died three years ago when a fellow passing through town in an automobile spooked the horse pulling her carriage. She was killed when it tipped over."

"Oh, I'm so sorry," said Myrtle, placing her hand on George's arm.

"Henri took it very hard. He and Lydia were engaged to be married."

Myrtle's eyes got big. "Henri? Is that why . . .?"

"Why he doesn't like automobiles?" said George. "I'm pretty sure that's the reason. Anyway, when Lydia died, her trust passed to me along with sole ownership of the house. Though I'm not much of a poker player, I hold my own often enough that I don't lose *too* much money."

By this time, they had arrived at the other end of the room. Myrtle ran her hand across the smooth oak finish of the table, about three and a half feet in diameter, and supported by four legs that ended in bear paws. She was surprised that, unlike other poker tables she had seen—and played at—the top of this one was wood, with no recesses for drinks or chips.

"Unusual table," she said.

"You're wondering why it doesn't look like an actual poker table," said George.

"You read my mind."

George unlatched a holder at one leg, then did the same with the opposing leg. Grasping the top, he spun it vertically in a one hundred and eighty degree arc, exposing a completely different surface, this one with six wells for chips and a bright beige covering.

"Beautiful," exclaimed Myrtle. "Tell me this: If I someday strike it rich, might I be able to join in then?"

George laughed. "Perhaps so," he said. "Perhaps so. One thing I could offer you now would be a game of billiards."

"Are you any good?"

"Not bad."

"Let's go."

An hour later, after Myrtle had beaten George three games in a row, she said, “Perhaps it’s time you took me home now.”

“Perhaps it is,” said George.

*****

At the door to the boarding house, George took Myrtle’s hand and gently placed a kiss on it.

“Miss Tully, it has been a pleasure. Might I see you again?”

“Perhaps, Mr. Salmon. We shall see.”

“I bid you good night, then,” said George. He quickly turned and walked back to the carriage.

As Myrtle went inside, she wasn’t sure if she should be relieved or insulted that George had not even tried to give her a real kiss.

CHAPTER NINETEEN

As Myrtle's car rolled into Marquette, she congratulated herself on getting lost only twice since leaving Booker Falls. The trip had taken most of the morning, but she'd enjoyed the ride, with the convertible top down, and a light breeze tousling the curly locks of her hair.

It was May, her first trip away from Copper Country since she'd arrived in Booker Falls the previous September, and only the second time she'd had a chance to drive the car since storing it in Mrs. Darling's barn early in November, before more than six feet of snow had covered the ground.

Altogether, more than one hundred and sixty inches had fallen over the winter, the most in sixteen years. But now, at last, spring seemed to have arrived.

She picked up the piece of paper on the seat next to her and checked the address again: 516 East Ohio Street.

Within minutes, she'd parked her car in front of a large, three-story home that had seen better days. Desperately in need of paint and missing a significant number of shingles, it paled in comparison to the houses on either side.

A knock at the door brought forth a short, heavy-set woman in her early seventies.

"Mrs. Sinclair?" said Myrtle.

"You're da young lady who wrote me?" said Elizabeth Sinclair.

"I am," said Myrtle. "Thank you for agreeing to see me."

As the two women passed through the living room, Myrtle was fascinated by the furniture, all of which, she was sure, was at least a half century old: a mahogany upholstered sofa, a walnut writing table, two rocking chairs, and a Willcox and Gibbs treadle sewing machine. Against one wall stood three, seven-foot high, tiger oak barrister bookcases, their shelves stuffed with books, bric-a-brac, and photographs.

It was obvious nothing had been dusted in months, if then.

Almost as fascinating was the number of cats that populated the place: Myrtle counted seven since coming through the front door. Even had she not seen them, the aroma that permeated the rooms would have been a giveaway.

Mrs. Sinclair led her to the parlor, a room that by all appearances had not undergone any change since the century just past. Hundreds of photographs, along with art work and a few mirrors, nearly obscured the faded, grime-covered wallpaper, with its fleur de lys design. More photographs filled the surfaces of every piece of furniture that had a flat top: the four small tables that flanked the two sofas facing each other across the room, one a Victorian dating back to the Civil War, the other more recent, only thirty or forty years old; a mahogany stand; and a Hallet and Davis Square Grand Piano. As with the furniture in the room they'd just come through, everything that could have collected dust, did. Two large chairs and three smaller matching ones completed the picture.

Mrs. Sinclair had brought in two cups of tea on a silver tray that she'd placed on the floor, as there was no room on any table. She shooshed away one of the cats who was curious to find out if this was a treat for him.

"I hope you like tea, dear," said Mrs. Sinclair, handing Myrtle a cup.

"I have come to appreciate it," said Myrtle. "Depending upon the flavor," she added quickly, keeping in mind Mrs. Darling's dandelion variety.

"This is thimbleberry."

"My favorite," said Myrtle.

"You said you were from Adelaide," said Mrs. Sinclair. "My daughter, Yvette, used to go there."

"I know. That's why I'm here."

Mrs. Sinclair looked puzzled. "You know she died almost thirty years ago—murdered?"

"I do," said Myrtle. "I work in the library: the assistant librarian—the same position Yvette held at the time of her passing. I recently found a box in the vault that contained some letters she had received from various people. I hoped you might be able to shed some light on who they might be."

"Me?" said Mrs. Sinclair. "I'm not sure how I can help."

Myrtle pulled a large envelope from the briefcase she had carried in, took out a batch of letters tied with a bow and handed it to Mrs. Sinclair.

"These were written by you. I thought you might want to have them back."

Mrs. Sinclair took the bundle and opened the first letter. Tears came to her eyes as she began to read.

"Yah, I remember these. So long ago . . . so long."

Myrtle pulled out the rest of the letters and handed them to Mrs. Sinclair. "How about these?" she asked. "Might you know who wrote them?"

Mrs. Sinclair examined the letters, looking at the signatures where there was one, but not bothering to read the contents.

"Only two," she said. "Paul, I'm sure, was da young man Yvette was seeing. And Cee-cee, of course, was her roommate."

"Cee-cee? You're sure that was her name?"

Mrs. Sinclair thought for a moment. "Yah, that's all Yvette ever called her—Cee-cee."

"And the 'W'? You don't know who that was?"

"I'm sorry," said Mrs. Sinclair. "I wish I could be of more help. Why are you asking about these letters? Are they important? Do they have something to do with my daughter's death?"

"I'm not sure," replied Myrtle, stuffing the letters back into the envelope. "Can you tell me more about your daughter?"

"Yvette was a wonderful girl," said Mrs. Sinclair. "A little wild, maybe . . . a little rambunctious."

So I gathered from the letters, thought Myrtle.

"But a good child. Very smart. And very pretty. One of her faults, though, was she always thought I was too nosy, that I was invading her privacy. That's why she was always hiding things, hiding them so I couldn't find them. Not that I was looking, anyway, you understand, but she thought I was. She thought her roommate was nosy, too."

"That explains where I found the letters," said Myrtle. "Did Yvette ever mention she was having trouble with anyone?"

"Trouble?"

"Had anyone threatened her?" Myrtle knew from the letters Yvette had been threatened by at least three people, but thought Mrs. Sinclair might know of others.

"Threatened her? Why, heavens no—everyone loved Yvette. She was a nice girl."

Myrtle took a sip of tea.

"Although there was that one man," said Mrs. Sinclair.

Myrtle almost spit the tea back into the cup. "What man?"

"I don't know who it was. Yvette referred to him as Mr. 'F.' Said she was afraid of him."

"Do you know why?"

Mrs. Sinclair shook her head. "No."

"But you don't know who he was?" said Myrtle.

"No, but I saw his picture."

Myrtle sat forward on the couch. "A picture? A photograph?"

"No, not a photograph—in da newspaper. Yvette brought a newspaper home with her and his picture was on da front page. It was a drawing."

"Like a sketch?"

Mrs. Sinclair nodded.

"Do you by any chance still have the paper?" asked Myrtle, hopefully.

"Oh, dearie, I'm afraid not. I don't know if Yvette left it or took it back with her."

"Did you mention this to the authorities?"

Mrs. Sinclair shook her head. "They never asked."

Myrtle was crestfallen. She knew more than she had before coming here—but how could she find out who Mr. 'F' was?

"When did Yvette show you the picture?" asked Myrtle.

"Da last time she got home, da week before she was killed. That's when she told me she was coming into some money."

Coming into some money? Things were getting interesting now.

"What did she mean she was coming into some money?" asked Myrtle. "Did she say from where—or whom? Or when?"

"No, I asked her and she said better I not know."

"Do you know if she got the money before she died?" Maybe Yvette's murder was over a robbery.

"I'm sure I don't know, dearie," said Mrs. Sinclair. "I never talked to her again after that visit." Then she added, "I'd hoped you were returning her watch."

"Her watch?" This was the first Myrtle had heard of any watch. First a scarf—now a watch?

"Yah, Yvette always wore it—on a nice silver chain around her neck. It had her initials on da cover: YMS. I was hoping it had been found."

"I'm sorry, no, I don't know anything about it." *But she was certainly going to find out.*

Myrtle looked at the photographs which covered every inch of the walls. "Are some of these of Yvette?"

"Oh, yah," said Mrs. Sinclair, her face lighting up. "Those are all family photographs."

"Do you mind if I look?" asked Myrtle.

"Not at all, dear. Here's a photograph of Yvette taken when she was seventeen, da year before she died. It's da last one we have of her."

Mrs. Sinclair picked up a framed photo from the end table and handed it to Myrtle. "While you're looking around, I'll take our cups back to da kitchen."

"She was quite lovely," said Myrtle, staring at the picture of an attractive, slender girl, dark hair falling to her waist.

When Mrs. Sinclair left the room, Myrtle stood and began to examine the other photographs, surprised at the dates written on scraps of paper attached to some of them, going back almost seventy years. She didn't realize cameras had been around that long.

She stopped short at one, bent down and studied it. It was a picture of Yvette with another girl—and Myrtle knew who the other girl was: Christiane de la Cruz!

"Here we are," said Mrs. Sinclair, returning to the room.

"Mrs. Sinclair," said Myrtle. "In this photograph—" she pointed to the one she'd been studying, "——this other girl with Yvette—was that her roommate by any chance?"

Mrs. Sinclair bent down and looked at the photograph, then straightened up. "Yah, yah it was," she said, "that was Yvette's roommate: Cee-cee."

*****

"I know who Yvette's roommate was. I know who Cee-cee is."

Daisy looked up from her book to find Myrtle standing there, her face lit up with a grin.

"Really? Who?"

"You won't believe this."

"I won't if you don't tell me. Come on—give," said Daisy.

"Christiane Picot."

Daisy sat back, a shocked look on her face. "Henri's mother? Are you sure? How'd you find out?"

Myrtle told Daisy about the photograph she'd seen at Mrs. Sinclair's home.

"Wow," said Daisy. "Well, he must not have known that. He had no idea who the Cee-cee was when you showed him the letters."

Myrtle went on to tell Daisy the other information she had uncovered: the missing watch, the expected money, and the mysterious Mr. 'F'.

"You going to tell Henri about all this?" asked Daisy.

"Not right away," said Myrtle. "Not until I know a little more. He wasn't too excited about the scarf. I think I'll do a little more digging."

CHAPTER TWENTY

Three months had passed since Myrtle had gotten the scarf from Claude. Though she'd told him at the time she would return it to him, she knew that wasn't likely: It was evidence.

He'd forgotten all about it, she thought.

She was wrong.

"Missus?"

Claude had been so quiet, Myrtle hadn't heard him approach the desk.

"Oh," she said, startled, first looking up from the book she'd been reading, then down to see the top of Claude's head peeking over the desk top.

"Sorry," Claude mumbled.

Myrtle stood so she could better see the little man. "Claude, what can I do for you?"

"My scarf," said Claude, reaching up his hand. "Can I have my scarf back?"

"Come around here," said Myrtle, motioning for him to come around the desk. "I'm sorry, but Constable de la Cruz has the scarf. He's keeping it as evidence in Miss Sinclair's death."

At first, Claude looked confused, then disappointed.

"I don't get it back?"

"No, I'm afraid not," said Myrtle. "Not as long as Miss Sinclair's murder remains unsolved."

"I'm sorry she's dead," said Claude.

"I know. Did you know her well?"

"She was a good girl—always nice to me."

"I don't suppose you saw her that day, did you?"

Claude nodded. "Yah, but I was home when she died."

"Oh?" said Myrtle, her curiosity piqued. "You know what time it happened?"

"After I saw her and Mr. Mitchell here in da library. They was still here when I left and went home, and she was still alive."

Now Myrtle's interest was *really* aroused!

"Wait! You saw Mr. Mitchell and Yvette here, together in the library, the same night she was murdered?"

Claude nodded.

"Did you tell anybody this?" asked Myrtle.

Claude shook his head. "Nobody never asked. They wanted to know where I was. I was home."

Myrtle was beginning to have her doubts about Constable Barnoble's competency.

"Did either of them see you?"

"No. They was in Mr. Mitchell's office. I was taking out trash."

"What time was this?"

Claude thought hard. "Maybe six—I think six."

"And they were both here when you left?"

Claude nodded and asked, "When do I get my scarf back?"

"I'll see what I can do."

Claude started to walk away.

"Claude, one more thing," said Myrtle.

Claude stopped and turned back.

"Miss Sinclair was wearing a watch . . . on a chain around her neck. Did you see it?"

Claude scratched his head, then shook it. "No, no watch. I didn't see no watch."

Then he turned back again and left.

*****

Henri was no more impressed with this bit of news than he had been with the discovery of the scarf.

"They worked together," he said. "What's so unusual about them being seen together at the library where they both work?"

"I checked the date Yvette was murdered," said Myrtle. "March 8th was on a Sunday. And according to Claude, the murder must have happened after six. The library's not open on Sunday. What were they doing there?"

"I don't know," said Henri. "I'm not sure it means anything. But if I think of it, I'll ask Frank about it."

"And what about the watch?"

Myrtle had decided to share what Mrs. Sinclair had mentioned about Yvette's watch with Henri. But not Mr. 'F'. Not yet. And certainly not the fact that his mother was Cee-cee.

"What about it?"

"Maybe whoever killed her took it."

"Maybe," said Henri. "If she even had it on that day."

"Okay, would you do me a favor?" asked Myrtle.

"What's that?"

"Can I borrow the scarf?"

"The scarf?"

"The scarf Yvette Sinclair was wearing when she was killed. May I borrow it?"

"Why?"

"I want to show it to someone," said Myrtle. "Then I'll return it."

"Who do you want to show it to?" asked Henri.

"Just someone. You don't think it's too important anyway, so what's wrong with loaning it to me for a few days?"

Henri shook his head. "Okay. I don't know what you're up to, but okay. I'll bring it home tomorrow—but I want it back by Friday."

"Deal," said Myrtle.

*****

"Where's Henri tonight?" asked Myrtle as she joined Daisy and Mr. Pfrommer at the dinner table.

"I saw him leef earlier," said Mr. Pfrommer. "But I don't know vere he vent."

"Myrtle, I've been thinking," said Daisy. "You said Mrs. Sinclair said Yvette showed her a newspaper with this Mr. 'F's picture in it."

"That's right."

"*The Rapids* has a copy of every paper they've ever published. We could check them out and . . ."

". . . and see if Frank, or anybody else we know whose first or last name began with an 'F' was in it."

"And," said Daisy, "that shouldn't take long, since the paper only comes out once a week. When did you say Yvette showed it to her mother?"

"The week before she was killed. We could start with the last paper before then."

*****

That evening, after searching through two months' worth of twenty-nine-year-old newspapers, Myrtle threw up her hands.

"Nothing!" she cried. "He's not here."

She and Daisy had found drawings of two males whose names began with 'F': five-year-old Floyd Nelson, who had been missing for three days; and Enrico Fernandez, a veteran of the War of 1812, who had celebrated his one-hundred and second birthday.

Neither seemed likely prospects.

"I don't know," said Daisy, shaking her head.

"I don't either," said Myrtle, disgustedly.

CHAPTER TWENTY- ONE

Myrtle rubbed her hands on her skirt, trying to wipe away the perspiration that had accumulated there.

Was she about to accuse Henri's mother, the Dean of Students at Adelaide College, of murder? Unless the woman could come up with a good explanation, she'd have no other recourse.

Knowing Christiane Picot was Henri's mother, Myrtle felt it best to confront the woman herself with the information she'd come across, rather than taking it to him.

"Miss Picot says you can come in now."

Myrtle looked up to see Christiane's secretary motioning towards the door.

"Miss Tully," said Christiane, as she stood and extended her hand. "Please, be seated. I remember you from the library, although we weren't actually introduced."

"You were Yvette's roommate." The words tumbled from Myrtle's mouth, not as a question, but rather as a statement of fact.

"Excuse me?"

"Yvette—Yvette Sinclair—the young woman murdered in the school library twenty-nine years ago—you were her roommate."

Christiane sat back in her chair, a look of puzzlement on her face.

"Who told you that?" she asked.

"Her mother—when I visited her last week."

"Elizabeth? How is she?"

"Mrs. Sinclair is fine. And very informative."

"Informative?"

"I saw the photograph of you and Yvette at the carnival. When I asked Mrs. Sinclair who you were, she called you Cee-cee, and said you were Yvette's roommate, which started me thinking about the letter."

"Letter?" said Christiane.

Myrtle pulled a letter from her purse and pushed it across the desk. "This one. The one where you said you were lovers, you were pregnant, and that you'd kill Yvette if she told anyone."

Christiane grabbed the letter, scanned it, then sat back in her chair. "My God, that was so many years ago. Where did you get this? From Yvette's mother?"

"Where I got it isn't important. What is important is you threatened to kill Yvette, and then she showed up dead."

Christiane squinted her eyes. "You think *I* killed her?"

"She threatened to tell the administration about you, and you wouldn't have graduated. But you did graduate. I looked it up in the records."

Christiane shook her head and sighed. "Yes, she did threaten to tell Wilfred."

"Wilfred?"

"Wilfred Forrester—the president of Adelaide?" said Christiane.

"But she didn't tell him?"

"Oh, no, she told him. She not only told him I was pregnant, but also that she and I had been lovers."

"But he didn't stop you from graduating?" said Myrtle.

"I'm not sure why you're asking me all these questions. And I'm not sure why I'm even talking with you."

Myrtle took the letter from Christiane's hand and started to get up.

"No, you're right. I should turn over all my information to Henri, and let him talk with you—if he wants to."

Christiane looked at Myrtle. "Sit down. I don't want Henri to know anything about any of this."

"Why didn't Mr. Forrester stop you from graduating?"

"I knew Wilfred wouldn't do anything, because I knew too much. For one thing, I knew that he and Yvette were lovers, although Yvette didn't know I knew.

"When Wilfred called me in and told me what she'd told him, I knew I was safe. I reminded him it wouldn't go well with either the administration or his wife if the truth about him and Yvette came out."

"But what did Yvette do when she found out Mr. Forrester wasn't going to do anything?"

"She never got a chance. I saw him on Friday. She was killed on Sunday."

"That's another thing. The library's not open on Sunday. What would she have been doing there?" Myrtle decided not to tell her what she'd learned from Claude—that Frank had been there, too.

"I have no idea."

Myrtle was starting to believe that perhaps Christiane had nothing to do with Yvette's death. But one question remained. Maybe more. She wasn't sure.

"How do you explain the scarf?"

"Scarf? What scarf?"

Myrtle pulled the scarf Henri had given her the night before from her purse and laid it on the desk.

"This scarf. The scarf Yvette was wearing when she was murdered. The scarf that was probably used to strangle her. I know it was yours. You had it on in the photograph I saw of you and Yvette."

"I remember that scarf," said Christiane. "I never did like it. I gave it to Yvette at Christmas. She liked to wear it as a head scarf. But I never heard anything about a scarf at the time when all this happened."

"It was never in the official police report, because Claude Amyx took it before he reported finding Yvette's body. You say Yvette wore this around her head, not her neck?"

"Yes. She didn't want to cover up her watch."

There was the watch again.

"What can you tell me about the watch?"

"It was very expensive, had a mother of pearl cover with her initials engraved on it: YMS. She always wore it. The only time I ever remember her taking it off was when she and I . . . well, she always wore it. Why do you ask?"

"It wasn't found with her body."

"Hmm. Perhaps Claude took it along with the scarf?"

"No," said Myrtle, shaking her head. "He told me he took the scarf, but he didn't know anything about a watch, and I believe him."

"Then I think there's but one conclusion that can be drawn: Whoever killed Yvette must have taken the watch."

"That's what I'm thinking, too."

"What did Henri have to say about it?"

"The watch? I haven't told him yet."

Christiane looked at Myrtle inquisitively. "Really? Well I suppose you have your reasons. I hope I've convinced you I had nothing to do with Yvette's death. And if I had, I certainly would never have come back here, in spite of that old saying."

"Old saying?"

"That the criminal always returns to the scene of the crime."

Myrtle laughed. "Okay, I guess maybe I'm convinced. And I'm sorry if I appeared accusatory."

"But that was why you were here," said Christiane. "I understand. If you want to find out who killed Yvette, I would start with Paul Momet, her boyfriend. He never was any good."

"We've talked with him—"

"We?"

Myrtle blushed. "Henri and I. We talked with him."

"I see," said Christiane. "But you did not tell my son you were going to talk with me."

Myrtle shook her head. "I didn't think it appropriate."

"I appreciate that," said Christiane. "And I trust what I've told you will be held in absolute confidence—at least the part about me and Yvette."

"So Henri doesn't know you and Yvette were roommates."

"No. And since he's read this letter, I don't want him to know. Have you told anyone else?"

Myrtle shook her head. She wasn't about to tell her that Daisy also knew.

Myrtle took out the letter signed 'W.'

"Do you think this might have been from Mr. Forrester?"

Christiane took the letter and read it. "I'd say so. It looks like his handwriting. And he wouldn't have wanted his wife to know about him and Yvette. Do you think this makes him a suspect?"

"Maybe," said Myrtle. "But as far as Paul Momet is concerned, he appears to be in the clear. He has an alibi: He was fishing at Lake Kennekuk when Yvette was murdered."

Christiane's brow furrowed. "No, he wasn't. He was right here in town."

"What do you mean?"

"I saw him that night. He was hanging around outside the dormitory. But when Yvette went out later, I didn't see him."

"You're sure?"

"I'm positive. I never understood why he wasn't charged."

"But his wife confirmed he was at the lake. Or at least, that he brought fish home from somewhere. Constable Barnoble seemed satisfied with his alibi."

Christiane snorted. "Constable Barnoble! The man was a drunkard. As I understand it from Henri, he didn't show up for work most days. Paul Momet could have told him he'd been *walking* on Lake Kennekuk, and Barnoble would have believed him. I'm telling you straight—Paul Momet was in Booker Falls the night Yvette was killed."

"Is it all right if I tell Henri about Paul being in town that night?"

Christiane hesitated. "I'm not . . ."

"I could tell him you were in the library and we got to talking, and it came up. You could have spotted him anywhere on the campus."

"I suppose so," said Christiane, still not convinced. "But that's all. Now, Miss Tully, is there anything else I can help you with."

"Just one thing. I'm curious—what *did* bring you back to Booker Falls and to Adelaide?"

Christiane smiled. "And why should I share my family history with you?"

"Because, as I said, I'm curious. And because I'm not sharing everything with Henri."

Christiane sighed and leaned back in her chair.

"Very well. After graduation, I returned to my home in French Guiana. I was four months pregnant with Henri. I met a nice man, a good man, Fernando de la Cruz. He married me, even though he knew I was carrying someone else's child. We had a good life together for six years until he died in a boating accident.

"He left me with a nice inheritance, so I decided to return to school to obtain my masters, and then I taught for eight years, until the school closed. About that same time I heard that Wilfred had become President here at Adelaide. Henri was ready to start college and I knew Wilfred's old position as Dean of Students, would be open. I wrote him and told him I wanted the job. I really left him no alternative but to give it to me and now, here I am, twelve years later. Now, Miss Tully, does that satisfy your curiosity?"

Myrtle stood up. "It does—thank you. And I believe I've taken enough of your time."

*****

Myrtle's half hour for lunch had not been quite enough time to allow her to get across campus to Christiane Picot's office and back, making her ten minutes late arriving at the check-out desk, a fact that did not sit well with her boss.

Myrtle watched as Frank approached, his steps a bit unsteady. About a dozen students were in the room, reading or working on various projects.

"Miss Tully," he said, when he reached the desk.

Myrtle smelled the alcohol on his breath: Southern Comfort.

"Mr. Mitchell," replied Myrtle.

"May I ask why you were not at your desk when you were supposed to be?"

The tone of his voice irritated Myrtle. "You may."

"Well?"

"I had an appointment with Miss Picot."

"Why was I not apprised of that?"

"It had nothing to do with the library. It was a personal matter."

"Miss Tully you are not being paid to take care of personal matters when you're working; you're paid to take care of this library." By now, Frank's voice was loud enough to be heard throughout the room. "And you goddamn well—"

Myrtle held an index finger up in front of Frank's nose, stopping him in the middle of his sentence. Then she turned her back on him and started off in the direction of his office.

He followed her.

When they were inside the office, Myrtle shut the door.

Eyes blazing, she looked up at Frank.

"You may chide me if you wish for being ten minutes late. You may even deduct money from my paycheck for those ten minutes. In fact . . ."

She reached into her sweater, pulled out a dime and slammed it down on Frank's desk, knocking his magazine to the floor.

"Here, here's ten cents, which more than covers my wages for those ten minutes. But you will never—I repeat, *never*—again berate me in public, and you will certainly never again curse me or take the Lord's name in vain in my presence."

Myrtle opened the door and started to leave. Then she turned back.

"And if you do, you will find yourself in need of a new assistant librarian."

This time, she left and closed the door behind her, leaving a dazed Frank wondering what had just happened.

*****

Later that afternoon when Claude came in to empty the trash, Myrtle motioned him over to the desk.

"Claude, when you took the scarf from Miss Sinclair's body, are you sure it was around her neck, and not her head?"

"Her head? No, missus, it was 'round her neck. Wrapped real tight, too. When do I get it back?"

"Soon, Claude, I promise—soon."

*****

The next morning when Myrtle arrived at the library, she was surprised to find it was already unlocked. She was sure she'd locked up the previous evening when she'd left.

Cautiously, she pushed open the door and saw the lights had been turned on. *There was no way she'd forgotten to turn them off.*

She looked around but the room was empty. She took her coat off and walked over to her desk. That's when she saw it: a beautiful arrangement of flowers—lilies, roses and carnations—in a cut glass crystal vase that had once belonged to someone's mother.

Propped next to the vase was a small envelope.

Myrtle opened the envelope and removed the card inside. She was surprised to see that the note had been written in red ink, in a long, flowery script.

She knew immediately where she'd seen that handwriting before.

Quickly, she read the note.

Dear Miss Tully,

I beseech you to forgive my behavior yesterday. I was rude and obnoxious and you were right to confront me. I promise I will never act in that manner again.

Yours,

Frank Mitchell

Myrtle laid the note down. So Frank Mitchell was the author of the two unsigned love letters she'd found, written to Yvette.

Interesting!

CHAPTER TWENTY-TWO

Myrtle arrived back at the boarding house that evening and found Henri sitting on the porch.

He stood as she approached.

"Miss Tully," he said. "Good evening."

"Good evening, Mr. de la Cruz. I was hoping to run into you."

"With your automobile?" asked Henri, smiling.

Myrtle returned the smile. "Nothing so drastic, I assure you. I have come across a bit of information I think might be of interest to you."

"Information?"

"Information that has come to my attention regarding the death of Miss Sinclair. Could we walk?"

Once clear of the house, Myrtle removed Frank's note from her purse and handed it to Henri.

"Does this look familiar?" she asked.

Henri read the note. "So Frank Mitchell was the other letter writer," he said, when he finished.

"Yes," said Myrtle. "And I think that makes him a suspect in Yvette's murder."

Henri looked at her. "Eh? What makes you think that?"

"I got a taste of how angry Frank Mitchell can be, how belligerent—especially when he's been drinking. While he expressed his love for Yvette in those letters, he also hinted that if he couldn't have her, well . . . unrequited love can sometimes lead to deadly results. I think it's at least worth questioning him—to see if he has an alibi."

Henri nodded. "All right, I'll talk to him."

"There's more," said Myrtle. "Paul Momet was in Booker Falls the evening Yvette was killed."

"What makes you say that?"

"Your mother."

"My *mother*?"

"She was in the library today, and we got to talking about the murder. I mentioned to her that you and I went to see Paul Momet and that he'd said he was fishing at that lake. Your mother said she saw him on campus that night. She knew who he was."

"How did she know him?" asked Henri.

"She knew Yvette, and knew she was dating him." No lie there. "How far is this lake from town, anyway?"

"Lake Kennekuk? Twenty miles, I'd say."

"How long would it take to walk that?"

"I'd say six hours. At a brisk pace. Maybe more."

"How long on horseback?" asked Myrtle.

"Not long at all, but twenty miles is quite a bit for a horse in one day. Then he'd have to ride back out to the lake again."

"But not necessarily that same night. He might have camped out near the campus, then rode back out on Monday. According to his wife, he didn't come home until Tuesday."

Henri thought about what Myrtle had said.

"I suppose you could be right. I'll talk with Jake and see what he thinks."

"I have more," said Myrtle.

"I bet you do," said Henri.

Myrtle pulled out the letter signed 'W.'

"I showed this to your mother to see if she might have any idea who wrote it. She said it looked like Wilfred Forrester's handwriting. She's familiar with it, because she gets a lot of correspondence from him."

"The President of Adelaide?" Henri's eyes narrowed. "I doubt that."

"And," Myrtle continued, "Mrs. Sinclair said Yvette told her she was afraid of a Mr. 'F'. Forrester's last name starts with an 'F.' And Frank's first name starts with an 'F.'"

"Now you have two suspects," said Henri, trying hard not to show his amusement. "Who's next—me?"

"You're not old enough," said Myrtle. "And your name doesn't start with 'F.'"

"Thank goodness for that," said Henri.

"One more thing," said Myrtle.

"Of course there is. And where does this come from?"

"Mrs. Sinclair."

"The two of you must have had quite a conversation."

"We did. She's a nice lady. There's the matter of Yvette's watch."

"Her watch?"

"Mrs. Sinclair said she always wore one." Myrtle wasn't about to tell Henri that his mother had confirmed that. "On a chain, around her neck. There's no mention of it being found with the body. I think whoever killed her took the watch."

"If there was a watch and it's missing, my guess is Claude has it. He took the scarf."

"By the way," said Myrtle. "Here."

She took the scarf from her purse and handed it to Henri.

"No," said Myrtle. "I don't think Claude took it. I asked him about it and he said no. I'm sure he didn't take it."

"Anything else?" asked Henri.

Myrtle shook her head. "That's all."

"That's a lot. Why are you doing all this, anyway?"

"I guess I'm just naturally nosy," said Myrtle. "But I also think we owe it to that girl and her mother to find out who took her life."

"Okay," said Henri, sighing. "I'll follow up on all of this."

"I'd like to go with you when you talk with Mr. Forrester and with Mr. Momet."

"Oh, you would, would you? And why would I allow that?"

"Because without me, you wouldn't have any of this information. I *deserve* to be a part of the investigation."

"And how about Frank? You don't want to be there when I speak with him?"

"I think it best I not be. But I'm sure you'll tell me what he says."

*****

The next morning Myrtle watched Henri enter the library and proceed straight to Frank's office. She strained to hear their conversation, but with the door shut she was unsuccessful.

She watched as Henri handed the two love letters to Frank—they'd both decided it best not to include his note to her, to keep her out of it—and the surprised look on his face as he read them.

Twenty-five minutes later, Henri left Frank's office, shaking his hand as he exited. Without looking at Myrtle, he walked to the front door and left.

He better have something good to tell me tonight, thought Myrtle.

*****

Myrtle could hardly wait to get back to the boarding house that evening to find out how Henri's talk with Frank went.

But he wasn't there.

"Mrs. Darling, do you know where Henri is?" asked Myrtle, tracking down her landlady in the kitchen.

"Why, dearie, he left before dinner. Said he was going over to his mother's."

Uh-o, thought Myrtle. *I hope I didn't get her in trouble.*

For the rest of the evening, Myrtle listened intently for the front door to open. Towards midnight, she gave up and went to bed.

The next morning, she hurried down the stairs and found Henri and Mr. Pfrommer at the table.

"Well?" she said, plopping down in her chair and looking at Henri.

"Well, what?" said Henri.

Myrtle didn't know what to ask him first: how his meeting with Frank went, or why he went to see his mother. She chose Frank.

"Your meeting with Mr. Mitchell. What did he have to say?"

Henri looked at Mr. Pfrommer, who was leaning back in his chair, eyes closed. He wasn't sure if he should talk in front of the old man or not. He decided that he probably wouldn't have any interest in the matter in any event.

"It was illuminating, to say the least," said Henri.

Daisy walked in. "What was illuminating?" she asked, taking her place at the table.

"You remember I told you about the note I got from Mr. Mitchell?" asked Myrtle.

Daisy nodded.

"Henri talked with him about it yesterday."

Now Daisy was all ears. "Okay, spill—what did he have to say?"

"He said he was with Miss Sinclair that evening," said Henri.

"I knew it!" exclaimed Myrtle. "Claude said he saw the two of them."

"He said she'd asked him to meet her at the library. When he did, about six o'clock, she told him she was expecting to come into a lot of money, and she wouldn't need the library job any longer."

"Money from where?" asked Daisy.

"She didn't say. Frank said the two of them left, but he returned about an hour later to get a book he'd forgotten. He'd extinguished his lamp and was getting ready to leave his office when he heard the front door open. He saw Yvette enter holding a lantern. The scarf was around her head, the way she always wore it. He started to call out to her but just then Paul Momet came in and he and Yvette walked back to the stacks.

"Frank heard some muffled conversation, and then noises as though they were engaged in a sexual activity, moaning and so forth."

Daisy and Myrtle both put their hands to their mouths.

"Oh, my!" said Daisy.

"Then he said Paul left and he was ready to do likewise when all of a sudden Paul returned and went back to the stacks. That's when Frank decided he'd had enough, so he slipped out and left them there. The next day he found out Yvette had been killed."

"Likely story," huffed Myrtle. "Why didn't he tell the police all this? I bet he killed her himself and made the rest of it up."

"No," said Henri, "I'm pretty sure Frank is innocent."

"What makes you say that?" asked Daisy.

"Because a couple of months before Miss Sinclair was killed, Frank fell and broke his right arm in three places. The doctor put a cast on it from the wrist to the armpit. It held the arm at a right angle. Frank couldn't bend his arm; he couldn't have used it to strangle Miss Sinclair."

"He couldn't have choked her with just one hand?" asked Daisy.

"Possible, I suppose, but not probable. Miss Sinclair would have put up a struggle. Besides, if Miss Tully's theory is correct, that Miss Sinclair was strangled with her scarf, it would have been virtually impossible."

"How do you know he's telling the truth—about his arm, I mean?" asked Myrtle.

"When I left the library, I drove over to Doctor Sherman's office. Frank told me he's the one who took care of him. He remembered the incident well. He confirmed what Frank had told me."

By now, Mrs. Darling had served breakfast. But no one had started eating except Mr. Pfrommer, who was busy working on his pancakes.

Myrtle turned to the old man and asked, "Mr. Pfrommer, what do you make of all this?"

Without looking up from his plate, Mr. Pfrommer took another bite of pancake, then replied, "I haff no opinion on da matter."

*****

Following breakfast, Henri stopped Myrtle in the hallway.

"I'm going to see President Forrester today. You want to come with me?"

Myrtle frowned. "I don't think Mr. Mitchell would let me off."

"I told him yesterday I might need your services."

Myrtle beamed. "My services! Of course, then. What time?"

"I'll meet you at his office at one."

"Did you have a nice time with your mother last night?" asked Myrtle, hoping to find out what she might have said to him.

Henri stared at her, a puzzled look on his face.

"Mrs. Darling told me you were visiting her," added Myrtle, quickly.

"She had invited me for dinner."

"Oh, I see," said Myrtle. "Okay, then, see you at one."

CHAPTER TWENTY-THREE

Precisely at one o'clock, Myrtle entered the office of Anna Gilmore, President Forrester's secretary. Henri was already there.

"President Forrester will see you now," said Anna. She stood and opened the door to his office.

The pungent odor of stale cigar smoke almost gagged Myrtle. Trying not to appear too obvious, she removed a handkerchief from her sleeve and brushed it across her face.

In his twenties, even early thirties, Wilfred Forrester had been a striking specimen of a man, sporting a handsome physique and a head full of curly blond hair. But forty years, thirty additional pounds and five cigars a day had not been kind to him. Now he was balding, over-weight, sixty-five-years-old with deep bags under his eyes.

"Henri," he said, coming around from behind his desk and shaking Henri's hand. "Good to see you again. And who might this lovely young lady be?"

"This is Miss Myrtle Tully," said Henri. "She's the assistant librarian. Been here since last September."

Wilfred stuck out his hand. Myrtle took it and noticed how strong it was.

"Miss Tully," he said.

"President Forrester," she answered.

"Sit down, sit down," said Wilfred, retreating back behind his desk. "What can I do for you?"

Henri slid the letters across Wilfred's desk, the ones signed 'W.'

"I believe you might have written these," he said.

Wilfred looked at the letters. His eyes got big.

"My God," he said. "Where did you find these?"

"It is your handwriting?" asked Myrtle.

"Yes, but—but, where did you find them?"

"In a cache of letters in the basement of the library," said Myrtle. "We know about you and Miss Sinclair."

"You threatened Miss Sinclair if she told your wife about the affair," said Henri. "I have to ask this—did you carry out the threat?"

"You think *I* murdered Yvette?" said Wilfred.

"You had motive," said Myrtle.

Wilfred looked at Myrtle. "I'm sorry, but why are *you* here?"

"Miss Tully is helping me with the investigation," said Henri. "Her contribution has proven to be quite valuable."

Myrtle swelled a bit with pride: It was the first time Henri had complimented her on what she'd uncovered.

"No," said Wilfred, "I did not kill Yvette. And, yah, she did tell my wife about the affair. But Wilma had already confronted me about it."

"That doesn't mean you didn't carry out your threat," said Myrtle.

"No, but the fact I was out of town at the time does."

"Out of town?" said Henri.

"The weekend Yvette was killed, Wilma and I were in Sault Sainte Marie, attending her sister's wedding. I wasn't in Booker Falls. Left on Friday, didn't return until Tuesday."

Myrtle sat back in her chair. With Frank apparently out of the picture, she'd been sure Wilfred Forrester was the Mr. 'F' Yvette had been afraid of, and thus, possibly, her killer.

"I'm assuming I could verify that if need be," said Henri.

Wilfred nodded. "You can check with the minister who performed the ceremony: my father-in-law."

*****

"Sounds as though you're out of suspects."

Myrtle had told Daisy about the meeting with President Forrester.

"Not quite," said Myrtle. "There's still Paul Momet. And I'd still like to know who Mr. 'F' is."

CHAPTER TWENTY-FOUR

Myrtle had just returned from her walk, now a regular Monday morning routine, when she ran into Mr. Littlefield, the mail carrier.

"Morning, Miss Tully," he said.

"Good morning, Mr. Littlefield. You have some mail for the house?"

"I do," said Mr. Littlefield, handing over a stack of mail. "Have a nice day, now."

"Perhaps I'll see you again on your afternoon rounds," said Myrtle.

"Perhaps," said Mr. Littlefield. "If you're here around three."

As Myrtle walked up the path to the house, she rifled through the envelopes. One in particular caught her eye, addressed to a Miss Gwen Farking. Myrtle checked the return address: Belle Farking, 1414 Winston Ave., Chicago, IL.

Myrtle shook her head. *Strange*, she thought.

Inside the house, she laid all the mail in a little tray on a table placed there for that purpose. As she was doing so, Daisy came tripping down the steps.

"Good morning, Myrtle."

"Good morning, Daisy."

"Where are you off to today?"

Myrtle shook her head. "Think I'll do some reading. I brought a new book home from the library on Saturday, *The Magnificent Ambersons*."

"Oh, who's it by?" asked Daisy, picking up the mail and sorting through it. She stopped short when she came to the letter addressed to Gwen Farking. Myrtle couldn't help but notice.

"Booth Tarkington, one of my favorite authors. It won a Pulitzer Prize last year. I named Penrod after one of his characters from another book, you know."

"That's nice," said Daisy, her attention still fixed on the letter. "Look, I've got to go."

Sticking the letter into her pocket she headed for the stairs.

"Daisy, wait a minute," said Myrtle.

Daisy stopped and looked at Myrtle.

"What's going on?"

"What do you mean?" asked Daisy, obviously flustered.

"Who is Gwen Farking?"

"You read my mail?"

"First of all, no, I didn't read your mail. I saw the name on the envelope when I brought the mail in. And you just now called it *your* mail? A letter addressed to someone else? I remember the time we went to Red Jacket to pick up your typewriter, some man called out *Gwen*, and I thought you were ready to respond. And I also noticed the name on the mail you received matches the initials on your flask: GF.

"One other thing: There was a reporter in the library a few weeks ago, passing through on his way up to Copper Harbor. Told me he worked for the *Detroit News.* I told him you used to work for the *Chronicle*. He said he'd never heard of any paper by that name in Detroit. I didn't think much of it at the time, but now I wonder . . ."

Daisy hung her head. "Come in the parlor," she said.

"I've wanted to tell you for a long time," said Daisy, once they were seated by the fireplace. "But I was afraid."

"Afraid of what?"

"First of all, my name isn't Daisy O'Hearn, it's Gwen Farking. Farking is my mother's maiden name. Mine too. I don't know who my dad was. The letter is from her, although I told her never to write me here, or if she did, not to use my real name. But she's getting old—she forgets.

"And I didn't work at any *Chronicle* in Detroit. In fact, I've never even been to Detroit. Before I came to Booker Falls I worked for the *Record Eagle* in Traverse City."

"Why all the mystery?" asked Myrtle. "And what—or who—are you afraid of?"

"Eight years ago, I was living in Chicago, working for the *Examiner*. I was married to Mike Fitzgerald. He also worked for the newspaper, as a pressman. When the union and the paper worked out a new contract, he had to take a twenty-five per cent cut in pay, so we were really struggling. Then they went on strike and he didn't have any money coming in at all, only my salary.

"Mike started to get more and more depressed and started to drink. A lot. It got to the point where we could hardly pay the rent. For the first time since we got married, I was glad we didn't have any children.

"The more Mike drank, the more abusive he became, mostly verbal at first, but then it also started to get physical.

"The strike was finally over in November of that year, except the pressmen didn't go for it, and their jobs were filled by non-union men. That pretty much pushed Mike over the edge.

"On Christmas Eve, he got as drunk as I'd ever seen him. He started beating on me, knocking me around the room. Then he pushed me down on the kitchen floor and tried to force himself on me. With all the knocking around, the block that held my kitchen knives fell on the floor. I grabbed one and I . . . I stabbed him in the back."

"Oh, no!" said Myrtle, taking Daisy's hand.

"His eyes got really big. I stabbed him again. I'm not sure how many times. Then I pushed him off of me. There was blood everywhere.

"I went to the bathroom and took off my dress, which was covered with Mike's blood. I washed up, got dressed and packed whatever I could take with me. On the way out, I put my dress in the chute that went down to the furnace.

"I found a cab and took it to my mother's house and I told her what I'd done. She said I'd have to leave town. I did that same night. I went to Traverse City—Mike and I had gone there on our honeymoon, and I kind of liked the place.

"I changed my name and got a job at the paper. Then, four years ago I thought I saw Mike's brother on the street. I was scared out of my wits that he'd tracked me there and had come to kill me.

"The next day I moved up here to Booker Falls. I'd read some old accounts in the archives at the paper in Traverse City about Yvette's murder, and thought maybe I could write a book. I was lucky enough to get hired on to the paper here. And that's what happened."

"You're afraid Mike's brother is still after you? Do you think that's who called out your name in Red Jacket?"

"I don't know," said Daisy. "I didn't look to see who it was. But, yes, I'm afraid Billy is after me."

"Does Leonard know about all this?"

Daisy looked away. "He did."

"He did?"

"I'm not seeing Leonard anymore," said Daisy.

"I wondered why I'd never met him," said Myrtle.

"He got transferred to Flint. We decided to call it quits as far as our relationship was concerned."

"But you're still getting your whiskey."

"He made sure a friend of his is taking care of that. Listen, you can't tell anyone about this."

"I promise."

"Good, because—"

Daisy was cut short by Henri's appearance at the doorway.

"I thought you might like to know—I've just arrested Paul Momet."

CHAPTER TWENTY-FIVE

On Wednesday, June 16, 1920, three weeks after Paul Momet had been taken into custody and charged with the murder of Yvette Sinclair, his trial began.

Ever since the arrest, the whole town of Booker Falls, as well as the surrounding area, had been abuzz with anticipation and excitement over the upcoming proceedings. Miss Madeline's Eatery had hired an extra waitress and increased its stock of food, especially the meats—beef, pork, chicken and moose—used in the pasties in which it specialized. Joker Mulhearn, who operated a speakeasy in the backroom of Alton Woodruff's barber shop—the existence of which was common knowledge to everyone in town, including Henri—scurried to procure additional inventory from his source in Canada.

And every store that sold goods of any type, figuring wives accompanying their curious husbands to town would take the opportunity to do some shopping, stocked the shelves in anticipation of a business windfall.

The only establishment, it seemed, not open for business, was the Adelaide College Library, as the last two weeks of June was the time it normally closed down during the year, a circumstance for which Myrtle was grateful, since it allowed her the opportunity to attend the trial.

As she climbed the stairs to the courtroom located on the second floor of the courthouse, Myrtle was surprised by the austerity of the building.

Dark, brown walls, devoid of any adornment—paintings, photographs, murals—presented a sense of solemnity, of severity: There was no doubt this was a place where serious business was transacted.

The handrails, concave and so oversized that Myrtle's hand couldn't fit around one, were an even darker brown than the walls. Myrtle wondered of what type wood they were made, and if they'd always been this color, or had the unwashed hands of countless visitors over several generations brought them to their current state.

Unpolished—*probably never had been*, thought Myrtle—they appeared dull and without any sheen whatsoever.

The original courthouse had been erected in 1854, shortly after the beginnings of the town. It had been sorely needed as a venue to arbitrate not only the lawsuits brought by feuding miners, but the physical conflicts that often accompanied them.

The present courthouse that, in addition to the second floor courtroom, also contained the offices of George Salmon and Henri, as well as the jail, was erected in 1880 to replace that original building that had been burned to the ground by a disgruntled—that is, losing—party of one of the trials.

Oddly enough, the trial about to begin this day would be the first ever in either courthouse that involved a murder charge.

When she reached the second floor, Myrtle encountered a large crowd gathered in the hallway, among them Daisy. The courtroom was not a spacious one, accommodating only about fifty spectators, so Henri had arranged for the two women to be included, Daisy as a reporter for the newspaper, and Myrtle because she'd been instrumental in bringing Paul Momet to trial.

"Isn't this exciting?" asked Daisy when Myrtle caught up with her.

"I'll say. Have I missed anything?"

"No, there's still ten minutes 'til they open the doors. I don't know who most of these people are." Daisy pointed towards a woman sitting on a bench. "Except that woman over there—that's Charlotte Momet."

Myrtle looked to where Daisy had indicated.

Charlotte Momet huddled in one corner, obviously trying her best to remain unnoticed. For a fleeting moment, Myrtle considered going over and telling her how sorry she was. Then she thought better of it, realizing Charlotte might know about her role in her husband's being charged with Yvette's murder.

"Have you seen Henri?" asked Myrtle.

"I doubt we will. I think he's the one who will bring Paul into the courtroom."

The ringing of a small bell indicated the time for the start of court. Two men, each dressed in suits, looking very official, opened the massive doors that separated the hallway from the courtroom.

Myrtle and Daisy forced their way into the crowd jostling to enter and found seats toward the back.

The courtroom itself was no more pretentious than the rest of the building with the exception of three items: To the right of the judge's bench, which rose about four feet above the floor, stood an American flag; to the left, the Michigan state flag; and on the wall behind the bench, a portrait of Woodrow Wilson, President of the United States.

A clerk's desk sat to the left of the bench, along with the jury box, while the witness stand was on the right. Between the bench and the spectator's section were two tables, each with two chairs.

Although the temperature outside had not reached sixty—normal for this time of year—the room felt stuffy. Perspiration formed on the back of Myrtle's neck.

A quick glance around revealed only two windows, both on the wall behind the jury box, and both closed. A large fan mounted in the middle of the ceiling turned slowly, as though reluctant to do so.

"It's going to get pretty warm in here," Myrtle whispered.

Daisy nodded, fanning herself with her notepad.

One man sat at the table designated for the defense, and another at the prosecutor's table. Myrtle presumed the prosecuting attorney was Jake McIntyre, but had no idea who the other, much younger, man was who would be representing Paul Momet.

"Do you know who Mr. Momet's lawyer is?" she asked Daisy. "He looks awfully young."

"I understand he's from Laurium," said Daisy. "Some big law firm there sent him over."

"I'm surprised Mr. Momet could afford someone from a big law firm."

"I hear they're providing the services for free."

"Why would they do that?"

"I think one of the partners was a good friend of his father."

"That's certainly nice of them," said Myrtle.

"Yes, but they might have sent someone with a little more experience. From what I heard out in the hallway, this is the man's first murder case."

As young as the lawyer appeared, Myrtle wondered if this might be his first case of any type.

She looked around at the spectators, mostly men, none of whom she recognized. They weren't big readers, thought Myrtle, as she'd never seen any of them in the library. She noticed the man sitting next to Daisy had his notebook open, a pen lying in it.

She nudged Daisy in her side and nodded towards the man. Daisy turned to him.

"Oh, hi," she said. "Are you a reporter?"

"I am," said the man. "Alan Greenmont—the *Mining Gazette."*

"Daisy O'Hearn," said Daisy. "*The Rapids,* here in town."

"Oh, right here in town," said Alan. "Do you know the accused?"

"No. But my friend here . . ." Daisy bent her head back towards Myrtle, ". . . she does. In fact, she's responsible for him being arrested."

Alan leaned forward to get a better look at Myrtle. "Really?" he said. "Do you suppose I might talk with you later?"

Before Myrtle had a chance to answer, the room got eerily quiet as Paul Momet, in handcuffs and accompanied by Henri, entered through a side door. The three weeks he'd been held in jail awaiting trial had been hard on him: He looked haggard, and tired. Dark circles under his eyes accentuated the stubble on his chin. His hair was unkempt, as though it hadn't had a comb or a brush in it since he'd been locked up.

Myrtle knew from Henri that Charlotte Momet had visited her husband every day, bringing him food from home to supplement the sparse meals provided by the county. And every day she'd taken most of it back home with her, Paul being too upset over his situation to eat anything.

Henri, on the other hand, was decked out in his official constable's uniform: tan slacks and jacket that buttoned up to his neck, with two hash marks adorning his left sleeve. His hair was parted in the middle; not like he normally wore it over to one side.

"Oh, my," said Daisy in a whisper. "Look at Henri. Doesn't he look handsome?"

Myrtle didn't answer, but secretly she had to agree: He did look handsome!

Stumbling, Paul barely made it to the table where his attorney waited for him. Myrtle thought it fortunate the table was the one closest to the door, for she doubted the poor man could have made it to the farther one.

Momet had just sat down when Judge Hurstbourne entered through a door behind the bench.

"All rise," said the bailiff in a commanding voice that reminded Myrtle of Mrs. Thackeray, her supervisor at the telephone exchange in France.

Among much rustling and shuffling, everyone came to their feet.

"Be seated," said the judge.

Judge Clarence Hurstbourne was an imposing man who stood some four inches over six feet and weighed over two hundred and sixty pounds. His face appeared to be as hard as the concrete of which the courthouse had been constructed, and his bushy beard, black, sprinkled with gray, more than compensated for the lack of same on his head. The black robe which he wore only enhanced the air of authority that seemed to infuse him.

A starting guard on the University of Michigan's inaugural football team in 1879, he later graduated from the school of law, then practiced as an attorney in Escanaba for over twenty years before being appointed to the bench in 1905.

His reputation as a firm, but fair, judge was well earned.

"In the case before us," said Judge Hurstbourne, "the State of Michigan has charged one Paul Momet with murder in the first degree. Is Mr. Momet present in court?"

Paul and his attorney stood.

"He is, your honor," said the attorney.

"Good," said Judge Hurstbourne. "Then we shall proceed. And you sir are . . .?"

"Gerald Lawrence, representing the accused, your honor."

"Welcome to my courtroom, Mr. Lawrence." The judge turned to the bailiff. "Let's bring in the jury."

One by one, twelve people, seven men and five women, selected the day before, filed into the room and took their place in the jury box.

"Mr. Momet," said Judge Hurstbourne, "how do you plead?"

Lawrence nudged Momet. "Not guilty your honor," said Paul.

"You may be seated," said Judge Hurstbourne. "Mr. McIntyre, you may proceed."

Jake McIntyre had been the prosecuting attorney representing this part of Michigan for the last eight years. Like Judge Hurstbourne, he had graduated from the University of Michigan Law School, although much more recently, having been admitted to the bar only twelve years ago.

In his mid-thirties, stretching to reach five foot seven in height, but more than compensating for that deficiency in girth, he looked as though he had slept the previous night in the same clothes he now wore in court.

What few strands of hair he had left on his head seemed to possess a mind of their own as to which direction they preferred to fall.

In spite of his appearance, Jake McIntyre was an excellent prosecutor, with considerably more victories to his credit than defeats.

Jake didn't stand right away. Instead, he took a cigar from his jacket pocket and started to light it.

"Do not light that cigar, Mr. McIntyre," said Judge Hurstbourne.

"Your honor, I mean no disrespect, but it is a man's God-given right to smoke a cigar," said Jake.

"Since you appear to be a religious man," said the judge, a thin smile on his face, "you are no doubt familiar with that famous phrase."

"What phrase might that be, your honor?"

"The Lord giveth, and the judge taketh away," said Hurstbourne. "Now, Mr. McIntyre, do not light that cigar. You may chew on it if you like, but it will not be lit—not today, not in this courtroom."

"Yes, your honor," said Jake, grinning and placing the cigar back in his pocket.

He stood and approached the jury. "Ladies and gentlemen, the State will prove to you that on the night of March 8th, 1891, the accused, one Paul Momet . . ."

Myrtle only half listened as Jake laid out the case for the jury, how he would proceed to prove Paul Momet's guilt in the death of Yvette Sinclair.

She was more interested in studying the twelve people who would determine Paul Momet's fate.

Since Michigan had abolished the death penalty in 1846, his future had but two possible endings: freedom, if found innocent, or life imprisonment if found guilty.

Myrtle wondered if she would ever be able to serve on a jury that held a man's future in its hands.

She had been absent the previous day when the jurors had been selected, a rather quick process that took little more than an hour. But at dinner that evening, Henri had shared with her and Daisy—and Mr. Pfrommer, though he evidenced no interest in the matter—what he knew from talking afterwards with both Jake and Gerald Lawrence as to why certain jurors had been rejected.

"There were three jurors the prosecution rejected because they owed money at the hardware store," said Henri. "Jake was afraid they'd vote Paul innocent, hoping he would forgive their debts. Then there was one older woman who babysat for him when he was a toddler.

"Mr. Lawrence rejected two people who were employed at the college at the time Yvette went there, although what their biases might be I haven't the foggiest, because they both said they didn't know her. And one woman who was in her eighties if she was a day, when Lawrence asked her why she wanted to serve on the jury said because when they found Paul guilty, the jury members might have the first choice to attend the execution. Then she asked, would they be hanging Paul or shooting him, and if it was the latter could the jurists do it."

Myrtle and Daisy both broke out laughing.

"And he kicked her off just for that?" asked Daisy, straining hard to get the words out.

"Just for that," said Henri. "Later I found out from someone who knows the woman that she was doubly disappointed; first, that she couldn't be on the jury and second that Michigan didn't have the death penalty."

Of the twelve jurors, Myrtle recognized only two, townsfolk who came into the library on a regular basis. She was surprised that one juror—a man—was black: She wasn't aware any coloreds lived in Booker Falls other than Henri and his mother.

". . . and so, ladies and gentlemen, in conclusion," said Jake, "you will have no recourse but to find Mr. Momet guilty and sentence him to be incarcerated in the Marquette Branch Prison for the remainder of his natural life. Thank you."

"Mr. Lawrence," said Judge Hurstbourne, when Paul's attorney made no motion to get up. "Would you like to make an opening statement?"

Flustered, Lawrence jumped to his feet, in the process sending papers flying from his table onto the floor. Quickly, he bent over, scooped them up and deposited them back on the table.

"That's not a good start," whispered Daisy.

Myrtle nodded.

"Yes, your honor," said Lawrence, "I would, thank you, your honor.

"Members of the jury," said Lawrence, sounding none too confident, "in our judicial system a man is presumed innocent until proven guilty beyond any reasonable doubt. That is the responsibility of the state to prove.

"From what I have seen and heard of what the state will present to you, their case is built on two things: circumstance and conjecture, neither of which is sufficient to prove guilt. For motive, they would submit that Mr. Momet murdered Miss Sinclair for one of two reasons: jealousy, or fear that Miss Sinclair would reveal their affair to Mrs. Momet. I mean, even the prosecution cannot decide which motive has more credibility, if any.

"We will show that neither of those motives has any merit, that indeed, Mr. Momet and Miss Sinclair were in love, and that they had planned to leave town together upon Mr. Momet's return from his fishing trip."

Myrtle turned to Daisy and whispered, "Leave town together?"

Daisy shrugged her shoulders.

Myrtle wondered if Charlotte Momet knew of this turn of events, and how she would react. She looked around to find her, but it didn't appear she was in the courtroom.

"We shall further show that at least one other person, a prominent member of this community, had reason to kill Miss Sinclair," said Lawrence.

Daisy shoved her note pad in front of Myrtle. On it she had written "WHO?"

This time it was Myrtle's turn to shrug. Clearly, President Forrester couldn't have done it: He was out of town. And Henri seemed sure Frank Mitchell would have been physically unable to, with his broken arm. While Claude was an original suspect, he hardly qualified as a "prominent" member of the community. Besides, as short as Claude was, if he were the second man Frank had seen enter the library, not Paul, he would have recognized him for sure.

And how would they even know about Christiane Picot?

Was there someone else they'd overlooked? And, if so, how had Lawrence found out?

"Once the facts have been made clear," said Lawrence, "we feel you will have no other recourse but to find my client innocent."

By the time he finished, Gerald Lawrence's level of self-assurance had evidenced a considerable increase.

"All right, then," said Judge Hurstbourne. "We shall adjourn for the day. Mr. McIntyre, please be prepared to call your first witness when we resume tomorrow at ten o'clock. And Mr. Wilkerson . . ." the judge, sweating profusely, looked at the bailiff, ". . . you will see to it that those blasted windows are open tomorrow, eh?"

CHAPTER TWENTY-SIX

Instead of discussing the case at dinner that evening, Henri, Myrtle and Daisy met on the front porch afterwards at Mrs. Darling's request. Unable to attend the trial, she was anxious to find out what was happening.

"Henri, will you be testifying?" asked Mrs. Darling.

"I'll be the first one the prosecution calls tomorrow morning," said Henri.

"Oh, I wish I could be dere!" exclaimed Mrs. Darling.

"We'll keep you informed," said Daisy.

"Henri," said Myrtle, "do you know anything about this 'prominent' member of the community Mr. Lawrence referred to?"

"I don't. And apparently Jake doesn't either. All he knows is there's a woman on the defense's witness list named Sylvia Strong. Jake says he has no idea who she is."

"You're sure Frank Mitchell couldn't have done it?" asked Myrtle.

"I can't say for sure, but I certainly don't see how."

In his room upstairs, Mr. Pfrommer sat next to the open window, listening. He had foregone his usual hour of playing the violin so that he might hear the conversation below.

"Who else will Mr. McIntyre call?" asked Daisy.

"Frank, my mother and probably Claude."

"Your mother?" said Mrs. Darling.

"She saw Paul on campus the night Yvette was killed," said Henri.

"What about President Forrester?" asked Myrtle.

"He's not on the list. I don't know what he could possibly contribute."

"And how about Mr. Lawrence?" asked Daisy. "Who is he calling?"

"Besides this Miss Strong, and at least one character witness, the only other one is Paul. He'll testify on his own behalf. Of course, witnesses can always be added to the list."

"Not Mrs. Momet?" asked Mrs. Darling.

"I would think she would be the last one Paul would want up there on the stand," said Henri.

*****

Myrtle spotted Charlotte Momet again the next morning, sitting hunched over on one of the benches in the hallway. She wore the same clothes she'd worn the previous day.

Myrtle wondered if she would be in the courtroom today, or absent as she was yesterday.

The bell rang, the doors opened and the fifty spectators pushed their way into the room. Once again, Myrtle and Daisy found seats in the back.

Myrtle was happy to see that Judge Hurstbourne's orders had been carried out: Both windows were wide open, though it seemed not to have had much effect on the temperature in the room.

At the entrance of Judge Hurstbourne, everyone stood, then sat back down at his command.

"Mr. McIntyre, are you ready to begin?" he asked.

"I am, your honor. I call Constable Henri de la Cruz to the stand."

Moments later, Henri was sworn in and seated.

"Constable de la Cruz, you were the arresting officer of Mr. Momet, is that correct?"

"It is."

"And this arrest was made after conferring with my office regarding information you uncovered during the investigation of Miss Sinclair's death."

"That is correct."

"Information *I* uncovered," muttered Myrtle.

"This crime is twenty-nine years old. What prompted you to look into the matter?"

"The discovery of a cache of letters written to the deceased shortly before her death."

"Where did you find these letters?" asked Jake.

"I was not the one who found them," answered Henri. "They were found by Miss Myrtle Tully, the assistant librarian at the college."

Myrtle sat up straight. *Thank you! It's about time you acknowledged me.*

"And were these letters written by Mr. Momet?"

"Six of them were."

"Your honor," said Jake, "I would like to submit as prosecution exhibit one, one of the letters written by Mr. Momet—the last one written."

"Has the defense had an opportunity to read these letters?" asked Judge Hurstbourne.

"We have, your honor," answered Lawrence.

"Proceed," said the judge.

Jake handed Henri a letter. "Constable de la Cruz, in this letter did Mr. Momet threaten Miss Sinclair?"

"He did."

"Would you read it to the court, please?" asked Jake.

"The letter is dated February 14th, 1891," said Henri. "That was three weeks before Miss Sinclair was murdered," he added, turning to the jury.

Myrtle leaned over to Daisy and whispered, "Valentine's Day."

"My dearest Yvette," Henri read. "You must know you are the one true love of my life. I cannot imagine a future without you. You are in my every thought, my every dream. I cannot escape the vision of your lovely face. It haunts me incessantly. I know you love me, too. But I also know that the desires of the flesh that torment you have led you to search for fulfillment with others, others who, I assure you, cannot love you even one one hundredth as much as I do. There will never be another for me but you. But if I cannot have you, I do not think I can allow you to belong to another. Please, for both our sake's, do not let it come to that. Yours, forever, Paul."

"And Mr. Momet admitted to writing the letter?" asked Jake, when Henri finished.

"He did, along with the others."

"Now, these letters were discovered last year, and shortly thereafter, you interviewed Mr. Momet. But you only recently made the arrest. Why is that?"

"When Mr. Momet was originally questioned by Constable Barnoble shortly after Miss Sinclair's death, he had an alibi: He said he was out of town, fishing at Kennekuk Lake. When I questioned him last December he gave the same alibi. Recently it came to light that Mr. Momet returned to town the night of Miss Sinclair's death, and had been with her that evening."

"And where did this information come from?"

"From two sources," said Henri. "My mother, Christiane Picot, was a student at Adelaide at the time and was familiar with Mr. Momet. She remembered seeing him on campus that evening."

"Objection, your honor," said Lawrence. "Heresay."

"I merely asked where the constable got his information," said Jake. "His answer does not imply as to whether Miss Picot actually saw the defendant or not. However, we will be calling her eventually as a witness."

"Overruled," said Hurstbourne.

"And the second source?"

"Mr. Frank Mitchell, the head librarian at the college, said he saw both Mr. Momet and Miss Sinclair in the library the night she was killed."

Lawrence started to stand to object, but Hurstbourne waved his hand. "Sit down, Mr. Lawrence, same reasoning as before."

Jake continued. "The same night, you say?"

"That is correct."

"How was Miss Sinclair killed?" asked Jake.

"According to the original file, she was strangled to death," said Henri.

"By hand, or was there a murder weapon?"

"The original file did not specify that. There is a suspicion, however, that Miss Sinclair might have been strangled with her own scarf."

Jake picked up the scarf from his table and held it up. "Is this the scarf?"

"It is."

"Your honor, I would like to submit this scarf as prosecution exhibit two."

Judge Hurstbourne nodded.

"I have no further questions of this witness, your honor," said Jake.

"Mr. Lawrence, your witness," said Judge Hurstbourne.

"Constable de la Cruz," said Lawrence, approaching Henri. "Has Mr. Momet confessed to killing Miss Sinclair?"

"No, sir, he has not."

"To even being in Booker Falls the night of the murder?"

"No."

"Has he denied killing Miss Sinclair?"

"He has."

"The scarf we just saw—was that part of the original evidence?"

"No, it was not," said Henri.

"Where did it come from, then?"

"It was in the possession of Claude Amyx."

"The college custodian who discovered the body?" asked Lawrence.

"That is correct."

"How did he come to have the scarf?"

"He said he took it from Miss Sinclair's body."

"But this was not discovered until recently?"

"Yes."

"Mr. Amyx was originally a suspect in this case, was he not?"

"According to the original file, he and your client were the only two suspects," answered Henri.

"But my client has an alibi," said Lawrence. "How about Mr. Amyx? Why was he not charged?"

"Claude did not have an alibi, but there was insufficient evidence to charge him. Plus, he had no motive."

"At that time," said Lawrence. "But once you discovered he had taken the scarf—a fact unknown twenty-nine years ago—did he not then emerge as a viable suspect?"

"Claude had no motive to kill Miss Sinclair—your client did."

"So you say. Now, Constable de la Cruz, in your updated report there was also a question of Miss Sinclair's watch, which the report states the victim always wore on a chain around her neck. Was the watch found with the body?"

"There's no evidence it was. The original report does not mention it."

"Is it possible that whoever killed Miss Sinclair also took her watch?"

"Objection," said Jake, rising. "Calls for speculation."

"I'll allow it," said Judge Hurstbourne. "Constable, please answer the question."

"Assuming Miss Sinclair had the watch on at the time," said Henri, "anything's possible."

"In fact," said Lawrence, "did you not ask Mr. Momet if he had taken the watch?"

"I did."

"And his response?"

"He denied it."

"He denied it because he also denied killing Miss Sinclair, is that not so?"

"Yes."

"Constable de la Cruz, did your department conduct a search of both Mr. Momet's home and his business?"

"Yes."

"And did you find the watch?" asked Lawrence.

"We did not."

"And did you ask Mrs. Momet if she had any knowledge of such a watch?"

"We did. She said she knew nothing about it."

"Constable de la Cruz, it's been established that Mr. Amyx removed the scarf from Miss Sinclair's body. Did you ask him if he also removed the watch?"

Henri hesitated, then answered. "I did not, but Miss Tully did, and he claimed to have no knowledge of it."

"But you didn't ask him yourself."

"No, I did not."

"Thank you. Now in your earlier testimony you said there were eighteen letters found, but only six were written by my client. Who wrote the others?"

"They were written by four different individuals," said Henri.

"And do we know who they are?" asked Lawrence.

"Six were from Miss Sinclair's mother. The normal kinds of correspondence one might expect. Three others were signed with the initial 'W,' one, written in French, was signed Cee-cee, and two were unsigned."

"Let me ask my question again: Do we know the *identities* of these writers?"

"Two of them."

It was obvious Henri was not going to be any more forthcoming than he had to be.

"Your honor, may I treat Constable de la Cruz as a hostile witness?"

"You may," said the judge. "Mr. de la Cruz, I believe Mr. Lawrence wants the identities of the letter writers. As do I. Please answer."

A look of resignation on his face, Henri said, "The unsigned letters were written by Frank Mitchell—"

"One of the prosecution's witnesses, as I recall," said Lawrence.

"Yes. And the ones signed 'W' were written by Wilfred Forrester."

The room was still, the only sound the gentle whirr of the ceiling fan overhead.

"That would be President Forrester, president of Adelaide College."

"That is correct," said Henri.

"And the letter writer named Cee-cee—do we know who she is?"

"We have not been able to determine that," said Henri.

Myrtle sank down into her seat. She knew who it was. Which made her guilty of withholding evidence, she figured.

Daisy glanced at her out of the corner of her eye, but said nothing.

"The letter you read previously, the one written by Mr. Momet—you said it contained a threat on Miss Sinclair's life."

"Yes, it did—you heard it," said Henri, testily.

"Yes, you're right, I did," said Lawrence. "What I have not heard, however, are any of the other letters. Did any of them contain threats on Miss Sinclair's life?"

Henri hesitated for a moment before answering. "Yes, two did."

"I believe these are the two you are referring to," said Lawrence, holding up the letters.

He handed one to Henri. "You did such a good job of reading Mr. Momet's letter. Would you please read this letter to the court?"

"Yvette," read Henri, "I am warning you—if you say anything to my wife about our relationship it will be the last thing you do. I am serious. Keep your mouth shut. W."

"Again, that would be President Forrester who wrote that, is that correct?"

Henri nodded.

"Your honor, I would like to add President Wilfred Forrester to our witness list."

"Noted," said Judge Hurstbourne, scribbling on a pad of paper on his bench.

"And now, this other letter, written by the mysterious Cee-cee. Would you please read that to the court?" asked Lawrence.

Henri read the letter Christiane had written.

"But we have no idea who this Cee-cee is?"

"No."

"Your honor," said Lawrence, "I would like to submit both of these letters as defense exhibits one and two.

"Constable de la Cruz—one final question: Other than the letter my client wrote to Miss Sinclair and what you claim will be the testimony of two people who said they saw Mr. Momet in town that evening, one who put him with the deceased in the library, is there any other evidence that implicates Mr. Momet in Miss Sinclair's death? Any physical evidence of any kind?"

"Not to my knowledge," said Henri.

"I have no more questions of this witness, your honor," said Lawrence, returning to his table.

"I think we'll adjourn for lunch," said Judge Hurstbourne. "And reconvene at two p.m."

"Mr. Lawrence is a lot sharper than I thought," Daisy whispered to Myrtle.

Myrtle nodded. "Yes, I'm not sure that went well for the prosecution."

CHAPTER TWENTY-SEVEN

Frank was the first witness to be called after the lunch recess. As he made his way to the box, Myrtle thought he seemed nervous. She hoped he hadn't been trying to settle those nerves with the help of his Southern Comfort.

"Mr. Mitchell," said Jake, "you are the head librarian at Adelaide College Library, is that correct?"

Frank nodded.

"Mr. Mitchell, we need you to speak to answer the questions," said Judge Hurstbourne.

"Yes, sir, sorry. Yes," said Frank, "I am."

"And you were in that position twenty-nine years ago when Miss Sinclair was murdered, is that correct?"

"Yes, sir."

"Can you tell us what happened that night?"

Frank commenced to recount the events of that evening as he had related them to Henri.

". . . and that's when I left," Frank said, finishing.

"Now when did you become aware of Miss Sinclair's death?" asked Jake.

"The next morning, when I came to work. Claude had notified President Forrester—of course, he wasn't the president then—anyway, Claude had notified him and he had notified Constable Barnoble."

"But you didn't tell the constable what you witnessed the previous night?"

Frank hung his head. "I didn't want to get involved. I thought somebody might find out how I felt about Yvette, and think I killed her."

"And you have no idea where Miss Sinclair was to receive the money from that she referred to?"

"No, sir."

"I have no more questions, your honor."

This time Lawrence didn't have to be reminded about questioning the witness. He jumped to his feet and strode to the witness box.

"How *did* you feel about Miss Sinclair?" he asked.

Frank lowered his head. "I loved her," he said, softly.

"And did you ever tell her that directly?"

Without looking up, Frank shook his head. "No. I was too afraid."

"But you did send her letters."

"I did. But I didn't sign them."

"Now," said Lawrence, "you testified you saw Miss Sinclair first enter with Mr. Momet. How did you know him?"

Frank looked at Paul. "I knew him from the hardware store," he said. "And I'd seen him in the library. I knew he and Yvette were seeing each other."

"Then, you say Mr. Momet left, but reentered the library a few moments later."

"Yes."

"How did you know it was Mr. Momet the second time?"

"What?"

"How did you know it was Mr. Momet who came back in? Miss Sinclair had not come back to the door carrying the lantern, had she?"

Frank shook his head. "No. She was still back in the stacks."

"So it was dark at the front door. There was no light there."

"I . . . I guess so," Frank stammered.

"So what you saw was a silhouette, the figure of somebody. You couldn't tell for sure if it was Paul Momet."

"I . . . I guess not."

"In fact, Mr. Mitchell," said Lawrence, "how do you know it was a man you saw enter the second time?"

"It . . . I thought it was a man."

"But it might have been a woman? It was dark, all you saw was a figure, isn't that correct?"

"I . . . I guess so."

"In fact," said Lawrence, "it's possible there wasn't a second person at all, isn't it?"

"What do you mean?"

"I mean that after that first person left—the one you identified as Mr. Momet—you might have gone into the stacks and strangled Miss Sinclair yourself in a jealous rage."

Jake McIntyre and Frank both raised their objections at the same time.

"Mr. Lawrence," said Judge Hurstbourne, "please refrain from speculating. Mr. Mitchell is not on trial here."

"I'm sorry your honor," said Lawrence. "I have no more questions for this witness."

"Wow," said Daisy. "Where is Mr. Lawrence going with all this?"

"He's making the case for other suspects," said Myrtle. "Other people who might have killed Yvette."

"Redirect your honor?" asked Jake, rising.

Judge Hurstbourne waved his hand in agreement.

"Mr. Mitchell," said Jake. "Did you murder Miss Sinclair?"

"Heck, no," said Frank. "I couldn't have."

"And why couldn't you have killed her?" asked Jake.

"I had a broken arm. It was in a cast. I couldn't bend the darn thing," Frank answered, extending his arm and bending it.

"Thank you," said Jake.

"Mr. McIntyre," said the judge, "we have time for another witness. Would you like to call the next one on your list?"

"I would, your honor. I call to the stand Mr. Claude Amyx."

In his unique gait, like a boat on a choppy lake listing first to one side, then the other, Claude ambled to the witness box.

"Mr. Amyx," said the bailiff, "do you promise to tell the truth, the whole truth, and nothing but the truth, so help you God?"

Claude looked at Jake, who nodded.

"Okay," said Claude.

"You may be seated, Mr. Amyx," said Judge Hurstbourne.

"Claude," said Jake, "you were the one who found Miss Sinclair's body, is that correct?"

"Da dead girl?"

"Yes, the dead girl."

"I found her in da morning. She was dead."

"And you immediately notified Mr. Forrester."

"Yah, Mr. Forrester."

"Had you seen Miss Sinclair the night she was killed?"

Claude nodded. "Her and Mr. Mitchell, they was in da library."

"And they were still there when you left for the day."

"Yah."

Jake picked up the scarf and showed it to Claude.

"Claude, did you remove this scarf from Miss Sinclair's body?"

"My scarf. When do I get my scarf back?"

"I'm not sure, but I do have a question for you; was this scarf around Miss Sinclair's head, or was it around her neck?"

"Her neck. 'Round her neck."

"Thank you, Claude. No more questions."

Claude stood and started to leave.

"Mr. Amyx," said Judge Hurstbourne, "perhaps Mr. Lawrence has some questions for you."

"Thank you, your honor," said Lawrence. "I do have one question."

Claude sat back down.

"Mr. Amyx, when you removed the scarf from around Miss Sinclair's neck, did you also take her watch?"

"Watch?" said Claude, looking confused. "No, I no take watch. Just scarf."

"Did you see a watch around Miss Sinclair's neck?" asked Lawrence.

"No, no watch. When I get my scarf back?"

"Thank you," said Lawrence. "No more questions your honor."

"Mr. Amyx, you are excused," said the judge.

Claude looked around, confused.

"You may go now," said Judge Hurstbourne.

Slowly, Claude stood and, led by Henri, exited through the side door.

"Your honor," said Lawrence. "I would request the court order Mr. Amyx's house be searched to determine whether or not the watch in question is there."

A murmur went through the crowd.

"Your honor . . ." said Jake, rising.

Judge Hurstbourne raised his hand. "So ordered. Constable de la Cruz, please carry out a search of Mr. Amyx's house this evening and report back to us tomorrow.

"Due to the lateness of the hour," the judge continued, glancing at the Giltwood clock hanging on the back wall, "we will adjourn until ten o'clock tomorrow morning. Mr. McIntyre, you may call your final witness at that time."

*****

"How does your mother feel about testifying tomorrow?" Myrtle asked Henri at dinner that evening.

"She doesn't want to. Doesn't understand why she has to."

"But she does, doesn't she?" asked Daisy. "I mean, she has to testify."

Myrtle had a good idea why Christiane Picot was reluctant to testify. There were things she certainly wouldn't want to come out in court, things only Myrtle and Daisy knew.

"Unfortunately, yes," said Henri. "And I don't know why she's so nervous. All she has to say is she saw Paul Momet on the campus that evening."

Let's hope that's all she has to say, thought Myrtle.

*****

Christiane sat at her kitchen table, a glass filled with Jack Daniels Old No. 7 in her hand. She had already refilled the glass twice.

What was going to come out tomorrow, she wondered. Would it just be whether or not she had seen Paul Momet the night Yvette was killed? Or would they go deeper? Would they ask about her relationship with Yvette? They couldn't know about Wilfred—could they?

It was so long ago, that part of her life. She'd been in love with Yvette Sinclair, there was no denying that. But she knew they had no future together. While Yvette might have loved her—and somewhere, in the back of her mind, Christiane thought she did—the girl liked sex too much, both with men as well as women, to ever settle down with one person.

Maybe the one night stand she'd had with that young guy from town—Christiane couldn't remember his name now, nor even what he looked like—that night she'd gotten pregnant with Henri, maybe that was what had forced her to consider a life apart from Yvette.

And it turned out to be a pretty decent life. She'd had a wonderful, though relatively short, marriage, a fulfilling career in teaching that eventually led to where she was now.

She no longer needed a man—or a woman—in her life for companionship. Life was good.

And then those damn letters had to turn up.

Christiane took another drink and leaned back. Why had she been so open with that woman, that Miss Tully? She knew she'd told Henri about Paul. Did she tell him anything more? She thought not, or he would have said something to her.

There was no way she was going to hang her dirty laundry out to dry in an open courtroom. She knew Jake wouldn't ask any questions that could embarrass her. She wasn't so sure about Momet's lawyer.

Well, she thought, *if he asks me anything I don't want to answer—I just won't.*

She drained the glass, picked up the bottle and poured another drink.

CHAPTER TWENTY-EIGHT

Stylishly attired in a turquoise dress that perfectly accentuated her coffee-colored skin, her hair flawlessly coiffed, Christiane sat in the witness box, waiting, as Jake approached her.

"God," Myrtle whispered to Daisy, "isn't she beautiful?"

"If I liked girls," said Daisy, "I could certainly go for her."

"Miss Picot," said Jake, "you were a student at Adelaide College in 1891, at the time Miss Sinclair also attended there, were you not?"

"I was," said Christiane.

Jake turned and faced the jury. "And you were familiar with both Miss Sinclair and Mr. Momet."

"Yes."

"In what context did you know Mr. Momet?"

"I knew he was Yvette's boyfriend."

"On the day of March 8th, 1891, did you see Mr. Momet on the campus?"

"Yes, around five that evening."

"But Mr. Momet says he was fishing at Lake Kennekuk that day."

"Not at five o'clock he wasn't."

"Thank you, Miss Picot. Your witness, Mr. Lawrence."

Myrtle watched as Christiane seemed to withdraw into herself, her hands clasped together in her lap.

"Miss Picot, what was your relationship with Miss Sinclair?" asked Lawrence.

"Pardon?"

"Your relationship—how did you and Miss Sinclair know each other?"

"We were both students at Adelaide," said Christiane.

"And more?"

"What do you mean?" Christiane knitted her brows.

"Weren't you and Miss Sinclair roommates? And weren't you and she also lovers? And aren't you the Cee-cee who wrote the letter to Miss Sinclair in which you threatened to kill her if she revealed to the administration that you were pregnant?"

If it seemed as though the room had gotten quiet two days earlier when Wilfred Forrester's name was brought up, the silence now was even more pronounced, as if even the ceiling fan had paused in its rotation to hear the answer to the question.

Oh my God, thought Myrtle, putting a hand to her mouth. How does he know that? She looked at Henri, who looked as though someone had punched him in the stomach.

"Miss Picot?" said Lawrence, when Christiane failed to answer.

Christiane stared at Lawrence and cleared her throat. "I am invoking my rights under the fifth amendment not to answer those questions," she said, her voice quivering.

No silence in the courtroom now. Instead it sounded as though a swarm of angry hornets had suddenly invaded.

Lawrence looked at Judge Hurstbourne, who was banging his gavel on the bench. "Your honor?"

"What?" said the judge, when the hubbub subsided. "Miss Picot has invoked her right not to answer. Do you have any further questions?"

Lawrence turned back to Christiane. "Miss Picot," he said, "how old is your son, Constable Henri de la Cruz?"

"Objection, your honor," said Jake, rising to his feet. "Relevance?"

"Sustained."

"Miss Picot," said Lawrence, "were you pregnant when you graduated from Adelaide?"

"I refuse to answer—" Christiane started to say, but Jake interrupted her.

"Objection!" he shouted.

"Sustained," said Judge Hurstbourne, obviously annoyed. "Another line of questioning if you will, Mr. Lawrence."

Lawrence nodded and turned back to Christiane. "Miss Picot, were you and Wilfred Forrester lovers?"

The room was deadly quiet again except for Jake McIntyre.

"Objection, your honor," he cried, jumping to his feet again. "Where is Mr. Lawrence going with this line of questioning?"

"My question, exactly," said the judge. "Mr. Lawrence?"

"Your honor, we believe Miss Picot and Miss Sinclair were lovers, that Miss Picot is the Cee-cee who wrote the letter the court heard previously, and that she had a motive to have Miss Sinclair dead."

Daisy scribbled furiously, trying to get all the information down. This was going to make one heck of a story!

"Miss Picot is not on trial here," said Judge Hurstbourne, now noticeably perturbed. "The objection is sustained and the jury is instructed to disregard Mr. Lawrence's unfounded conjectures.

"Mr. Lawrence, do you have any more questions that pertain to the innocence of your client?"

Rather than the guilt of someone else, thought Myrtle.

"No more questions, your honor," said Lawrence, returning to his table.

"Miss Picot, you are excused," said Judge Hurstbourne.

Myrtle watched as a visibly shaken Christiane headed towards the side door. As she was leaving, she glanced at Henri and mouthed the words, "I'm sorry."

"Mr. McIntyre," said the judge, "do you have any other witnesses to call?"

"No, your honor."

"Constable de la Cruz," said Judge Hurstbourne, "did you complete the search of Mr. Amyx's home as I ordered?"

Henri stood up. "I did your honor. Miss Sinclair's watch was nowhere to be found."

"Very well, then, we shall adjourn until Monday at ten o'clock. Mr. Lawrence, please be prepared to call your first witness at that time. Court adjourned."

*****

"I don't know where the defense got their information," said Myrtle, "except it wasn't from me. I didn't even know about Henri's mother and Mr. Forrester. But I don't see how Christiane can think it came from anybody else."

She and Daisy had stopped at Miss Madeline's for a cup of tea following the court session. Daisy was going on to the newspaper office from there to type up her report, while Myrtle was returning to the boarding house to tell Mrs. Darling what had happened, hoping Henri would not be there.

"You think so?" asked Daisy.

"I have to go see her, to tell her I didn't do it." Myrtle looked at Daisy. "*You* didn't tell anyone what I told you she told me, did you?"

"Me? No, I haven't said anything to anyone, swear to God!"

"Well, at least she didn't admit to any of it."

Daisy grunted. "She might as well have. When someone takes the fifth, it's as good as admitting to whatever they're being accused of. Golly, I can't believe how juicy this all is. I'm going to have a best seller when this gets published.

"Not to change the subject—okay, to change the subject: I haven't seen George Salmon at any of the sessions. I thought he would have been there."

"He's out of town," said Myrtle, sipping her tea. "In Jackson."

"Jackson? And how do you know this?" asked Daisy.

"He told me. But he's returning this evening. Tomorrow we're going to Red Jacket."

Daisy raised her eyebrows. "Oh?"

"We're going to a show at the theatre—Harvey's Greater Minstrels."

"I hear they're very good," said Daisy.

"Have you ever seen them?"

"No, but I've read some reviews. I assume *you'll* be driving?"

Myrtle sighed. "I suppose so. You'd think some of the more enlightened men in this town would join the twentieth century and buy a car."

*****

Christiane played with the glass of bourbon in her hand while Henri paced the floor of his mother's kitchen.

"Is it true?" he asked. "Were you and President Forrester . . . you know . . ."

"Lovers?" said Christiane. "Yes, Wilfred and I were lovers."

"And you and Miss Sinclair—Yvette?"

Christiane took a drink, then sighed.

"Yes, Yvette and I were lovers also. You have to understand—it was a different time in my life."

"And you wrote the letter threatening her life. So, is President Forrester my . . .?"

"No, Henri, he's not your father. I'm not even sure who your father was."

"Why didn't you tell me all this? I wouldn't have let Jake put you on the stand."

She looked at him. "Why didn't I tell you? Tell you about my lovers, what kind of person I was?" She looked away. "Jake would still have had to call me as a witness. And it wouldn't have made any difference, anyway. I saw the witness list—Sylvia Strong. I'm sure she's the one who gave that Mr. Lawrence all that information."

"Who is she?" asked Henri. "I've never heard of her."

"She was in college with Yvette and me. Had the room next to us. I'm sure Yvette told her about us sometime and I'm afraid I'm the one who told her about Wilfred and me."

"But why did Lawrence bring it up at all? What's the purpose?"

"Don't you see what he's doing?" asked Christiane. "He knows the jury will believe Paul was with Yvette that evening, no matter how much he might deny it. But Mr. Lawrence is trying to put the idea into the jury's mind that someone else, someone who had a reason, like me and Frank, maybe even Wilfred—maybe even Claude—could have committed the crime, to instill reasonable doubt."

"But it won't work, will it? I'm sure Paul Momet killed that girl."

"Stranger things have happened," said Christiane, taking a long drink. She handed her glass to Henri and nodded towards the bottle sitting on the sink.

CHAPTER TWENTY-NINE

As soon as Myrtle finished lunch, she hurried upstairs to get dressed. George was coming at one, as they were planning to attend the matinee, then have dinner afterwards at the Michigan House.

Looking at herself in the mirror, even she was impressed by what she was wearing: a black, V-neck sleeveless dress with a pleated skirt, under a gold sequin wrap cape. She wished Henri could see her in it so he would know that she was, indeed, a woman, not a girl. But he had skipped lunch and was nowhere to be seen.

She had just finished running the brush through her hair when the blare of an automobile horn shattered the afternoon stillness.

Rushing down the stairs, she opened the front door to find a grinning George Salmon at the road, standing next to a shiny new automobile the color of a robin's egg.

Myrtle was as impressed by George's attire as she had been by her own: a white linen suit, straw boater hat, and a bow-tie that matched the color of his car.

"George?" she called out. "Is that yours?"

"Yah, it is," said George. "Isn't she a beaut? Come take a look."

"George, it's gorgeous," said Myrtle when she reached the car.

By now both Daisy and Mrs. Darling had come out from the house and were on their way to see George's new acquisition.

"What kind is it?" asked Myrtle. "And where did you get it?"

"In Jackson—I bought it in Jackson while I was down there. It's a Briscoe, manufactured by the Briscoe Company that's located there. This is the touring model. Cost me eleven hundred and eighty-five dollars."

Daisy, who was now walking around the vehicle, running her hand over its shiny side, let out a whistle.

Four-door, it had a convertible top like Myrtle's Model N, with leather covered seats, headlights and, of course, the horn that George had proudly beeped when he drove up.

"I didn't know you could drive a car," said Myrtle.

"They gave me a half hour lesson at the factory."

Myrtle rolled her eyes. "And you're driving us to Red Jacket?"

"I drove here from Jackson, didn't I?"

"Did you come across the straits on a ferry?" asked Daisy.

"I sure did. On the *Algomah.* And it was pretty rough, let me tell you, the ship bobbing up and down. I don't want to have to make that trip again anytime soon."

"All right," said Myrtle, "Let me get my bonnet and a jacket and I'll be ready to go."

Myrtle started for the house, then stopped and turned back.

"Does Henri know about this?" she asked.

"You mean the car?"

Myrtle nodded.

"Nope. Haven't seen him yet."

"He's not going to be happy," said Myrtle over her shoulder as she continued toward the house.

*****

Myrtle had to admit that George wasn't half bad as a driver.

It had been a pleasant trip to Red Jacket. At Myrtle's request, George left the convertible top down. She'd removed her bonnet and reveled at the feel of wind in her hair. Puffy white clouds broke up a sky so blue Myrtle thought it must have been painted expressly by God.

"Look there," said George, pointing to a tall white pine next to the road.

Myrtle looked up, shielding her eyes from the sun with her hand. About a hundred feet up in the tree she saw a large bird with a white head on a nest about eight feet in diameter.

"Is that . . .?"

"Yah, an eagle."

A slight movement a dozen feet higher revealed a second bird.

"They're magnificent," said Myrtle, marveling at the majestic creatures as George drove on by.

"Did you know they mate for life?" asked George.

"If one of them dies young it must be hard on the other one," said Myrtle. She remembered Mrs. Darling telling her she had been widowed at thirty-five, and never re-married.

"Eh, here's the thing," said George. "If one dies, the other looks for another mate. Survival of the species, you know."

Thirty minutes later, they were treated to another site when two does, accompanied by three fawns, leisurely crossed the road in front of them, disappearing into the woods.

"I love the wilderness of this place," said Myrtle as she watched them go. "There's always something new."

When they arrived in Red Jacket, they found the streets so crowded with cars, buggies and pedestrians that it was difficult to make their way down Sixth Street. Spaces to park the Briscoe were non-existent.

Eventually, they found themselves at St. Anne's Catholic Church at the other end of town from the theatre.

"I'll drive back to the theatre," said George, "and let you out. Then I'll find a place to park the car."

"Absolutely not," said Myrtle. "I'm perfectly ca—"

Just then Myrtle spotted an empty space. "There! Park there, George. We can walk from here easy."

Myrtle was happy they'd ended up parking on the other side of town. Walking up Fifth Street past massive buildings—the John Green Block, the Calumet Block, the Holman Block, Baer Brothers Building, and the Ruppe Block which contained the Ruppe department store where Daisy had purchased her typewriter—structures that housed myriad stores selling groceries, millinery, meat, shoes, confectionaries, pastries, drugs; and others that provided services: barber shops, undertakers, photography—allowed her to window shop, in awe at how cosmopolitan the town was.

"Look," said George, nodding towards a tall, well-built man in his mid-twenties, walking on the other side of the street. "That's George Gipp."

Myrtle looked at the man, then at George. "Who's George Gipp?"

"You've never heard of George Gipp? The All-American football player from Notre Dame?"

Myrtle was never one for football—or any other sport, for that matter. George Gipp might as well have been the man in the moon as far as she knew.

"He's probably the most famous football player in the world. And he lives right here—or right here in Laurium."

"Do you know him?" asked Myrtle.

"Met him once, that's all," said George as they continued up the street. "Shook his hand."

Myrtle thought she noted a sense of pride in George's voice.

They turned left at Oak Street, then took a right onto Sixth Street at the Michigan House. A block later, they stood in front of the Calumet Theatre.

"You haven't been here?" said George.

"Not inside," said Myrtle. "Daisy and I drove by it when we here last fall. She said sometime we'd come over for a play. But we never did."

As Myrtle entered the hall, her eyes were drawn to the five colorful murals—each one representing one of the five muses of the arts—that flowed in a semi-circle around the proscenium-arched stage that stood thirty-two feet wide, twenty-six feet deep, and twenty-six feet high.

Although the theatre could seat nearly twelve hundred people, only a portion of that number were present for this matinee performance.

George escorted Myrtle to their seats in the first row of the second balcony, for which he had paid the premium price of a dollar and a quarter each. They read through the program and settled back to watch the show.

For the next two hours, they roared and howled as white performers in blackface danced, sang, played musical instruments, presented skits and told jokes.

"What did you enjoy best?" asked George later, as they wound their way out of the theatre.

"I think my favorite was 'Spareribs' Jones," said Myrtle. "He was funny. Although I thought some of his jokes a little risqué."

"I liked 'Slim Jim' Austin," said George. "There aren't too many musicians who can play the glissando trombone that well. You ready for some food?"

"Absolutely!" said Myrtle.

*****

It was no surprise the Michigan House was crowded. Saturdays usually brought throngs of people into town. After a wait of about twenty minutes, George and Myrtle were seated and had placed their orders: beef tenderloin for Myrtle and pork loin chops for George.

"I like a woman with a good appetite," said George.

"Then you would love Daisy," said Myrtle. "I swear, that woman can eat like a longshoreman."

"And you're familiar with longshoremen?" said George.

"Only by reputation," Myrtle answered, smiling.

From where they sat they had an unobstructed view of the bar. Suddenly Myrtle spotted the man she thought had called out to Daisy from the window when they'd come to town to pick up the typewriter.

She laid her hand on George's arm.

"George, I need you to do me a favor."

"Of course. What is it?"

"See the man at the bar with the bowler hat?"

George turned to get a better look.

"Yah."

"I'd like for you to find out his name."

George turned back to Myrtle, a curious expression on his face.

"Why in the world would you want to know who he is?"

"I can't explain it," said Myrtle. "But it's important. Would you?"

"You expect me to walk up to the bloke and ask him his name?"

"No, not directly. You go up to him and say, 'Aren't you Mr. so and so?' Then, hopefully he'd say 'No, I'm Mr. so and so,' and you'd apologize, come back here and tell me what you found out."

"And if he said 'no' and turned back to his beer? Should I whack him one with my cane to regain his attention?"

"You'd still apologize, stick out your hand and introduce yourself. He'd almost have to introduce himself so as not to appear rude."

"Or I could go up and say, 'The young lady I'm with would like to know your name.'"

"No!" said Myrtle. "You absolutely cannot say that!"

"This is important to you?"

"It is."

George folded his napkin, laid it down, stood up and walked over to the bar. Myrtle turned so the man couldn't see who she was and peeked over her shoulder, but couldn't tell what was being said. She watched as the two men exchanged words, then shook hands.

George returned to the table and took his seat.

"Well?" she said.

"He was very nice. Said his name was Billy Fitzgerald, and that he worked at the Ahmeek mine over in Hubbell."

Fitzgerald—so it was *Mike's brother who called out to Daisy,* thought Myrtle. And he lives right here in the area. *But the question is: Is he here looking for Daisy?*

*****

Daisy was upset at the news Myrtle brought back from Red Jacket, that the brother of her late husband—whom she'd stabbed to death—was now no more than thirty miles away.

"I'm going to have to go," she said through the tears streaming down her cheeks. "Leave town. If he finds me, he'll kill me, I know it."

"Maybe you should talk to Henri," said Myrtle.

"And what—tell him I killed someone?"

"You're right. That might not be a good idea. But I don't think you should run, either."

Daisy stood and began pacing the room. "What else can I do?"

"First of all, you don't know he's here looking for you. He works at a mine. Maybe it's merely a coincidence he ended up here."

"Coincidence or not, he's here. And he saw me in Red Jacket. That means whenever I go there, or anyplace else for that matter, there's a chance he'll see me and recognize me."

"Let's sleep on it tonight," said Myrtle. "Maybe we'll come up with an answer tomorrow."

Daisy shook her head. "I don't know what it will be except for me to leave town. Leave the state. Shoot, maybe leave the country."

*****

Myrtle tossed and turned all night, worrying about Daisy. What options *did* the poor woman have other than running again?

When she awoke in the morning, she had come up with a plan. Not a perfect plan, but at least a plan.

"We'll disguise you," she told Daisy on the porch after breakfast.

"As what—a man? No, wait, a nun!"

"Nothing that drastic. We'll dye your hair. You'll start using makeup: lipstick, eye shadow, rouge. We'll buy you new clothes, not like what Billy would think you'd wear. We'll make a new you."

"And what happens if that doesn't work?" asked Daisy.

"Let's cross that bridge when we come to it," said Myrtle. "*If* we come to it," she added, quickly correcting herself.

Myrtle enlisted Mrs. Darling's help to cut and color Daisy's hair.

"Why does she want to do all dat?" asked Mrs. Darling. "I tink she looks beautiful just da way she is."

"She just wants to," answered Myrtle. "You know, sometimes a woman just wants to look different."

Mrs. Darling shook her head.

Later, at lunch, Henri stopped when he entered the dining room and saw Daisy.

"Very nice," he said, taking his seat.

*****

That afternoon the two women walked downtown. Myrtle wasn't sure where they could find what they needed to jazz up Daisy, but she'd seen Isabell Dougherty, the owner of de Première Qualité Women's Wear shop in the library on a number of occasions and was always impressed by how attractive the woman appeared. Myrtle was positive it was due in no small part to what had to be very good makeup.

Fortunately, the shop was one of the few in town that was open on Sundays.

When Myrtle explained what they wanted to accomplish—but not why—Isabell looked at Daisy and said, "We're going to make you beautiful."

An hour later, when Daisy looked in the mirror, she couldn't believe the face that stared back at her.

"My God!" she exclaimed. "You *did* make me look beautiful—or at least as close as you could, considering what you had to work with."

It was true. Daisy not only looked ten years younger than her forty-six years, but Isabell had successfully gotten rid of the dark circles under her eyes, and re-shaped her lips so they appeared, not vulgar, but certainly appealing.

"Okay," said Myrtle. "Next stop: dresses."

CHAPTER THIRTY

A light drizzle greeted Myrtle and Daisy as they made their way downtown to the courthouse. The day was overcast, the sky a smudgy gray, with dusky clouds swirling about. There was a chill in the air, uncommon for the Upper Peninsula that time of year. The two women chitchatted, speculating on what the trial proceedings might bring.

Myrtle had suggested they drive but Daisy insisted on walking. She wore one of the new dresses Myrtle had picked out for her the day before, and she wanted anyone they might pass to be able to see it.

"Besides," said Daisy, brushing raindrops from her sleeve, "today's the first day of spring. This rain won't last."

Fortunately, Mrs. Darling had loaned them her umbrella, which helped keep them at least partially dry.

Myrtle was relieved that, although Henri had showed up for all the meals over the weekend, he hadn't mentioned his mother's testimony.

Maybe she didn't say anything to him, thought Myrtle. *Maybe she doesn't think I'm the one who spilled the beans*.

When they entered the courthouse, people were milling about in the lower hallway. There were still twenty minutes before court was scheduled to begin. Myrtle spotted Henri deep in conversation with Jake McIntyre and beyond them Paul Momet's attorney talking with a woman who looked to be in her late forties. When Lawrence spotted Myrtle, he quickly ended his conversation and walked over to her.

As he drew near, the scent of Bay Rum lotion, a not altogether unpleasant fragrance, and one that Myrtle associated with fond memories of her father, preceded him. *It suited Mr. Lawrence well,* she thought.

"Miss Tully?" he said.

"Yes?"

"Might I have a word with you? In private?"

Myrtle arched her eyebrows. "Why . . . why, I suppose so."

Lawrence took her arm and led her into an empty room. As he did so, Myrtle glanced back at Daisy, who stood with a questioning look on her face.

Once inside the room, Lawrence closed the door and turned to Myrtle.

Should I be worried? she wondered.

"Miss Tully, I understand you met with Mrs. Sinclair last month," said Lawrence.

Myrtle relaxed. Lawrence's demeanor was so polite and placid, any concern she might have had melted away.

"That is true, I did," said Myrtle.

"I wonder if she told you anything, shared anything with you that might have a bearing on this case."

Myrtle hesitated. Should she be telling Paul Momet's lawyer anything that might help him get his client off? On the other hand, shouldn't all the pertinent information and facts about this case be known?

"Several things, actually," said Myrtle.

"Can you tell me what they were?"

"First of all, she confirmed that Miss Picot was Yvette's roommate, and that she went by Cee-cee. There was a photograph of the two of them hanging on the wall."

Lawrence nodded. "And?"

"She also told me Yvette always wore her watch on a chain around her neck."

Lawrence nodded again. "Which Constable de la Cruz detailed in his report."

Myrtle began to wonder why, since he already knew all of this, she was bothering to tell him.

Then she remembered. "Oh, and two more things. She said Yvette told her she was afraid of someone, a Mr. 'F,' but she didn't know who it was—Mrs. Sinclair, that is. And, Yvette showed her a picture of the man."

At this bit of information, Lawrence's eyes lit up. "Are you sure about that?"

"Yes, she said Yvette showed her a newspaper with a sketch of the man's face."

"Did she still have the newspaper?"

"Mrs. Sinclair wasn't even sure Yvette had left it there. And she didn't know where it might be."

"You said there were two more things."

Myrtle thought for a moment. "Oh, yes, the other thing—Mrs. Sinclair said Yvette told her she was coming into some money. Oh, but you knew that, too."

"Yes, but did she say how or when? Or who was giving her the money?"

"Mrs. Sinclair said Yvette wouldn't tell her."

"Miss Tully, as much as I would love to call you as a witness, everything you've told me would be hearsay. But this is extremely valuable information. Thank you."

"What did he want?" asked Daisy, when Myrtle rejoined her in the hallway.

"He wanted to know what Mrs. Sinclair told me when I visited her."

"Do you think he can use any of it?"

"Well, he already knew everything—except about Mr. 'F.' So, if he's as curious about Mr. 'F' as I am, he might pursue that."

*****

Lawrence's first witness was Sylvia Strong, the woman Myrtle had seen him conversing with earlier.

"Did Mr. Lawrence tell you who this woman was?" Daisy whispered to Myrtle.

"No, but I'm sure we're about to find out," Myrtle whispered back.

"Mrs. Strong, you were a student at Adelaide College in 1891, were you not?" asked Lawrence.

"Yah, I was."

"And what was your relationship with the deceased, Miss Yvette Sinclair?"

"I had da room next to her and Cee-cee."

"By Cee-cee, are you referring to Christiane Picot?"

"Yah," said Sylvia. "That's what everyone called her back then. She and Yvette were roommates."

"And were they lovers also?" asked Lawrence.

"Objection," said Jake, looking up from his notes. "Relevance?"

"Mr. Lawrence?" said Judge Hurstbourne.

"Your honor, there are letters from two persons other than my client who threatened harm to Miss Sinclair. I believe Miss Picot to be one of them, the writer named Cee-cee."

"I'll allow it," said Judge Hurstbourne. "With some reservations," he added.

"Mrs. Strong?" said Lawrence.

"Yah," said Sylvia, "da two of them were lovers."

"And how do you know this?"

"Yvette told me. And Cee-cee told me she and old man Forrester was lovers, too."

"Objection, your honor!" cried Jake, this time rising to his feet.

"Mrs. Strong, please limit yourself to the questions asked of you," said the judge. Then he turned to the jury. "The jury will disregard that last statement by Mrs. Strong."

"As if they could," muttered Myrtle.

"Thank you, Mrs. Strong," said Lawrence. "Your witness, Mr. McIntyre."

Jake stood, hesitated for a moment, then decided he had nothing more. "No questions, your honor," he said.

"Mr. Lawrence, your next witness?" said Judge Hurstbourne.

"We call Mr. Wilfred Forrester to the stand, your honor."

When Wilfred entered the witness box, Myrtle thought he looked as nervous as Christiane had when she'd been called by the prosecution. No wonder. A lot of dirty, little, thirty-year-old secrets were coming out in this trial.

"President Forrester," said Lawrence, "in 1891 you were, at that time, Dean of Students at Adelaide College, is that correct?"

"Yes, it is," said Wilfred, his voice obviously strained.

"And were you at that time in a relationship with the deceased, Miss Yvette Sinclair?"

Wilfred hesitated, then answered. "I was."

"You were lovers, is that correct?"

"Yes."

"And Miss Sinclair threatened to tell your wife about the affair?"

"Yes." Drops of perspiration began to creep down Wilfred's brow.

"And you sent Miss Sinclair a letter threatening her in turn if she did tell your wife?"

"Yes, but I didn't kill her. I couldn't have. I was in Sault Sainte Marie the night she was murdered."

"So I heard. Did you hire someone to kill her while you were out of town?"

Lawrence's directness was like an electric shock running through the courtroom.

This time Jake didn't have a chance to object before Lawrence spoke. "I withdraw the question."

"Mr. Lawrence," said Judge Hurstbourne, pointing his finger at Lawrence and wagging it, "my patience is wearing thin. I have warned you several times over the past week about this approach you seem to persist in taking. It is your client who is on trial here, and no one else. Is that clear?"

"It is, your honor. My apologies."

"If it happens again," said the judge, "I will hold you in contempt."

"Yes, your honor. No further questions."

Jake stood and walked over to Wilfred. He pulled a handkerchief from his pocket and handed it to Wilfred, who took it and wiped his brow. He made as if to hand it back, but Jake waved it off.

"President Forrester, Miss Sinclair threatened to tell your wife about the affair. But hadn't your wife already found out?"

"She sure had," said Wilfred, somewhat more composed. "And she was ticked off, I can tell you."

A snicker ran through the crowd.

"So you had no reason to kill Miss Sinclair, since your wife already knew about the affair."

"That's right."

"No more questions, your honor," said Jake.

"Your next witness, Mr. Lawrence?" said Judge Hurstbourne.

"Your honor, we would like to add a witness to our list, Mrs. Elizabeth Sinclair."

The stirring of voices filled the courtroom.

"The victim's mother?" said Judge Hurstbourne, not sure he had heard correctly.

"Yes, your honor. We believe Mrs. Sinclair may be aware of certain information that casts doubt on my client's guilt. And, as Mrs. Sinclair lives in Marquette, we request a continuance until tomorrow so she may be brought here."

"Mr. McIntyre, your thoughts on this?" said the judge, looking at Jake.

"Your honor, I think it highly inappropriate that the victim's mother be called to testify for the accused."

"I agree. However, if Mrs. Sinclair does indeed have information pertinent to Mr. Momet's innocence . . . or guilt," said Judge Hurstbourne, lowering his gaze at Lawrence, "I think it should be heard. I'll grant both of your requests, Mr. Lawrence. You may call Mrs. Sinclair, and we will adjourn until one p.m. tomorrow."

"Wow, was that a surprise," said Daisy as they walked down the stairs to the first floor. "What do you suppose he's going to ask Mrs. Sinclair?"

"I'm pretty sure he plans to ask her about this Mr. 'F' Yvette said she was afraid of. That's certainly one piece of this puzzle that I haven't figured out," said Myrtle as she opened the door to exit the courthouse . . . and groaned.

It was raining harder now.

CHAPTER THIRTY-ONE

Myrtle and Daisy each cradled steaming cups of coffee in their hands as they sat on the front porch of the boarding house and listened to the rain beating a steady tat-a-tat-tat on the roof above their heads. Penrod lay curled up at the feet of Mrs. Darling, who had joined them.

Myrtle ran over in her mind the testimony they had heard the day before. Was Mr. Lawrence succeeding in raising doubts in the minds of the jurors about Paul Momet's guilt by implying there were other, just as worthy, suspects?

She herself, at one time or another, had thought any of the letter writers other than Yvette's mother, especially the three who'd threatened Yvette, could be guilty. But they all seemed to have either good alibis or no reason to have killed her.

Until Paul Momet's alibi went out the window.

Even now, there was a nagging doubt in Myrtle's mind about his guilt.

Daisy, wrapped up in her cardigan to ward off the chill, was deep in her own thoughts, anxious about the fact that Mike's brother had followed her here to Copper Country. How much longer would it take him to find her? And what would he do when he did? Kill her? She'd never known Billy Fitzgerald to be a mean person, but people who are out for revenge can sometimes become someone they aren't.

She shivered. Not so much from the dampness in the air as at the uncertainty that lay ahead.

Mrs. Darling's thoughts were more mundane. She was planning that night's dinner: lamb chops with new potatoes and green beans. What she hadn't decided on yet was dessert. Should she bake a pie? Or make a custard?

She took off her glasses and wiped them on her apron. Pie . . . or custard?

*****

Myrtle and Daisy hurried through lunch in time to make the resumption of the trial at one o'clock. Henri had not appeared to eat with them.

The rain had not let up. This time Daisy was all too ready to take Myrtle up on her offer to drive downtown.

They parked across the street from the courthouse, behind a basic, black Model T Ford, not nearly as elegant as either Myrtle's Model N or George's Briscoe.

"Who do you suppose that belongs to?" asked Daisy.

"My guess would be either that reporter from Houghton, or Mr. Lawrence," said Myrtle.

Daisy nodded. "Mr. Lawrence. He seems the type."

*****

Myrtle watched as Henri assisted Mrs. Sinclair to the witness box. She looked much older, more frail, than Myrtle remembered when she'd seen her a month ago.

In a weak voice, Mrs. Sinclair vowed to tell the truth, the whole truth and nothing but the truth.

"Mrs. Sinclair," Lawrence began, "first of all, thank you for making the trip here from your home. You understand you're testifying for the defense, for the man accused of murdering your daughter?"

"I do," said Mrs. Sinclair.

"I'd like to ask you about Yvette's watch. She always wore it on a chain around her neck, is that correct?"

Mrs. Sinclair nodded. "It was a gift from her father..." Mrs. Sinclair crossed herself, looked up, then back at Lawrence, "...on her twelfth birthday. She always wore it."

"And do you have the watch?"

Mrs. Sinclair looked confused. "Me? No. I don't have it."

"And you don't know its whereabouts?"

Mrs. Sinclair shook her head.

"If it please the court, let the record show Mrs. Sinclair answered in the negative," said Lawrence. "Now, Mrs. Sinclair, this photograph you brought with you—it's a picture of your daughter and her roommate at Adelaide, Cee-cee, is that correct?"

Mrs. Sinclair looked at the photograph that Lawrence held out before her.

"Yah, that's dem."

"Your honor, I'd like to submit this photograph as defense exhibit three, which corroborates the testimony previously heard by Mrs. Strong that Christiane Picot, known as Cee-cee, was indeed Miss Sinclair's roommate."

Judge Hurstbourne nodded. Lawrence walked over to the clerk and handed the photograph to her. Then he returned to Mrs. Sinclair.

"Mrs. Sinclair, I assure you once this whole matter is settled, your photograph will be returned to you."

Mrs. Sinclair broke into tears. Taking a handkerchief from her pocket, she wiped her eyes. "Won't make no difference. I don't reckon I'll be around by den anyway."

"How long does she think this trial's going to last?" Daisy asked, lowering her voice.

"I think she's dying," muttered Myrtle. "That's why she looks so bad."

Lawrence stepped back, stunned. “I’m so sorry, Mrs. Sinclair.” He hesitated for a minute, then asked, “Do you feel well enough to continue?”

Mrs. Sinclair nodded.

“Did your daughter ever confide to you she was frightened by anyone?” asked Lawrence.

“Yah, she did. She said she was afraid of Mr. ‘F.’ She showed me a picture of him in da newspaper.”

“Did she say who this Mr. ‘F’ was?”

“No.”

“So you don’t know who he was, either.”

“No.”

“Mrs. Sinclair, do you still have the newspaper your daughter showed you?” asked Lawrence.

“No,” said Mrs. Sinclair. “I’m not sure if she left it at da house or took it back to school with her.”

“Mrs. Sinclair, one last thing: Did your daughter tell you she was about to come into some money?”

“Yah, she did. Last time she was home, when she brought da newspaper. Said she was going to come into some money.”

“Did she say from where, or from whom, this money would come, or how much she would be getting, or when?”

“No, she didn’t tell me nothing about none of that, just that she was getting it.”

“Mrs. Sinclair, again, I appreciate your taking the time to appear here today. No more questions, your honor.”

“Mr. McIntyre?” said Judge Hurstbourne.

“No questions, your honor.”

“Mr. Lawrence, you may call your next witness.”

“Your honor, we call Mr. Paul Momet to the stand.”

A murmur swept through the crowd of spectators. At last, they’d be hearing Paul’s side of the story.

Myrtle looked around the room. She wondered if Charlotte Momet had shown up today for her husband's testimony. She'd been in the hallway outside the first two days, but hadn't come in. And Myrtle hadn't seen her on Friday or yesterday.

She spotted her, seated in the back row, next to the wall. She looked pale and drawn.

"Mr. Momet," said Lawrence, "you've been charged with the murder of Yvette Sinclair. Did you kill her?"

Paul shook his head. "No! I loved Yvette. I'd'a never hurt her."

Myrtle glanced back at Charlotte. Her face was emotionless.

"You claimed previously, twice in fact, in 1891 and again last December, that on the evening Miss Sinclair was murdered, you were fishing at Lake Kennekuk. Were you telling the truth both times?"

Paul hung his head. "No," he said, his voice almost inaudible. "I wasn't. I was here in town dat night."

The swarm of angry hornets returned to the room.

"Quiet!" yelled Judge Hurstbourne, banging his gavel. "Quiet, or I'll have the room emptied!"

"So," said Lawrence, "you were in Booker Falls. And were you with Miss Sinclair that evening?"

Paul looked up at Lawrence. He appeared so pitiful Myrtle almost felt sorry for him.

"Yah," said Paul. "Me and Yvette, we met up at da library."

"And you were intimate," said Lawrence.

"Yah, we were."

This time only a murmur made its rounds of the room.

"Now, Mr. Mitchell testified he saw you and Miss Sinclair together in the library that night, which you have confirmed. He also testified he saw you leave, and minutes later return. Is that true? Did you return?"

"No!" Paul answered, more sure of himself now. "When I left I went straight over to Andy's house and spent da rest of da night dere before I went back to da lake next morning."

"Andy?"

"Andy Erickson, a friend of mine."

"And will Mr. Erickson verify you spent the night at his home."

"He sure better."

"And when you left the library, was Miss Sinclair still alive?"

"She sure was."

"I'd like you to walk us through what happened that evening if you would."

"Okay, den. I seen Yvette in town earlier dat week. She wanted to meet up with me; she had something exciting to tell me, she said. I told her I had dis fishing trip planned, but I'd slip back Sunday evening and we'd hook up at da library.

"So, Sunday comes and I get back to town. Yvette and me, we meet up in da grove . . ."

"The grove next to the library?" said Lawrence.

"Yah, dat one. Den she says, let's go on in, so I says well, okay, den. Now, it's darker'n a skunk's a—well, it was really dark in dere, but Yvette, she's got dis lantern, so we could see okay. She leads me back to da stacks and I'm thinking we're going to do it, but she says, wait, she's got something to tell me. Well, I sure din't feel like waiting, but I did.

"Then she says she's going to come into a lot of money real soon. I said, how soon? She said dat night."

"That night? She said she was getting the money that night?" asked Lawrence.

"Yah, dat's right—dat night."

"And did she say where this money was coming from?"

"No," said Paul, shaking his head. "I asked her, but she din't want to say."

"Go on."

"Den she says she wants to run away with me."

"Run away with you?"

"Yah, says she really does love me and wants to run away with me."

"Run away to where?"

"New York. Says she wants to try her hand at show business."

"And did you agree to this?" asked Lawrence.

"Heck, yeah, I agreed. I was in love with Yvette. I only married Charlotte 'cause I taut Yvette was done with me. We was going to leave town on Tuesday after I got back on Monday."

"I hope you burn in Hell, you rotten bastard!" shouted Charlotte from the back of the room, jumping up from her seat.

Everyone turned to look.

"I hate you!" Charlotte shouted again, tears streaming down her face as she climbed over people on her way to the aisle.

Judge Hurstbourne banged his gavel. "Order, order!" he cried.

But by then Charlotte was out the door.

A visibly shaken Paul Momet sat glued to his seat.

For a moment, Lawrence was speechless. Then he turned back to Paul. "Uh, Mr. Momet, what happened next?"

"Huh?" said Paul, still stunned by Charlotte's outburst.

"What happened after Miss Sinclair told you about the money?"

"Den we made love," said Paul.

"And then you left?"

"I din't want to, but Yvette looked at her watch . . ."

"The watch she wore around her neck?"

"Yah, dat watch. She looked at it . . ."

"How could she see it in the dark?" asked Lawrence.

"Da lantern was still lit. We never turned it off."

"So she looked at her watch . . ." said Lawrence.

"She looked at her watch," said Paul, "and said I had to go, like she was expecting somebody. I left and went straight to Andy's."

"And you didn't go back inside."

"No, sir, I did not."

"One more question—was Miss Sinclair still wearing her head scarf when you left?"

"Yah, she had da dern thing on da whole time we was . . . well, yah, she still had it on when I left."

"No more questions, your honor."

Jake stood and took his time walking to the witness box.

"That's quite a story, Mr. Momet," he said when he stood before Paul. "And very believable—right up to the point where you say you didn't go back in the library and you didn't kill Yvette Sinclair."

"But I din't," Paul protested. "I din't. I loved Yvette. We was going away together."

"So you say," said Jake. "Can anyone else verify you and Miss Sinclair planned to run away together?"

"Andy. Andy can. I told him all about it when I got to his house."

"*After* you got to his house. Of course, that would have been after the fact, wouldn't it, after the fact that Yvette Sinclair was already dead because you'd just killed her."

"No, dat's not true! I din't kill her. She was alive when I left her."

"Mr. Momet, you've already lied twice, once twenty-nine years ago when you said you were fishing at Lake Kennekuk, and again last December when you were interviewed by Constable de la Cruz. The only reason you finally admitted you were in town the night Yvette Sinclair was killed is because two witnesses put you there. Why should we believe you now, when you say you didn't kill Yvette Sinclair?"

"Because I din't! I loved her!"

"I have no more questions of this witness, your honor," said Jake, turning and walking back to his table.

"Mr. Momet, you are excused," said Judge Hurstbourne. He looked at the clock. "I see our time has grown short. We will adjourn until ten o'clock tomorrow morning, at which time, Mr. Lawrence, you may call your final witness. Do you anticipate his testimony will take long?"

"A few moments only, your honor."

"Then we will commence with closing arguments immediately thereafter," said the judge.

CHAPTER THIRTY-TWO

Jake took a long drink of scotch from his glass and started drumming on the table with his fingers. He was uneasy. George and Henri had joined him in his office to discuss how the trial was going.

"I'm still concerned about the other things," he said.

"You mean the watch and the money?" asked George.

Jake nodded. "Yeah, and that blasted reference to some mysterious Mr. 'F.' I'd sure like to know who that was."

"I don't know how we'll ever find out," said Henri. "And as far as the watch and the money is concerned, I think Momet took the watch and sometime later pawned or sold it, either here or over in Red Jacket or Houghton or Hancock or somewhere."

"And the money?" said George.

"I think Yvette made that up," Henri answered. "She wanted to get out of Booker Falls and figured if she told Momet she had money, he'd take her."

"But it wasn't only Momet she told; she also mentioned it to her mother, as well as Frank," said George.

Henri shrugged. "I don't know then. What do you think this Erickson fellow's going to say tomorrow?" he asked Jake.

"I think he's going to corroborate Momet's story, that he spent the night with him. But I'm going to make him out to be a liar, and get his testimony discredited."

"How you plan on doing that?" asked George.

Jake smiled. “You’ll see.”

He picked up the bottle of scotch and refilled all three glasses.

*****

Andy Erickson was one of three men employed by the town of Booker Falls to push a wheeled barrel through the streets, cleaning up the droppings of the numerous horses that provided transportation to its citizens.

He looked the part: scruffy, unkempt, grubby—Daisy ran as many words through her mind as she could to describe the man while she scribbled her notes.

“Mr. Erickson, you and Mr. Momet are friends, is that correct?” asked Lawrence.

“Since we was kids,” said Andy. He looked at Paul and grinned. “My pa owned da barber shop next to da hardware store.”

“On the night in question, March 8th, 1891, the night Yvette Sinclair was murdered, did Mr. Momet spend the night at your home?”

“He sure did. Spent da whole night there.”

“And what time did he arrive?” asked Lawrence.

“’Bout eight o’clock.”

“Did he discuss with you what transpired between him and Miss Sinclair earlier that evening?”

“Sure did,” said Andy. “Said him and old Yvette got it on in da liberry.”

“And what else did he tell you?” asked Lawrence.

“Said him and Yvette was planning on running away after he got back from fishing. Said she was getting some money.”

“He didn’t seem like a man who’d just killed his girlfriend?”

“Heck no! He seemed like a man who’d just . . . who’d just, you know, had a really good time.”

“Thank you. Your witness, Mr. McIntyre.”

"Now, you and Paul Momet are good friends," said Jake, as he approached Andy.

"Yep, that's right. Best friends."

"Mr. Erickson," said Jake, leaning on the front railing of the witness box, "do you know what the term *perjury* means?"

"Huh?" It was clear from Andy's expression he had no idea what Jake was talking about.

"Perjury is when you tell a lie under oath. An oath, such as the one you took a few minutes ago."

"Okay," said Andy, shrugging. "So?"

"Have you ever perjured yourself?" asked Jake.

"What do you mean?"

"Have you ever told a lie while under oath?"

Andy scrunched his brows. "Shit, no!"

"Mr. Erickson," said Judge Hurstbourne, "please watch your language in my courtroom. Otherwise, you will find your wallet considerably lighter than when you arrived."

"Sorry, your honor," said Andy. Turning back to Jake, he said, "I might of told a lie or two in my time, but not in no courtroom."

Jake walked back to his table and picked up a sheet of paper. "Mr. Erickson, were you and Mr. Momet good friends in 1903?" He turned to look at Andy.

"1903? Yeah, like I said, all our lives."

"Do you recall that in 1903 you spent nine months in jail?"

"Objection, your honor," said Lawrence. "Relevance?"

"Your honor," said Jake, "goes to the witness's credibility."

"I'll allow it," said the judge. "But let's get to it."

Jake turned back to Andy. "1903? Nine months in jail? Remember that?"

"Well, I been in jail a couple times," said Andy, "but if you say so, I'll go along."

"In January of 1903, Mr. Momet was charged with robbing your father's barber shop on a Sunday morning. You testified you saw him leaving the shop with a bag of money and a jug of whiskey. But when two other witnesses, including a priest, testified that at the time of the robbery Mr. Momet was in church having his baby baptized, you recanted and admitted that you took the money yourself. Seems you and your friend, Mr. Momet, had gotten into an argument a few days earlier and you wanted to get him in trouble.

"Your father declined to press charges, but you were still found guilty of giving false testimony and served nine months at Marquette. Remember that now?"

Andy sank back in his chair. "Yeah, okay, I remember it. So what?"

"So you're a proven liar, and you've lied under oath. Are you lying now? Are you lying to make up for trying to get Mr. Momet in trouble seventeen years ago?"

"No! I ain't lying. I'm a' tellin' da truth!"

"Mr. Erickson, do you do business at Momet's Hardware?"

"Yeah, some."

"In fact, didn't you have a balance there last week of some one hundred and twenty-one dollars and forty-seven cents?"

"Maybe. I ain't exactly sure of da 'mount."

"And did Mr. Momet tell you he would wipe that amount off the books if you testified here today?"

"Well, yah," said Andy. He glanced at Paul and started to squirm. "He did. But I'm still telling da truth. I ain't lying. He spent da night at my house da night Yvette got killed."

"Thank you, Mr. Erickson; no further questions," said Jake.

Lawrence stood. "One more question, your honor. Mr. Erickson, Mr. Momet forgave your debt, but you would have testified anyway, isn't that correct?"

"Yah, I guess so," said Andy, sounding not all that convincing. "Probably."

Lawrence frowned, considered asking another question to overcome the uncertainty of Andy's answer, then decided to let it go.

"No more questions, your honor."

As Andy left the witness box, Jake stood.

"Your honor, I would like to recall two of the defense's witnesses, Mrs. Strong and Miss Picot."

"Very well. Are either of the ladies present in the building?"

"They both are, your honor."

"Then let's have the first one," said the judge.

Sylvia Strong wasn't sure what she could tell the court that she hadn't already, but she sat quietly in the witness box, waiting for Jake McIntyre's question.

"Mrs. Strong," said Jake, "did you see the deceased, Miss Sinclair, on the day she was murdered?"

"Sure," answered Sylvia. "We ate breakfast together."

"And did Miss Sinclair make any mention of her plans to run away with Mr. Momet?"

"No, she told me she was going to see him that evening, but that was all."

"Thank you."

Christiane had heard Jake's questions and Sylvia's answers, and was pretty sure she'd get the same.

"Miss Picot, did you see the deceased, Miss Sinclair, on the day she was murdered?"

"Several times," said Christiane. "We both rose about the same time that morning. I went to Mass and Yvette was still in our room when I returned."

"And did she say anything about running away with Mr. Momet?"

"No, she did not. Nor did she say anything about meeting him later that day."

"Thank you, Miss Picot. Your honor, I have no more questions."

"Mr. Lawrence?" said the judge.

"No questions, your honor."

"I see it is ten minutes before eleven," said the judge, "and I am hopeful we will be able to conclude with the closing arguments today. Therefore, let's adjourn and reconvene promptly at noon, at which time we will hear Mr. McIntyre."

A mad rush for the doors ensued, as everyone wanted to make sure they found a nearby place in which to eat, then make it back in time for the start of arguments.

Daisy and Myrtle shoved right along with the crowd and in minutes found themselves on the sidewalk outside the courthouse.

"What now?" asked Daisy. Any thoughts of getting served on time at Miss Madeline's, located across the street from the courthouse, were gone, as that was where most of the spectators had headed. No one was going into The Polar Bear, which was right next door.

"There," said Myrtle, pointing as she dashed across the street.

"Ice cream for lunch?" shouted Daisy, hurrying to catch up with her.

"I've had worse. Besides, they have hot dogs, too."

"Okay, then, sounds good to me," said Daisy.

CHAPTER THIRTY-THREE

When Myrtle and Daisy got back to the courthouse, it was apparent they'd chosen wisely in foregoing Miss Madeline's. More than half of the previous spectators were still absent.

This time they squeezed as close to the doors of the courtroom as they possibly could, and were rewarded by nabbing seats in the second row.

Myrtle spotted Henri and waved him over.

"How long will it take for the jury to come to a decision after the closing arguments?" she asked.

"I know for a fact the judge is going home for the night right afterwards," said Henri. "Even if the jury was to decide within ten minutes, he won't hear their decision until tomorrow morning."

Judge Hurstbourne entered and the normal process of standing up, then sitting back down, commenced as he took his seat.

"Mr. McIntyre," he said, once he was settled in, "you're up."

"Thank you, your honor," said Jake. He stood and walked slowly to the jury box, lingering there for a moment, as he studied each of the jurors.

"Ladies and gentlemen, you have a tremendous responsibility here. The state has charged Paul Momet with voluntary manslaughter. What does that mean? It means the state does not believe Mr. Momet went to the Adelaide College Library on the night of March 8th, 1891, with the intention of killing Miss Sinclair, but that something happened to cause him to want to take her life. We believe that something was a jealous rage.

"Only weeks before the day in question, Mr. Momet wrote a letter to Miss Sinclair, threatening her life, warning her that if he couldn't have her, no one else would. And even though, within the next week, he married another woman, he continued to harbor the hope that Miss Sinclair would be his.

"By his own admission, he was with her the night she was murdered, in the very location where the crime took place. He would have you believe he and Miss Sinclair conspired to run away together, yet Miss Sinclair did not share that information with anyone, including either her roommate, or her close friend, Mrs. Strong. The only other one who has spoken to that is Mr. Erickson, and his testimony, if truthful—and I remind you he is a convicted perjurer—was what was supposedly told to him by Mr. Momet.

"Mr. Lawrence has tried to raise the possibility of guilt of other individuals, including two who, like Mr. Momet, wrote threatening letters to Miss Sinclair. But, unlike Mr. Momet's motive—namely, jealousy—the other letter writers' reasons were resolved before Miss Sinclair was killed, and therefore no longer existed. Also, unlike Mr. Momet, these other individuals all had alibis.

"The state believes this is what transpired that night: Mr. Momet returned from his fishing trip for a pre-arranged meeting with Miss Sinclair at the library, where they engaged in sexual activity. Miss Sinclair then told Mr. Momet it would be the last time—that she wanted nothing more to do with him. Mr. Momet left the library, then, becoming enraged by Miss Sinclair's rejection, returned and strangled her, using her own scarf.

"He then left the library a second time, went to Mr. Erickson's home, told him a cock and bull story about him and Miss Sinclair running off together. The next morning, Mr. Momet returned to Kennekuk Lake, continued fishing, and returned home that evening.

"All the facts are in evidence. There can be no doubt that Mr. Momet did, indeed, strangle and murder Miss Yvette Sinclair, and it is your duty to find him guilty as charged. Thank you."

Jake turned and walked back to his table.

"Mr. Lawrence?" said Judge Hurstbourne.

Lawrence stood, but didn't move out from behind the table.

"Mr. McIntyre has laid out for you the scenario of what happened that night twenty-nine years ago when a young girl lost her life. And we do not dispute his account . . ."

Lawrence buttoned the middle button of his suit coat, then leisurely made his way to the other side of the table.

". . . right up to the point after which Mr. Momet left the library. Assuming there was someone who entered shortly thereafter, Mr. Mitchell all but admitted he couldn't be sure it was my client. In fact, he couldn't say for sure it was a man. And—please bear this in mind—we have only Mr. Mitchell's word there even was another appearance by anyone.

"Now," said Lawrence as he approached the jury box, "Mr. McIntyre says all the facts are in evidence. But is that so?

"On the night she was murdered, Miss Sinclair was wearing a watch on a chain around her neck, the same watch she always wore. My client testified to that. What happened to that watch? Did the murderer take it? There's been no connection of the watch to Mr. Momet. Officers searched both his home and his store and did not find it. His wife said she never saw it. Where did it go? The police don't know.

"Miss Sinclair told three different people—her mother, Mr. Mitchell and my client—she was coming into some money. Mr. Mitchell and Mr. Momet were told she would be getting it that night, the same night she was murdered. From whom? Where was the money coming from? What was the money for? The police don't know.

"Weeks before she was killed, Miss Sinclair told her mother she was afraid of some man, a Mr. 'F.' She showed her mother a newspaper with the man's sketch. Who was that man? Where is the newspaper? The police don't know.

"There seems to be a lot the police don't know, doesn't there?

"Ladies and gentlemen, here's the thing: If you believe my client's story that he and Miss Sinclair did actually plan to run off together, then he was left with no motive for killing her. And if he did not return to the library after he left—at which time Miss Sinclair was alive and well, according to both my client and Mr. Mitchell—and a second person then entered the library, in all likelihood it was that second person who committed the crime and took Miss Sinclair's watch.

"Now, who might that be? In spite of what Mr. McIntyre would have you believe, we have no lack of suspects, not only those individuals who sent threatening letters, but possibly others who Miss Sinclair might have been intimate with or associated with.

"Or, consider this. Miss Sinclair was expecting to come into some money. Was it from someone about whom she knew something they didn't want known? In other words, was she blackmailing someone? If so, might she have been meeting that person that night expecting to be paid, but instead ended up dead? And might that person have been the mysterious Mr. 'F'?

"In a few moments, Judge Hurstbourne will give you instructions to consider in your deliberations, one of which is that should you believe my client to be guilty, it must be beyond a reasonable doubt."

Lawrence shook his head. "I don't know about you, but I believe the whole case presented by the state is rife with reasonable doubt, and you will have no recourse but to find my client innocent. Thank you."

Lawrence turned and strode back to his table and sat down.

"Mr. McIntyre," said Judge Hurstbourne, "anything further?"

"Thank you, your honor." Jake stood, but didn't move. "That's quite a story Mr. Lawrence has concocted, about a mysterious stranger who's being blackmailed. Unfortunately for him and his client, there is not a shred of evidence to support it. The facts are simple: Mr. Momet had motive and he had opportunity. All other scenarios are but conjecture. You must find Mr. Momet guilty."

"Thank you, gentlemen," said Judge Hurstbourne.

Over the next ten minutes, Myrtle listened as the judge instructed the jury, stating the issues and defining several terms that he thought might be foreign to them, as well as the standard of proof they should apply.

"You are the sole judge of the facts that have been presented, and of the witnesses' testimony. Your conclusions must be based solely on the evidence that has been given, bearing in mind the closing statements by Mr. McIntyre and Mr. Lawrence are not evidence. You are now instructed to retire to the jury room where you will debate and ultimately reach a conclusion as to the innocence or guilt of the accused.

"When you have reached a decision, you will notify the bailiff, who will then notify me. Until then, we are adjourned."

As the jurists exited the jury box, the spectators spilled out from the courtroom, amidst a great deal of chatter.

"What now?" asked Daisy, as she and Myrtle reached the sidewalk outside the courthouse.

"Like Henri said, nothing's going to happen until tomorrow. Let's go home."

*****

Mrs. Darling had mentioned she would like to be at court to hear the jury verdict, so Henri had arranged for her to be admitted to the courtroom along with Myrtle and Daisy. She had brought out her finest earrings for the occasion: dangly, gold, with natural pearls and rose-colored diamonds, giving them a brownish-pink glow. Daisy and Myrtle both enthused over them, which pleased Mrs. Darling to no end.

Myrtle noticed that in addition to her landlady, at least two dozen more new spectators were present than had been at the previous sessions, lined up against the two side walls.

She was surprised to see Mr. Pfrommer among them. She nudged Daisy. "Look," she whispered, "there's Mr. Pfrommer over there."

"Where?" asked Daisy, casting her eyes around the room. "Oh, I see him now." She turned to Mrs. Darling. "Did you know Mr. Pfrommer was going to be here?"

Mrs. Darling shook her head. "He didn't say nothing to me."

"Please rise," said the bailiff, as Judge Hurstbourne entered the room.

"You may be seated," said the judge once he was in his chair. "Bailiff, please bring the jury in."

One by one, the jurists entered and took their place in the jury box. Once they were seated, Judge Hurstbourne said, “Has the jury reached a decision?”

“We have, your honor,” said the foreman, rising and passing a scrap of paper to the bailiff, who transported it to the judge.

Judge Hurstbourne scanned the note, then handed it back to the bailiff, who returned it to the foreman.

“What say you?” asked the judge.

“In the matter of the state versus Paul Momet,” said the foreman, “we find the defendant, Paul Momet . . . guilty.”

CHAPTER THIRTY-FOUR

The room was so silent following the announcement of the verdict that Myrtle was sure she could hear Daisy's eyebrows twitching.

Then bedlam broke loose.

Reporters, along with everyone else, rushed for the doors, the former in a hurry to file their stories, the latter to tell theirs to friends, neighbors, relatives—anybody who would listen: Paul Momet was guilty—a three-decades-old murder case had been solved.

Myrtle, Daisy and Mrs. Darling decided hanging back from the rampaging crowd was the prudent—safest—thing to do. By the time they exited the room, the courthouse halls had emptied, except for Mr. Diffledon, the custodian, who was cleaning up the clutter left by the mob that had just departed.

"Where to now?" asked Daisy. "Miss Madeline's or The Polar Bear?"

"I feel like a banana split," said Myrtle.

"What's a banana split?" asked Mrs. Darling.

Daisy and Myrtle stared at her.

"You've never had a banana split?" asked Daisy.

Mrs. Darling shook her head. "Never heard of it," she said.

"Come on," said Myrtle, taking her landlady by the arm and starting off. "You're going to enjoy this."

The Polar Bear had been a fixture in Booker Falls for over forty years. A copper-colored tin ceiling set with two glass chandeliers, each eight feet in diameter, ran the length of the room. The floor was parquet, a deeper brown than the ceiling. An oak counter on one side of the room accommodated ten bar stools, while the opposite side held half a dozen booths, deep enough to seat three people on each side. Metal tables down the middle provided additional seating.

At the room's far end, a pianola, with over a hundred songs in its collection, was playing "My Bird of Paradise," by the Peerless Quartet.

"I've never been in here before," said Mrs. Darling, looking around. "This is very nice."

"All the years you've lived here, and you've never been to The Polar Bear?" asked Daisy.

Mrs. Darling shook her head.

"Hi, my name is Sally," said a young girl, no more than eighteen, who had approached their booth, pad and pencil in hand. "What can I get for you ladies?"

"Banana splits all around," said Myrtle.

"You want the Bananapalooza?" asked the girl.

"That's the one with everything, right?" asked Daisy.

"Yep," said Sally, nodding.

"Bring it on," said Myrtle, a twinkle in her eye.

Five minutes later, the waitress arrived with their order.

"Oh, my," said Mrs. Darling, eyeing the giant concoction before her. "Dat is a lot. I'm not sure I can eat all of it."

"I'm betting on you, Mrs. Darling," said Myrtle.

"Me, too," chimed in Daisy, as she spooned a sinful bite of vanilla ice cream and banana dripping with pineapple syrup into her mouth. "But if you need any help, I'm available."

Mrs. Darling took a tentative bite of chocolate on chocolate. Her eyes opened wide.

"My, dat is tasty," she said, taking another bite.

Ten minutes later, all three women leaned back in their seats, their dishes scraped empty. Mrs. Darling patted her stomach, contentedly.

"See," said Myrtle. "I knew you could do it."

"What did you think of the verdict?" asked Daisy, picking up her water glass. "We haven't talked about that yet."

"I was surprised," said Myrtle. "I thought Mr. Lawrence brought up enough points to cast some reasonable doubt on Paul's guilt."

"I guess the jury didn't agree with you," said Daisy. "But I think I do. Somehow, I don't think he did it. What do you think, Mrs. Darling?" asked Daisy, turning to the old woman.

But Mrs. Darling, her head resting against the seat back, was fast asleep.

*****

"I don't see how you can disregard the evidence," said Myrtle, her arms folded defiantly as she leaned against the door of her room. "I mean, the watch, the money."

For the past twenty minutes, she and Henri had been arguing—or at the very least, vigorously discussing—the jury's decision regarding Paul Momet.

"They found him guilty," said Henri, starting down the stairs, Myrtle close on his heels. "That's all I need to know. Apparently they were convinced with the evidence."

"Yes, but how about—"

Myrtle's shoe caught on the stair runner: She found herself tumbling forward, falling. Desperately, she tried to stop her plunge by grabbing the railing, but to no avail. The next thing she knew she had crashed into Henri, propelling both of them down the last of the steps, ending in a tangled heap at the bottom.

Henri's face was inches from Myrtle's; close enough that he barely had to move his head to kiss her. It wasn't a hard kiss, but not a soft one, either: It was perfect. Myrtle wasn't sure what surprised her more: that Henri was kissing her . . . or that she was kissing him back.

And it lasted the perfect time, too, ending just as Mrs. Darling, alerted by the commotion, came racing down the hallway.

"Oh, my!" she exclaimed. "Are you two alright? Are you hurt?"

Henri and Myrtle quickly disentangled themselves and got to their feet.

"I'm okay," said Henri. "Miss Tully, are you hurt?"

Myrtle looked down at her skirt, which now showed a big rip in the front.

"No . . . yes—I'm afraid I've ruined my skirt," she said.

No one said anything for a moment, then they all burst out laughing.

"I'm going to make some tea," said Mrs. Darling as she scurried away.

"Not for me. I have to go now," said Henri, as he turned and rushed out the door, leaving Myrtle standing by herself, looking confused, wondering what had just happened.

"Go on out on da porch," yelled Mrs. Darling from the kitchen. "I'll be right out. Don't worry none about your skirt. We'll take care of it later."

*****

Myrtle was still in the rocking chair, holding a cup of cold dandelion tea when Daisy came strolling up the path to the house.

"Well, look at you," said Daisy, plopping down next to Myrtle. "Sitting out here like the Queen of Sheba, taking life easy, enjoying some liquid refreshment. Is that dandelion?"

Myrtle nodded.

"Don't you need something to make it a little more tasty?"

"No, it's gotten cold, anyway."

Daisy looked at the cup in Myrtle's hand. "How long you been out here, anyway?" she asked.

Myrtle shrugged. "An hour? I'm not sure."

"Okay, give. What's going on?"

Myrtle turned to Daisy. "Henri kissed me."

Daisy looked as though she'd been kicked by a horse. "What? When?"

"And I kissed him back."

"What?" Daisy nearly jumped out of the chair at this news.

Myrtle told Daisy what had happened earlier. When she finished, Daisy asked, "Was it good?"

"The fall?" said Myrtle. "No, it hurt and I ripped my skirt." She pulled the skirt around to show Daisy.

"You know what I mean, darn it! Was it good kissing Henri?"

Myrtle grinned. "It wasn't bad."

"You devil, you. You going to do it again?"

"No," said Myrtle. She sipped her tea and scrunched up her face. "One time falling down the stairs is enough."

"Darn it, you know what I mean!" exclaimed Daisy. "Are you going to kiss Henri again?"

"I don't know," said Myrtle. "Don't know if we'll ever fall down the stairs together again."

"I give up," said Daisy, as she stood and headed for the door. "You're hopeless."

*****

That night, Henri was the last one into the dining room.

He sat down and turned to Myrtle. "About earlier today . . ."

"Yes, about earlier today," said Myrtle.

"I'm sorry. It won't happen again." Henri turned back to his meal, picked up his glass of water and took a drink.

Myrtle was stunned. *That's it?*

"Yes," she said, finally, "it won't happen again." *But why not?* she thought.

Daisy turned to Myrtle but didn't say anything.

Throughout dinner, the debate continued as to the innocence or guilt of Paul Momet.

"You really think Paul is guilty?" Myrtle asked Henri.

"Yes," said Henri, "if for no other reason than there is no other viable suspect."

"What about Mr. Lawrence's theory that Yvette was trying to blackmail someone?" asked Myrtle. "And he—or she, I guess it could be a she—killed her rather than pay up?"

"Pure conjecture—nothing to back it up."

"Except she told everyone—okay, three people—she was expecting to come into some money."

"As Jake said, she could have been saying that to get Paul to run away with her. If he thought she had money, he'd leave his wife, his kids, his store—after all, he was crazy in love with the woman."

"Which tells me it wouldn't have made any difference if she had money or not," said Myrtle.

"Mr. Pfrommer," said Daisy, turning to the old man, "you were there today. What do you think?"

"It vas good dat justice vas served," replied Mr. Pfrommer without looking up, nor pausing in his assault on the pile of fried potatoes in front of him.

"Well, all right then," said Henri.

"Well, all right then," echoed Daisy.

CHAPTER THIRTY-FIVE

Myrtle was looking forward to the next three days before the library reopened and she had to go back to work. Her plan was to catch up on her reading, and spend more time with Penrod. She was afraid he was becoming Mrs. Darling's dog, rather than hers.

Then again, she thought, *would that be so bad?* Her landlady certainly relished the dog's company. The old lady was the one who fed him, bathed him and let him out to do his business.

Both Henri and George had invited her to a concert at the theatre in Red Jacket on Wednesday, the Mountain Ash Welsh Male Concert Choir, but she had declined both offers.

"I'm not so much into music," she'd told each of her suitors.

After breakfast, she settled in on the porch, wrapped up in the Norfolk jacket she'd brought back with her from Europe. The rain that had plagued them the past few days had stopped, but there was a chill in the air.

She had just opened her book when Daisy came running up the path.

She was crying.

"Daisy, what's wrong?" asked Myrtle, jumping up.

Daisy didn't answer. Instead, she held out a piece of paper to Myrtle and sank into the other rocker.

Myrtle took the paper from Daisy's hand. It was a telegram.

"Mother passed. Stop," read Myrtle out loud. "Funeral set for Wednesday 10 a.m. Stop. Saint Henry's. Stop.

"Oh, no," continued Myrtle. She looked at Daisy, her face now buried in her hands. "I'm so sorry."

"I don't know what to do," sobbed Daisy.

"Why, you must go, of course," said Myrtle. She sat down and placed her arm around Daisy's shoulder. "You have to."

"I can't," said Daisy. "They're still looking for me for killing Mike."

"The police," said Myrtle, nodding.

"And Mike's family, too."

"But Billy's up here. He probably doesn't know about your mother's death."

"There are other family members, cousins. They'll know about it. And they could be there, waiting for me to show up."

Myrtle thought for a moment. "No, you're going," she said. "And so am I. I'm going with you."

Daisy looked up for the first time. "What do you mean?"

"I mean, you're going and I'm going with you. I can be your lookout. I don't have to go back to work until Thursday. You already look a lot different than you used to, since we disguised you. And we'll get you a wig."

"A wig?"

"We'll go see Isabell and get you a wig, a gray one, so you look a lot older. You'll wear a veil, but I won't. We can do this."

"How will we get there?" asked Daisy.

"It's too far to drive. We'll take the train. We'll go downtown now and get your wig and funeral dresses for both of us. We can catch the train tomorrow, get to Chicago, go to the funeral on Wednesday and come back that day. There's no passenger train out of here, is there?"

"No, just freight. I guess Houghton would be the closest."

"Once we get to Chicago we'll find a hotel to stay at."

"A cheap hotel," said Daisy.

"No, not a cheap hotel—an inexpensive hotel. There's a difference. Who sent you the telegram, anyway?"

"Mrs. Winterstreet. She was my mom's best friend. I guess Mom told her how to get in touch with me if anything happened."

Daisy started crying again. "And it did. I can't believe she's gone."

"It'll be okay," said Myrtle, snuggling in closer. "Everything will be okay."

*****

The next day, after departing Houghton early in the morning on the Duluth, South Shore and Atlantic Railway line, Daisy and Myrtle reached Nestoria, where they transferred to another line which ran to Bessemer. There they boarded a Chicago & Northwestern train, bound for Chicago. Late that evening, they arrived at the new C&N passenger terminal.

"This was built the year before I left here," said Daisy as she and Myrtle disembarked. "I remember Mike tried to get a job on the construction crew."

"Amazing," said Myrtle, as she eyed the cavernous structure, flabbergasted by the enormity of the complex, which contained sixteen tracks elevated above the street, sheltered by a train shed that extended almost nine hundred feet. The upper level consisted of a concourse and other facilities, including baths, dressing rooms, and medical facilities. An imposing waiting room some forty thousand square feet in size served as the centerpiece of the upper level. All of it was covered by a tunnel-type ceiling over seven and a half stories high.

Down at the street-level concourse, they hailed a cab that took them to the Lincolnshire Hotel, not far from the church where the Mass was to be held.

Shortly before midnight, they sank into bed, exhausted from their day-long trip, and within minutes were sound asleep.

*****

St. Henry's Catholic Church was a massive, red brick structure which featured a tower at one end. Large clocks were displayed on each side below where the spire began its ascent to the heavens.

The interior was what Myrtle had come to expect from every Catholic church, at least the ones she'd been in: myriad stained glass windows, high arching ceiling and a great deal of what she thought of as filigree.

She loved it all.

Two large portraits hung above alternate sides of the altar. Myrtle thought one might have been of the Blessed Virgin Mary—although it didn't look like other representations of her she'd seen—and she had no idea who the man was in the second painting.

"That's Blessed Alojzije Stepinac," said Daisy, when Myrtle asked her.

"Who's he?"

"No idea. The other painting is the Queen of Croatia."

They had planned to arrive at the last minute to lessen the possibility that Daisy might encounter anyone she knew, especially members of Mike's family who might be attending.

But of the several dozen people seated in the front rows of pews, only a few were familiar to Daisy, older women who had known her mother, among them Mrs. Winterstreet. With her disguise, especially her gray wig, Daisy could easily have fit in with them.

Following the hour-long Mass, Myrtle and Daisy watched as the casket was carried down the aisle by four men and out the door of the church.

Daisy kept her head down as the mourners passed by, following behind the casket. She and Myrtle took up the rear and trailed behind as they exited the church and proceeded to the cemetery, which was adjacent to the church.

When the graveside service concluded, Daisy wanted to talk with Mrs. Winterstreet, but Myrtle cautioned against it.

"No sense taking a chance anyone might recognize you. Send her a letter after we get back home."

*****

Myrtle had been surprised at Daisy's lack of tears. She discovered in the taxi on the way to the train station that she'd been saving them, as they now flowed freely.

Myrtle didn't say anything. She knew it best to just allow her friend to grieve.

CHAPTER THIRTY-SIX

Although it was only July 1, classes were set to start at Adelaide for a three-month term that ran until the end of September, a time set aside for incoming freshmen students to get prepared for the rigorous schedule demanded of them.

Over the next three days, Frank kept Myrtle busy putting the shelves and stacks in order, cataloging and filing new books, papers and other material that had come in while the library had been closed for two weeks.

She was always happy when Sundays came, but especially so this week, as Daisy had spent the whole time on the train ride back from Chicago touting the upcoming Fourth of July festivities scheduled for the day.

"I'm so excited I think I'm going to pee my pants," said Daisy, as she and her fellow boarders each dug into the special breakfast Mrs. Darling had prepared for them: sizzling bacon, fried potatoes, poached eggs and the *pièce de résistance*—a plate-sized pancake with blueberries, thimbleberry jam and whipped cream.

All except for Mr. Pfrommer.

The bacon, potatoes and eggs were fine; but he preferred plain maple syrup on his pancakes.

"Not very patriotic," Daisy mumbled under her breath.

"What time does the parade start?" asked Myrtle, between mouthfuls of her second pancake.

"Two," said Henri. "The best place to watch will be at the corner of Caldwell and Main. Then it will continue on out to the college."

"What happens at the college?" asked Myrtle.

"Oh, didn't I tell you that part?" said Daisy. "There'll be a big picnic, with food and games and lots of fun."

"Will you be in the parade?" Myrtle asked Henri.

"No, but I'll be there to make sure nothing happens."

*****

Myrtle stood next to Daisy, each waving a small American flag as the parade passed by. All the buildings were festooned with red, white and blue banners, American flags bearing forty-eight stars flying over every doorway.

A large banner reading, "FOURTH OF JULY—BOOKER FALLS—1920" stretched across Main Street from the top floor of the Jorgeson Building to the third floor of the Walther Building.

After so many days of cooler weather, a warming spell had hit, with the temperature edging over eighty degrees where they stood, with no shade to ward off the heat. Myrtle wasn't sure who she felt sorrier for: the men in their suits and blazers and ties; or the women, equally overdressed. She had opted to wear her plaid slacks, her newsboy cap, and an oversized white tee shirt with the word *France* across the front.

"Where in the world did you get that shirt?" asked Daisy.

"A sailor on the ship that brought me back from Europe," said Myrtle. "The *France*. It was a present."

"And what did you give him in return?"

"A kiss."

"I think the sailor got the better of the deal. Oh, look," said Daisy. "There's George."

George Salmon, decked out in a red and white striped blazer along with a straw hat sporting a similarly colored hatband, maneuvered his new Briscoe down the street, steering with one hand and waving to the crowd with the other. When he saw Myrtle, he waved more vigorously.

"I think that was a special wave for you," said Daisy.

Myrtle didn't say anything.

"Have you told him about you and Henri?" asked Daisy.

Myrtle looked at Daisy. "No. It's none of his business."

"I think it is if he still has designs on you."

"Let's just watch, okay?"

For the next hour, along with throngs of people gathered along each side of the street, they watched and cheered as the parade passed by: veterans of both the Civil War and the recently concluded conflict in Europe, proudly wearing their respective uniforms; Booker Falls' two horse-drawn fire engines, bells clanging, exciting the crowd—"Let's trust we don't have any fires right now," whispered Daisy—; the Miners Brass Band entertaining the crowd with patriotic songs, such as "Welcome Home," "That's What The Red, White and Blue Means," "Pack Up Your Troubles in Your Old Kit Bag," and, of course, "The Star Spangled Banner." Following close on their heels was the newly formed Boy Scout Troop Number 27, proudly sponsored—as the banner proclaimed—by St. James Lutheran Church.

Numerous floats, paid for by local businesses and decorated with banners, ribbons, flags, flowers and who knew what else, made their way slowly past where Myrtle and Daisy stood.

The final entry included a company of riders on horses, the mounts adorned with flowers and ribbons much as the floats had been. At the very end strode the old man with the wheeled barrel Myrtle had seen her first day in town. Today a young boy assisted him.

"What did you think of it?" asked Daisy.

"It was fun," said Myrtle. "What now—off to the picnic?"

"Let's go," said Daisy, taking off without waiting on her companion.

*****

Although Mrs. Darling had passed on attending the parade—"You see one parade, you've seen them all," she'd told Myrtle and Daisy when they asked if she was going—there was no way she would miss the picnic.

This was her main opportunity all year to see friends and acquaintances, other than those she saw at church on the rare times she attended.

Rather than having her landlady drive the two miles to the college in her carriage, Myrtle convinced her to accompany her and Daisy in the Model N.

She was delighted to discover that, just as Mrs. Darling had never been in The Polar Bear until she and Daisy took her there, her landlady had also never ridden in an automobile.

"You're kidding," said Daisy.

"No," said Mrs. Darling. "We didn't have them when I was growing up. And, as you know, there aren't that many even now in Booker Falls."

"Yeah, just two," said Daisy.

"Well, hang on," said Myrtle, "'cause here we go."

Myrtle decided she'd drive as fast as the car would allow, in order to give Mrs. Darling a memorable ride. When she looked over to see how the older woman was doing, Mrs. Darling was holding on desperately to whatever she could find, earrings swinging excitedly to and fro.

By the time they arrived, a large crowd had already gathered. Myrtle decided to park the car a little distance from where the carriage horses were tethered, so as not to alarm them.

"Oh, my," said Mrs. Darling, when Myrtle finally stopped the car.

"Did you enjoy that?" asked Daisy.

"Oh, my," said Mrs. Darling again.

"I think we'd better get you down," said Myrtle.

Carefully balancing the pot of beans Mrs. Darling had cooked, Myrtle made her way to where a dozen tables had been set up end to end to hold the cornucopia of food the townsfolk had brought. Daisy assisted their landlady, still unsteady from the experience she'd just been through.

Following two blessings, the first by the newly installed pastor at St. James, the Reverend Albrecht, and the second—the one that actually counted, as far as most of the crowd was concerned—by Father Fabien, lines formed on both sides of the tables, the children shoving and pushing to be first.

Daisy spread out a blanket under a large oak tree where she, Mrs. Darling and Myrtle settled down to enjoy their food. It wasn't long before George showed up.

"Ladies," he said, tipping his hat. "Wonderful day for a picnic, isn't it?"

"Mr. Salmon," said Mrs. Darling. "Won't you join us? We've plenty of room."

"Why, Mrs. Darling, don't mind if I do," said George, plopping down next to Myrtle.

Daisy noticed her housemate made no effort to move away from George.

"You sure looked spiffy in your machine," said Daisy, "with your patriotic blazer and all."

"Why, thank you, Miss O'Hearn. And you look pretty spiffy today, too."

Daisy had chosen a red dress for the occasion, topped by a navy blue jacket and a white bi-corn hat with two ribbons, one red, the other blue, dangling from the back.

George turned to Myrtle. "And Miss Tully," he said, "may I say you also look lovely today."

"Thank you, Mr. Salmon. If nothing else, I was comfortable."

For the next half hour, the four of them chit-chatted, comparing the various floats and other entries from the parade, as well as a critique of the two graces said prior to the meal.

"Father Fabien gave an excellent blessing," said Mrs. Darling. "He's such a gifted speaker, a real man of God."

"I agree," said George. "The man has a way with words."

"And Reverend Albrecht?" asked Myrtle.

"What about him?" asked George.

"Don't you think he did a great job, too?"

George shrugged. "He got all the words right, I suppose."

"I thought he did an excellent job," said Myrtle.

"Look," said Daisy. "Here comes Henri."

Dressed in the same official constable uniform he'd worn during the trial, Henri strode up to the quartet.

"Looks as though you're all having fun," he said.

"We are," said Myrtle. "Why don't you join us?" she added, ignoring the scowl on George's face.

"I wish I could, but I have to go inspect the arrangements for the fireworks. Can't have anyone getting killed accidentally, you know."

"Or on purpose," said George.

"Or on purpose. Anyway, I'll see you all later back at the house." He looked at George. "Well, most of you, I suppose."

With that he was off.

The rest of the evening was spent watching the children play games. George, Myrtle and Daisy each got into the swing of things by engaging in some adult games: sack races, three-legged races, wheelbarrow races, egg toss, horseshoes, and *pétanque*, a game especially popular with the French residents of Booker Falls, where the goal was to throw hollow metal balls as close as possible to a small wooden ball called a *cochonnet* while standing inside a circle with both feet on the ground.

"This is kind of like bocce," said Daisy. "We used to play that in Chicago."

By the time sunset arrived, everybody was worn out from all the eating and playing and eating again. But no one dared leave before the fireworks display.

At nine thirty precisely, the first of the pyrotechnics went off, and for the next twenty minutes the whole crowd—children and adults alike—watched enthralled, oohing and aahing, as rockets, sparklers, pinwheels and other explosive devices blanketed the night sky in dazzling colors—red, white, and blue dominating.

At ten o'clock, Myrtle, Daisy and Mrs. Darling loaded everything back into the Model N and headed for home.

Mrs. Darling declined Myrtle's invitation to ride with her and rode back instead with Henri in his carriage. She'd had far too much excitement for one day.

CHAPTER THIRTY-SEVEN

After two trips to Red Jacket, the first with Daisy, the second with George, Myrtle finally made the trip on her own.

She parked her car in front of Italian Hall, which housed the Great Atlantic & Pacific Tea Company at one end of the building. Mrs. Darling had ordered a number of imported items, chief among them bananas—she had gotten hooked on banana splits—which at that time were not available in Booker Falls, and Myrtle had volunteered to make the trip to pick them up. She'd hoped Daisy would accompany her, but she'd begged off, citing a headache.

Myrtle suspected, though, it was more a case of her fear of running into Billy Fitzgerald, the brother of Daisy's late husband, for whose death she'd been responsible.

As she left the store carrying a bag containing her purchases, Myrtle saw a man coming out of Vairo's at the other end of the block. Operating as a saloon until Michigan had banned the sale and consumption of alcohol the previous year, the establishment still met the needs of thirsty patrons, though not as openly as before.

When the man saw Myrtle, he started walking briskly towards her.

Myrtle's heart sank; she almost dropped the bag of groceries.

It was Billy Fitzgerald.

*****

Daisy lay stretched out on her bed, reading, when Myrtle's head popped around the door.

"Daisy, I need you to come downstairs with me."

Daisy laid the book down and looked at Myrtle. "Downstairs?"

"There's something you have to see."

Daisy looked puzzled. "Can't you bring it up here?"

"No," said Myrtle. "Come on. This is important."

Daisy climbed out of bed and followed Myrtle down the stairs. When they entered the parlor, she saw a man standing there, his back to them. When he turned around, Daisy let out a shriek: it was Billy Fitzgerald.

"Nooo!" she cried, covering her mouth and backing up towards the door Myrtle had just shut behind them.

She started to turn, but Myrtle stopped her. "It's all right, Daisy, it's all right."

Daisy looked at Myrtle, her eyes unbelieving. Had her friend brought this man into the house, this man she was sure was looking to wreak vengeance on her for killing his brother?

"Gwen," said Billy.

"Don't touch me," cried Daisy. "The constable lives here and he's upstairs right now."

In truth, Daisy had no idea where Henri was at the moment.

"I'm not going to hurt you," said Billy.

Daisy wrapped her arm around Myrtle, as though she were a shield.

"What are you doing here? How did you get here?"

"I brought him," said Myrtle.

Daisy let go of Myrtle and backed away from her. "*You* brought him? I told you he was looking for me because I killed Mike."

"That's just it," said Billy. "You didn't kill Mike."

Daisy stared at Billy, trying to fathom what game he was playing. Of course she'd killed Mike—she'd stabbed him to death.

"You didn't kill him," said Billy again.

"He's . . . he's alive?" asked Daisy.

Billy hung his head. "Well, no, he ain't exactly alive, neither. He died a couple years back."

"I don't understand," said Daisy.

"Why don't you sit down," said Myrtle. "Let Billy explain."

Daisy sank into the nearest chair. Billy sat down across from her on the sofa while Myrtle stood, her arm around Daisy's shoulder.

"That day—the day you thought you killed Mike—I was on my way over to your house to tell him I got him a construction job with me at the River Center. When I got to your place I found him on the kitchen floor, bleeding like a stuck pig.

"I called a neighbor and we got him to the hospital. All the way there he kept asking for you, saying he was sorry.

"He was in surgery for four hours and then in and out for 'bout a day and a half. Kept calling for you every time he woke up. When he finally come to, he told me what happened, said you wasn't to blame, and that it was all his fault.

"They kept him in the hospital another two weeks before they let him go. Soon as he got out he started looking for you, said he wanted to apologize, make it up to you, start all over."

Daisy wiped a tear from her eye.

"But it was like you'd disappeared off the face of the earth. He tried to find out from your ma where you was, but that old gal, she wouldn't tell him a blessed thing.

"He still had a job waiting for him, so he went back to work. But every spare minute he had, he tried to find you. Gave up drinking, started going to church—he turned his life around. That guy—he loved you so much. And he was so sorry 'bout what he'd done."

Billy paused for a minute.

"You said he's no longer alive," said Myrtle.

"Yeah, that's right. After the River Center was finished, we both got other construction jobs. One day we was a'workin' and this beam slipped and smacked right into Mike, knocked him on his ass. Had a big gash in his head. We all thought he was dead right then and there. But he weren't.

"We got him to the hospital, but the doc said there weren't nothing they could do 'cept make him comfortable. I was with him when he went. The last thing he said was, he said I should keep looking for you to let you know you didn't kill him, and that it weren't your fault in the first place and he was sorry and he loved you. Then he closed his eyes and that was it."

By now, tears flowed freely down both women's cheeks.

"And you finally found me up here," said Daisy, through her sobs.

"Just luck, that's all," said Billy.

"But didn't you come up here looking for me?"

"Heck, no. I did try to find you for about two years, but there weren't no trace. I tried your ma again, too, but by then she said she didn't know where you was. I had a feeling she wasn't telling me the truth, but weren't nothing I could do 'bout it."

"Then how did you end up here?" asked Daisy, more composed now.

"I met this gal, Mary Sue's her name, met her in a bar. She was from Lake Linden and visiting a cousin in Chicago. We kind of hit it off, and ended up getting hitched. But she didn't like big-city life, wanted to move back home, so I said okay, and we did. I got me a job at the mine. And now we got a little boy—named him Mike.

"I didn't know you was up here in these parts until that day I saw you and Miss Myrtle over in Red Jacket. I couldn't believe my eyes. I called out to you but you didn't answer and by the time I got down to the street, you was gone.

"I kept on the lookout for that snazzy car Miss Myrtle drives, and today when I spotted it in front of the A and P, I knew I had to talk to her, find out what was going on with you."

"So I didn't kill Mike," said Daisy, the news now starting to sink in.

"Nope, you sure didn't," said Billy, shaking his head.

He stood up. "Look, I got to go now, it's a drive back home."

"Did you drive here?" asked Daisy.

"Miss Myrtle brung me, but Mary Sue followed us. She's waiting for me downtown."

Daisy jumped up, raced over to Billy and flung her arms around him.

"I'm so glad you found me," she said. "Thank you."

Embarrassed, Billy put his arms around Daisy. "Heck, me too. I hope you can rest easy now."

Myrtle walked Billy to the front door. When she returned to the parlor, she found Daisy bent over, tears streaming down her face. She sat down next to her and put her arm around her.

"Why the tears?" asked Myrtle. "This is good news."

"He really loved me," Daisy managed between sobs. "He really did. If I'd only known . . . I would have gone back. We could have had a good life."

"I know," said Myrtle, soothingly. "I know. But at least now you can get on with your life without looking over your shoulder."

After a few minutes, Daisy stood up.

"Come on," she said, taking Myrtle's hand. "I've got something for you now."

"What is it?" asked Myrtle.

"Lipstick, rouge, makeup—I'm tired of being someone I'm not. I'm going back to being plain old Daisy O'Hearn."

"You're not going to go back to your real name now that you know no one's looking for you anymore?"

Daisy stopped. "I hadn't thought about that," she said.

"And your new clothes?" asked Myrtle.

"Oh, I'm keeping those," said Daisy. "I don't want the 'complete' old me back."

They started up the stairs, giggling as they went.

"Maybe I'll keep one tube of lipstick, too."

CHAPTER THIRTY-EIGHT

"How's the book coming?"

Daisy looked up from her typewriter to see Myrtle standing in the doorway.

"Well, I'm making progress," answered Daisy.

Myrtle spotted a photograph lying on Daisy's bed. She went over and picked it up.

"What's this?"

Daisy turned around to look. "Oh, remember I told you I had a photograph of the crime scene? Well," she added sheepishly, "I told you it was from Detroit. It was actually from when I was in Traverse City."

"And this is it?"

"Yeah. You can see the body's still laying on the floor."

Myrtle squinted, studying the photo.

"Daisy, you have a magnifying glass, don't you?"

Daisy opened the drawer to her desk, pulled out a magnifying glass and handed it to Myrtle.

Holding the glass close to the photograph, Myrtle put her face so that it was almost touching.

"That's what I thought," she said, without looking up.

"What?"

"Here," said Myrtle, handing both the magnifying glass and the photo to Daisy.

Daisy took them and studied the photo. "I'm not sure what I'm supposed to be seeing," she said.

"Isn't that Mr. Mitchell there on the left?"

Daisy looked again. “I think you’re right. A lot younger, of course, but that’s definitely him.”

“And what do you see? Or, better yet, what don’t you see?”

Daisy looked again, then shook her head. “I don’t know what I’m supposed to see or not see.”

“No cast. He doesn’t have a cast on either arm.”

Daisy looked at the photo again, then at Myrtle. “You’re right—he’s not wearing a cast!”

“And his alibi, why he couldn’t have killed Yvette Sinclair,” said Myrtle, “was because he had a broken arm and it was in a cast.”

“Are you going to show this to Henri?” asked Daisy.

Myrtle shook her head. “Not right away. There’s someone else I need to talk to first.”

“Who’s that?”

“Doctor Sherman, the one who Henri said confirmed Mr. Mitchell’s alibi.”

*****

“I don’t understand,” said Doctor Sherman, looking up from the photograph. “He did have a broken arm. I know he did—I set it myself, and put the cast on.”

Myrtle had confronted the doctor with the photograph, and reminded him that he had confirmed Frank’s situation with Henri.

“Well, when did you take it off?” asked Myrtle.

The doctor thought for a moment. “Now that I recall, I never did take that cast off. Frank must have taken it off himself—or had someone else do it.”

*****

Ten minutes later, Myrtle stood in Henri’s office.

“Look at this,” she said, laying the photo on his desk.

“What is it?” asked Henri.

"A photograph of the original crime scene of Yvette Sinclair's murder. Look at the man standing to the right."

Henri looked at the photo, then at Myrtle. "Frank Mitchell," he said.

"With no cast on his arm," said Myrtle.

Henri looked again. "My God, you're right. But how can that be?"

"I think it's time you asked Mr. Mitchell that very question."

"You don't want to go with me? You're always wanting to be involved whenever I question someone."

"Not Mr. Mitchell," said Myrtle. "He's my boss. I think it best if I just stay out of the picture."

"When have you ever just stayed out of the picture?"

*****

"Oh, I can explain that," said Frank, after glancing at the photograph. "I'd taken the cast off myself that morning before I went into work. I'd had it on for almost two months and it was getting rather shabby. Besides, my arm was beginning to itch something fierce. So I got a pair of shears and just cut it off. I figured my arm should have healed by then. And I was right."

"You told me it was still in a cast when I questioned you," said Henri.

Frank's brows furrowed. "Yes, that's what I said. And it *was* in a cast the night Yvette was killed. I didn't take it off until the next morning."

"Very convenient."

"Well, it's the truth," said Frank, defensively.

*****

"And you believe him?" asked Myrtle, when Henri told her Frank's explanation.

"Whether I do or not, there's no way I could disprove it," said Henri.

"Are you going to search his home? His office? See if he has Yvette's watch?"

Henri chuckled. "No, I am not. First of all, the crime's already been solved. Paul Momet was found guilty, if you recall."

Myrtle snorted. "Well, I'm still not convinced he did it."

"And secondly," Henri continued, ignoring her, "I'd have to get a search warrant, and I doubt very seriously if any judge would give me one just based on this photo. Oh, and did I mention—the killer's already in jail?"

"You can believe the real killer's in jail if you want," said Myrtle, "but I'm going to keep looking. If Frank Mitchell is the Mr. 'F' Yvette was afraid of, I think the case is going to have to be reopened."

Henri shrugged. "Do what you have to do, then. Just don't bother me with it."

Myrtle turned and left Henri's office, slamming the door behind her.

*****

Daisy watched as Myrtle ground the Model N to a stop in front of the house, and stormed her way up the path to the house.

"I take it your meeting with Henri did not go well," she said.

"That man is . . . well, he's . . . not very proactive, that's all I can say."

"Proactive?"

"I mean, he doesn't seem to *want* to look for the truth: too much of a bother. I almost want to say he's just plain lazy."

Myrtle sank down into the rocker next to Daisy.

"So, what did he say?" asked Daisy. "Was he surprised by the photograph?"

"Surprised? Maybe. But he didn't seem to care much. He said somebody's already in jail for having killed Yvette Sinclair. Why waste time by looking any further."

"Well," said Daisy, sneaking a puff on her cigarette, "he is right. Paul Momet was found guilty."

Myrtle glared at Daisy. "That doesn't mean he did it. It only means twelve people *thought* he did it. And they could have been wrong."

"Why wasn't Mr. Mitchell a suspect to start with?"

"It wasn't until the letters came to light and we found out he wrote two of them that there was any reason to suspect him. Plus, until he testified in court, no one even knew he was in the library that night."

"So, what are you going to do?" asked Daisy.

"Go snooping."

"Go snooping?"

"Go snooping."

*****

Saturday was Frank's day off from the library.

Myrtle arrived early and locked the door behind her. She'd unlock it in thirty minutes at the regular time so that anyone waiting outside could get in. Going straight to Frank's office, she unlocked it and went in. For the next twenty minutes, she went through his desk, as well as all four drawers of the file cabinet.

No luck: Yvette's watch was nowhere to be found.

Myrtle wasn't too surprised: she thought it would be a long shot. If Frank had killed Yvette and taken her watch, he probably would keep it at his home. But Henri wouldn't even try to get a search warrant to go there.

She wondered what her chances were of sneaking into his house herself.

And then she thought better of it.

CHAPTER THIRTY-NINE

Myrtle approached Henri as he was leaving St. Barbara's the next morning after Sunday Mass.

"Henri, might I have a minute?"

Henri looked at her suspiciously.

"You're not going to go into this whole 'Frank Mitchell is the killer thing' again, are you?" he asked.

Myrtle sighed. "No, not that. Claude came to talk to me yesterday. He wanted to know when he was going to get his scarf back."

Henri chuckled. "He's never going to let that go, is he?"

"I think not. Is there any chance he can have it?"

"Sure," said Henri. "Why don't you stop by the office with me and we'll get it."

*****

Although Myrtle had been in Booker Falls for almost ten months, it was the first time she'd been in Henri's office.

Rather small, it was large enough only for a desk, two chairs and a filing cabinet. Aside from a brass postmaster desk lamp, the only illumination came from a double-bladed ceiling fan with two lights attached to the base.

A window at the front of the room looked out onto Blanchard Street, while a door on one wall led to a storage area and the two-cell jail where Paul Momet had spent the four weeks before and during his trial. Next to the door was a telephone on the wall.

The blandness of the room was broken by two pictures, one a photograph of President Wilson, the other a water color painting of the Booker Falls waterfalls, dominated by lots of dark green areas.

Myrtle studied the painting while Henri searched the adjacent storage area for the scarf.

"Mr. Mitchell has a painting almost exactly like this in his office," she said, when Henri returned. "Who's the artist?"

"Frank is," said Henri.

"Mr. Mitchell? The Frank Mitchell I work for? The one I think killed Yvette Sinclair?"

"One and the same."

"I didn't know he could paint."

"Well, he did graduate from Adelaide with two degrees: one in art history, the other in fine arts."

"He's not a very good artist," said Myrtle. "It's so dark. Does he work in oil at all?"

"Nope. Strictly water color. And Booker Falls is about his only subject. I've only seen two or three other pictures of anything else he's done."

Henri handed the scarf to her. "Here. You can give this to Claude the next time you see him. I'm going to send Mrs. Sinclair's photograph back, too."

"Oh," said Myrtle. "You suppose I might take it to her? I'd like to see how she's getting along. She looked so frail at the trial."

"That's a long trip to Marquette just to return a photograph," said Henri.

"I'm off tomorrow. It will be a nice drive. Perhaps Daisy will accompany me."

Myrtle started for the door.

"Wait," said Henri. "I . . . I want to ask you something."

Myrtle stopped and turned back. "Yes?"

"I . . . I was wondering if you might like to have dinner with me tonight."

Myrtle's eyebrows arched. This was unexpected! Though not altogether unwelcome.

"We have dinner together every Sunday evening," she said. "Except when you don't show up."

"Yes, I know. But I meant—you know—you and me."

"You and me?" said Myrtle.

"You and me."

"Where would you be taking me—Miss Madeline's?"

"No, I was thinking of Marinucci's."

"Marinucci's?" Myrtle had never heard of the place.

"It's in Houghton. A very nice restaurant. I think you'd enjoy it."

"And how would we get there? Would I drive?"

"I was thinking of asking George if I might borrow his car."

"George? You do know I've been out with him?"

"I know, but he's a good fellow. I think he'd say yes."

"Do you even know how to drive an automobile?" asked Myrtle.

"How hard can it be?"

"I'll drive," said Myrtle, laughing. "What time shall we leave?"

*****

Henri was right: Marinucci's was an excellent restaurant.

Situated on the south bank of the Portage River that separated Houghton from Hancock, it was a typical Italian restaurant. Red and white checked tablecloths covered all the tables, on each of which sat a small candle and a vase holding a single daisy.

Their dinner of roast leg of lamb served with roasted potatoes, peas and carrots, was followed by tiramisu.

"This is delicious," said Myrtle, licking the last of the dessert from her fork.

"You've never had it before?" asked Henri.

Myrtle shook her head. "No, but I'll certainly look forward to having it again."

What impressed Myrtle as much as the quality of the food was the delightful playing of the violinist who circulated among the various tables.

"He's as good as Mr. Pfrommer," said Myrtle.

"A little different style, though," said Henri.

"You picked a beautiful place," said Myrtle. "I love it."

*****

Later, back in Booker Falls, Myrtle parked the car in front of the boarding house and waited for Henri to come around to help her out. She had come to decide that since he felt it the chivalrous thing to do, she shouldn't be so determined to prove it wasn't necessary.

"I'm having a drink before I go up," said Henri, when they were standing in the foyer. "Would you care to join me? Mrs. Darling keeps a bottle or two down here for the use of her guests."

"What are we drinking?" asked Myrtle.

"Sherry? Or whiskey?" said Henri.

"Sherry. I can't remember the last time I had a sherry."

When Henri returned from the kitchen with their drinks, he found Myrtle standing next to the piano.

"Don't you want to sit down?" he asked, handing Myrtle her glass.

"I've been sitting for hours. I need to stand a bit. Thank you for dinner. I really enjoyed Marinucci's."

"Maybe we can go again some time," said Henri.

"Yes, I think I'd like that."

"You're still uneasy about the outcome of the trial, aren't you?" asked Henri.

"There are things that bother me. Things left unresolved."

"Like the mysterious Mr. 'F.'"

"You mean Mr. Mitchell? Yes, that is a bother."

"And you and Daisy didn't find any pictures of him or any other likely suspects when you went through the newspapers?"

"No, but there weren't that many to look at, since *The Rapids* only publishes once a week."

"What about the others?"

"The others what?" asked Myrtle. She had no idea what he was talking about.

"The other newspapers—you checked those, didn't you?"

"What other newspapers?"

"All the ones that come from Canada, especially from Quebec. Yvette Sinclair was a student, so I think it unlikely she spent much time reading *The Rapids*. But one of her jobs, as I understand it, was to receive and catalog the out of town newspapers."

"Of course!" exclaimed Myrtle. "If she saw a picture of Mr. Mitchell, it could have been in one of those newspapers! He goes to Quebec every Christmas to see his mother. That's the time Yvette might have seen his picture in the paper. Henri, I could kiss you!"

"Why don't you?"

Myrtle looked surprised. "What?"

"Why don't you kiss me?" said Henri.

Myrtle placed her glass on the doily atop the lamp table stand, then walked over to Henri and, taking his face in her hands, kissed him—a long, lingering kiss, unlike the one they had shared at the bottom of the stairs.

Still holding his glass, Henri embraced Myrtle and returned the kiss.

For a few moments, they stood, looking at one another.

Then Myrtle slipped out of Henri's grasp and started for the stairs.

"Thank you for a very nice evening, Mr. de la Cruz," she said, glancing back over her shoulder and smiling.

As she mounted the stairs, Henri stood in the parlor, glass still in hand, a grin covering his face.

CHAPTER FORTY

At breakfast the next morning, neither Myrtle nor Henri spoke to one another, unsure of what should be said.

Mrs. Darling finally broke the awkward silence. "Where you off to this morning, dearie?" she asked as she poured coffee into Myrtle's cup. "I see you got your driving gear hanging on da hall tree."

Along with a broad-brimmed hat with sash she could tie under her chin to keep it from flying away, Myrtle had recently bought a duster to wear when driving the Model N on the dirt-covered roads that blanketed the area.

"Daisy and I are off to Marquette," said Myrtle, "to see Mrs. Sinclair. We're going to return the photograph she loaned Mr. Lawrence to use in the trial."

"That's a long way to go," said Mrs. Darling, filling Henri's cup.

"That's what I said," said Henri.

"But we're making a day of it," said Daisy. "We're going to stop at Hogan's Place for lunch."

"You'll be back in time for dinner?" asked Mrs. Darling. "Meatloaf tonight."

Daisy nodded. "Definitely. Do not want to miss your meatloaf."

"And tomorrow," said Myrtle, "I have a special project I'm going to work on."

"What's that, dearie?" asked Mrs. Darling.

"Henri mentioned that when I was looking for a picture of Mr. 'F' in those old newspapers, I should not have confined myself only to *The Rapids*, but since Yvette spoke fluent French, it stands to reason that it might have been one of the papers from Canada where she saw the picture. Tomorrow, I'm going to go through the old copies of those papers to see what I can find."

"But why would you do dat?" asked Mrs. Darling.

"Because I'm not convinced Paul Momet killed Yvette Sinclair. Ordinarily, you would think the local constabulary would check that out . . ." she glanced at Henri, who was ignoring her, busily studying the bowl of oatmeal sitting in front of him, ". . . but since that apparently isn't happening, I shall take it upon myself to do so."

"Oh, well, good luck, den," said Mrs. Darling.

"I won't be back until dinner time either," said Henri.

"Oh, and where you off to?" asked Mrs. Darling.

Henri grinned. "It's a surprise."

*****

It had been raining all during breakfast, but by the time Myrtle and Daisy were ready to start out, the skies had cleared.

They had barely gotten out of town when Myrtle could no longer refrain from telling Daisy what had happened the previous night.

"It happened again."

Daisy turned to look at Myrtle. "What happened again?"

Myrtle stared straight ahead at the road. "Henri kissed me."

"Oh my God," said Daisy, sitting straight up in the seat. "This is getting serious."

Myrtle smiled. "Although to be honest—I guess I was the one who did the kissing."

"Okay, spill," said Daisy. "Tell me what happened."

Myrtle recounted the whole evening: the drive to Houghton, the dinner at Marinucci's, the late night drink in the parlor, concluding with Henri's suggestion of looking at other newspapers that led to the kiss.

"And then I went to bed," Myrtle concluded.

"Alone?"

Myrtle turned and looked at Daisy, a shocked look on her face.

"Of course alone—what would you think?"

Daisy shrugged. "I don't know—that you got lucky? Or someone got lucky?"

Myrtle shook her head. "What a mind you have on you, Miss O'Hearn. You should be ashamed of yourself."

"Oh, I am, I am—very ashamed of myself," said Daisy, giggling.

"You're terrible," said Myrtle, laughing, as she turned her attention back to the road.

"Okay, seriously," said Daisy. "How far do you see this going? And what about George?"

"George? What does he have to do with this?"

"You have gone out with him, too."

"Yes, but I didn't kiss him. And I don't know I would—if we were to go out again, I mean. And as for Henri." Myrtle shrugged again. "I have no idea. But enough of this. Let's talk about something else."

"Okay. Did you hear about Mr. Folger and Mrs. Finnegan?"

"Agnes Finnegan?"

"That's the one," said Daisy.

"And Mr. Folger—the attorney?"

"Yep."

"Okay, tell me everything you know."

For the next hour, Daisy kept Myrtle enthralled, not only with the nefarious tale of Mrs. Finnegan, but all the other gossip that came her way at the newspaper office.

". . . and that's when they found out the manager stole the money," she finished.

"You certainly are in the know of what goes on in town," said Myrtle, duly impressed.

"I do keep my ear to the ground. Look, here's Negaunee coming up. Let's stop and get a bite to eat. I'm ravenous."

"When aren't you?" said Myrtle, teasingly.

"When I'm asleep," said Daisy. "Except then I dream about eating."

After a brief lunch, they were on their way again.

Shortly, they came to a sharp curve in the road.

"This is Dead Man's Curve," said Daisy. "See that white stripe down the middle of the road?"

Myrtle looked at the stripe, not unlike many she had seen on other roads, though few in Michigan.

"That was the first white line ever painted down the middle of a road in the United States," said Daisy, sounding very authoritative. "Three years ago."

"How do you know that?" asked Myrtle.

"Because when I came to work for *The Rapids* three years ago, that was the first story I was assigned to. 'Write about the stripe down the middle of the road between Negaunee and Marquette,' Mr. Whitfield told me. I looked at him, wondering if he was spoofing me. But he wasn't. That was a big deal back then. I even got to interview Mr. Sawyer. He was the guy who was in charge of getting the line down. 'Course, lots of roads have stripes now. But this was the very first one."

"You amaze me with your knowledge," said Myrtle, shaking her head.

"Yeah, me, too," said Daisy.

*****

When Mrs. Sinclair opened the door, Myrtle was shocked at how much she appeared to have failed in the few weeks since the trial.

The older lady invited them in and Myrtle found herself in the same parlor where she had first talked with Yvette's mother months earlier. True to form, Mrs. Sinclair excused herself to go prepare some tea.

"This place is like a museum," whispered Daisy, after their hostess had left the room.

"I know. It's as though it's been frozen in time," said Myrtle.

After Mrs. Sinclair returned and served the tea, Myrtle held out the photograph.

"Oh, thank you," said Mrs. Sinclair. She took the picture and held it up to study it. "She was such a beautiful girl. I'm glad they put that horrible man away who took my baby from me."

Mrs. Sinclair started to cry. Neither Daisy nor Myrtle knew what to do.

After a few minutes, Mrs. Sinclair was able to compose herself and the weeping stopped. She dabbed her eyes with a handkerchief.

"Did you ever find out who that Mr. 'F' was?" she asked.

"No, we never did," said Myrtle. "I looked at all the Booker Falls editions from the time just before the . . . just before it happened, but not with any luck. But tomorrow when I go back to work, I'm going to check the out of town papers starting with Christmas of that year. Constable de la Cruz suggested that I do so."

Mrs. Sinclair nodded. "Yah, that sounds like a good idea. Yvette enjoyed reading those newspapers. It gave her an opportunity to use her French. One of those might have his pictures in it—though I don't suppose that makes any difference now, now that they found da man who killed my little girl. He's in jail, isn't he?"

"He is," said Myrtle. "Right here in Marquette."

"Excuse me," said Daisy, "but did you say pictures? Mrs. Sinclair, was there more than one?"

Myrtle's eyebrows went up. *Pictures?*

"Oh, yah, didn't I tell you that before?" asked Mrs. Sinclair, speaking to Myrtle. "Da newspaper had two pictures, one of da front of his face, and da other was a side view."

"You didn't remember much about how the man looked when I was here before," said Myrtle. "Do you remember any more now?"

Mrs. Sinclair thought for a moment. "No," she said finally, "I guess I don't. I'm sorry."

"That's all right," said Myrtle. "Knowing that I'm looking for a page with two pictures is helpful."

For the next hour, Mrs. Sinclair reminisced about her deceased daughter.

"I think I must be boring da two of you," she said, at last. "I'm sure you have better things to do than listen to an old lady's stories of time gone by."

Myrtle and Daisy said their goodbyes and soon were on their way out of town, and back to Booker Falls.

"I'm looking forward to digging into those old archives tomorrow," said Myrtle. "I'm going to see if I can find Mr. Mitchell's pictures."

*****

As Myrtle and Daisy pulled up in front of the boarding house, they were surprised to see Mrs. Darling running out to meet them, looking distraught, earrings flying from side to side.

"Oh, my, oh, my," she said, breathing hard as she reached the car. "Something terrible has happened."

"What? What is it?" asked Myrtle, scrambling out from behind the driver's wheel. What had gotten Mrs. Darling so worked up?

"It's Penrod," said Mrs. Darling, trying to catch her breath.

Myrtle took Mrs. Darling's arm. "Penrod? What about Penrod?"

"He's . . . he's been poisoned," said Mrs. Darling.

CHAPTER FORTY-ONE

Myrtle's hands sprang to her mouth. "Is he...is he..?"

"He's not dead," said Mrs. Darling, hurrying the two women up the path to the house. "But he is awful sick. Doc Simpson says he tinks he'll make it."

Entering the house, the three of them rushed to the kitchen, where Penrod lay curled up in his box next to the stove. His eyes were open, but he appeared listless.

Myrtle hurried over, kneeled down and stroked his head.

"Poor dear," she said.

Looking up to Mrs. Darling, she asked, "What happened?"

"Doc Simpson says it was arsenic."

"Arsenic?" said Daisy. "Where would he have gotten arsenic?"

"Someone did it on purpose," said Mrs. Darling. "I'd tied him up out in da yard after I give him a bath. When I went out later, he was just a'layin' there, real still. There was some kind of meat on da ground close by—I could see he'd eaten some of it. I could tell he was sick, 'cause usually when I come out to let him in, he's all jumpy and bouncy and ready to race inside.

"Lucky for us, Henri had come home a little earlier. I called him to come out and he knew right off someting was wrong, so he picked him up and off we went to Doc Simpson's. Henri said we should take da rest of da meat with us—it turned out to be ground beef. Doc Simpson knew right off what it was—said he'd seen dogs poisoned before with arsenic.

"He gave Penrod something that made him vomit, said he should be all right, to take him back home and keep an eye on him."

"Where's Henri now?" asked Myrtle.

"He took off down to da pharmacy to find out who bought arsenic lately. Said he'd be back as soon as he could. Girls, I'm going to fix some tea. Why don't you all go change and I'll serve you out on da porch in a few minutes. He's resting okay now; he'll be okay."

*****

Myrtle and Daisy watched as a car pulled up and parked behind the Model N. Neither was sure of what was more surprising: that there was a new automobile in town—heretofore only Myrtle's and George's had been driving the streets of Booker Falls—or the driver sitting behind the steering wheel: Henri.

Daisy jumped up and ran out to the road, Myrtle following close behind.

"Whose car is this?" asked Daisy, when she got there.

"Mine," said Henri, grinning broadly.

"Yours?" said Myrtle. She couldn't believe it! The man who hated automobiles now owned one?

"When did you get it?" asked Daisy, walking around the vehicle, sizing it up.

"Today," said Henri. "George drove me down to Iron Mountain. I had it shipped in by train from a dealership in Dayton, Ohio."

Myrtle hopped up into the driver's seat. "What kind is it?" she asked.

"It's a Packard Town Car, but fitted as a police car. See the bell in the front?"

The bell to which Henri referred was hard to miss. About a foot high, it was attached by a chain to a lever next to the steering wheel.

"When there's an emergency and I need to go someplace in a hurry," said Henri, "I can ring the bell and other vehicles have to get out of the way."

"Other vehicles?" said Myrtle. "You mean such as my car and George's?"

"Carriages, horses—whatever's in the way." Remembering Myrtle's account of her first day coming into Booker Falls, Henri added, "and moose," eliciting a round of laughter from the three women.

"Why, Henri, I do believe you might have a sense of humor," said Myrtle.

"What happened to your dislike of these 'infernal machines'"? asked Daisy.

Henri shrugged. "As George reminded me, they're the coming thing. Besides, the next time I ask Myrtle to go someplace out of town, she won't have to drive. Oh, I almost forgot—how's Penrod?" he asked, hoping to change the subject.

"Feeling better, I think," said Myrtle. "Thank you so much for taking him to the veterinarian. But what makes you think I'd be going out of town with you again, anyway?"

"I'm a born optimist. Besides, you said you would."

Myrtle shrugged. "I guess I did, didn't I?"

Daisy was more interested in what Henri had learned at the pharmacy. "Did you find out who bought the arsenic?" she asked.

"No," said Henri. "No one has purchased any for over a month, according to Alexander. He doesn't keep a record of who does and said he didn't remember who had before then, either."

"Someone did this on purpose," said Myrtle.

"And the question," said Daisy, "is why?"

"Wait a minute!" exclaimed Myrtle. "Isn't arsenic sometimes used in the paint that artists use?"

"Why, as I recall from my art appreciation class when I was at Adelaide," said Henri, "it was used in green paint at one time. Cézanne, especially, liked to use it. There's some suspicion even that it might have contributed to his death."

"Is it in oil or watercolor?" asked Myrtle.

"Watercolor for sure. I know Cézanne did watercolor. I'm not sure about oil. Why?"

"Mr. Mitchell is an artist," said Myrtle, "who paints in watercolor. And he told me Cézanne was his favorite artist. He would know about arsenic."

*****

"Was Mrs. Sinclair grateful to get her photograph back?" asked Henri, as he and the two women sat down to join Mr. Pfrommer.

"She was," said Myrtle. "And I found out something interesting, too. She remembered the newspaper Yvette brought had two pictures of Mr. 'F,' one from the front and one from the side."

"And you're going to start looking for it tomorrow?" asked Henri.

Myrtle nodded. "Yes, I am. And if I find—*when* I find—Frank Mitchell's picture, I will be sure to tell you. And this time I *will* go with you when you arrest him."

*****

After dinner, Myrtle decided to take Penrod for a walk. He'd seemed to perk up some, and she thought the fresh air would be good for him.

They'd go to the city park where they could sit and watch the ducks in the pond. Afterwards, they'd walk on into town and look at the merchandise in the store windows, maybe stop in Mr. Abramovitz's pawn shop: he always stayed open later than the other stores. The old man didn't mind that Myrtle brought Penrod in with her—in fact, he always had a treat of some sort to give him.

When Myrtle and Penrod stepped out onto the porch, they saw Daisy in one of the rockers.

"Daisy," said Myrtle, "we're going for a walk. Want to come along?"

Daisy sprang up. "Sure. Let's go."

This particular evening was delightful, with the temperature hovering around forty-five. They walked in silence for a while before Myrtle spoke.

"Did it seem to you that Henri and Mr. Pfrommer were particularly non-cordial to each other tonight?"

"Oh," gushed Daisy, "I've been meaning to tell you."

"Tell me what?"

"Henri told me that yesterday he went into the bathroom—the one he and Mr. Pfrommer share at the other end of the hall—and he was shaving his head."

"Shaving his head? Mr. Pfrommer? I thought he was naturally bald."

"Me, too. Anyway, he got very irate that Henri had burst in on him, started yelling about respecting his privacy, and to get out. Henri tried to apologize and explain he wouldn't have come in if Mr. Pfrommer had locked the door, as he should have. But the old man just got angrier and angrier, and started waving his straight razor around, so Henri got out as quick as he could.

"He said something else, too."

"What was that?"

"He said the old man was in his undershirt—first time Henri had ever seen him without a dress shirt on. Said he had some sort of scales on his arms and shoulder."

"Scales?"

"Henri said he'd seen something like it before. Thought it was psoriasis."

"That's horrible," said Myrtle. "Poor man."

When they got back to the boarding house, the two women found Mrs. Darling in the kitchen.

"Mrs. Darling," asked Myrtle. "has Mr. Pfrommer always been bald?"

Mrs. Darling looked at Myrtle as if it were a strange question to ask—which indeed it was. She thought for a moment.

"No," she said, "when he first got here he had a lovely head of hair, as I recall."

"When did he go bald?" asked Daisy.

"Why, maybe about two months after he moved in. But he didn't go bald—he shaved it off."

"Shaved it off?" said Myrtle. "Shaved his hair off? Why would he have done that?"

Mrs. Darling ran her hand through her hair. "Said someting about some sort of rash or someting. I hated to see his hair go—like I said, it was lovely."

"And he never let it grow back?" asked Myrtle.

Mrs. Darling shook her head. "No, I guess he had to keep it off because of da rash. I'm surprised it only affected da top of his head."

"What do you mean?" asked Daisy.

"Well, about da same time he shaved his head, he started growing his beard. 'Course, maybe that was to hide da scar."

"Scar?" said Daisy.

"A long jagged scar down da right side of his face." Mrs. Darling ran her hand down her cheek. "Funny, I hadn't thought any more 'bout that scar 'til right now."

"And how long has he been with you?" asked Daisy.

"Ever since he came to town—more than thirty years ago now."

*****

"Mr. Mitchell," said Myrtle, nodding as she walked past Frank on her way to the check-out desk.

"Miss Tully," said Frank, "can you come into my office, please?"

Uh, oh, thought Myrtle. *Does he suspect I'm on to him?*

"I have two projects I need you to work on. First of all, we've just received the new tenth edition of the Dewey Decimal System. I need you to check and make sure all of our catalog files are in accordance with it."

Myrtle let out a sigh of relief. It was just work.

"Then," continued Frank, "I want to re-do the display upstairs. There are a number of old photographs, books, maps and other papers downstairs in the archives that we haven't had out for several years. I'd like you to ferret them out and get them cataloged.

"I imagine those two jobs will take you most of the morning. This afternoon we'll start replacing the current material. I doubt we can finish by the time we close. If I have dinner brought in, do you suppose you could work late?"

That certainly wasn't how Myrtle had envisioned her day would go. This meant she'd have to wait until tomorrow to look for Frank's pictures.

"Of course," she said. "That will be fine."

When she reached her desk she found a folded up copy of the latest edition of *The Rapids*. As she picked up the newspaper, a scrap of paper fell out and fluttered to the floor. Myrtle picked it up and read the four words printed in red ink in large, bold, block letters: LAST WARNING STOP LOOKING.

Myrtle's eyebrows furrowed. Stop looking? Stop looking at what? Or stop looking *for* what? And if this is the last warning, what was the previous one?

Myrtle felt her stomach start to tighten. Was Penrod's being poisoned a warning? And was this a warning to . . . she couldn't believe what she was thinking . . . to stop looking for Mr. 'F'—for Mr. Mitchell, as she was now convinced it must have been him Yvette was afraid of?

Frank liked to write using red ink. Myrtle knew that, from the letters he'd written to Yvette and the apology note he'd written to her.

She hurried to Frank's office and, without knocking, barged in.

"Do you know anything about this?" she demanded.

Frank looked up, startled by the intrusion.

"What?" he said. "Anything about what?"

"This," said Myrtle, tossing the note onto the desk.

Frank read it and looked up. "I have no idea. Did you think I wrote it? What does it mean?"

Myrtle didn't know which emotion was churning her insides most: fear or rage.

"Never mind," she said, grabbing up the paper and darting out from the office. From the surprised look on Frank's face, he either had nothing to do with it or he was a very good actor.

She scanned the nearly deserted room. Only two other people were there, both female students whom she recognized. She hurried over to the two girls who were seated together, whispering.

"Ladies," she said, "have you noticed anyone around my desk this morning?"

The girls looked up. "No, Miss Tully, I haven't," said one of them. "The only other person I remember seeing is Mr. Mitchell."

"Me, too," said the second girl.

Myrtle glanced back at Frank's office. He was watching her. She thanked the girls, then returned to her desk. Now she was more determined than ever to discover the identity of Mr. 'F'—either Frank or someone else.

*****

Myrtle devoted the rest of the day to the two tasks Frank had given her. While searching through the material in the vault to be used in the revised display, it was all she could do to stop from walking over to where the old copies of the out of town newspapers were stored and going through them.

Tomorrow, she thought. *Definitely tomorrow*.

By the time Myrtle arrived back at the boarding house late that evening, she was only too happy to fall into bed.

*****

The rain that had fallen constantly earlier in the week was back.

Myrtle debated whether or not to take the Model N to work. At breakfast she'd shared with Henri and Daisy the note she'd found on her desk the day before. Henri thought it was a joke someone was playing.

"Who have you told you were going to be searching through the newspapers besides us?" he asked.

"Only Mr. Mitchell," Myrtle replied. "That's why at first I thought it might have been him who'd written the note, especially since it was in red ink."

"But now you don't think so?" asked Daisy.

"Well, I'm just not sure."

"Maybe Henri's right," said Daisy. "Maybe someone is playing a joke."

"Penrod being poisoned was no joke," Myrtle retorted.

"No, you're right," said Daisy. "It certainly wasn't."

*****

It was almost five before Myrtle got away from the desk and started looking through the old, out of town newspapers. She'd told Frank she'd noticed yesterday when she was working on his project that they needed attention.

In the 1890s, Adelaide College Library had received a dozen different French-language newspapers, some weekly, some daily, some published two or three times a week. They came from a number of cities in Canada and France, as well as New Orleans and even one from French Guiana, and were primarily for use by the French-speaking students at Adelaide, as well as those students who were learning the language, so that they might have as much practice as possible. In addition, members of the community were also welcome to come in and read them.

Yvette's mother had told Myrtle that the last time her daughter was home before she returned the week prior to her murder, was at Christmas. Myrtle assumed the newspaper with Mr. 'F's pictures must have been received sometime within the first two months of the year.

What Mrs. Sinclair wasn't sure of was if the pictures had been on the front page of the paper or somewhere within.

Myrtle elected to start with the last issues received shortly before Yvette had gone to see her mother. She would take a different newspaper at a time, search back as far as December 27 and if nothing turned up, try another publication for the same period of time. If, after going through all the papers, she hadn't found anything, she'd start again with the first publication and go back even further.

She'd been diligently searching for four hours—interrupted three times by Frank calling her to run errands—and by six-fifteen, fifteen minutes until the library closed, had gone through only the first ten sets of periodicals, with no success. Only two remained: the *Quebec L' Action Libérale* and *Le Journal de Montréal*. She decided to try the former.

The first three issues she looked at were like everything else she'd seen that day. But when she picked up the fourth paper from the pile her mouth fell open.

"I don't believe it," she muttered.

Myrtle stared at the two pictures on the front page of the newspaper, one a front view, the other a profile.

It was the face of a man with whom she was well acquainted.

But not the one she was expecting.

CHAPTER FORTY-TWO

"Are you serious?" Daisy looked up from the front page of the newspaper Myrtle had laid in front of her. "Really? Mr. Pfrommer? That nice old man?"

"Shh," said Myrtle, holding a finger to her lips. She lowered her voice. "Now you tell me that's not him."

Daisy looked at the sketches again. "No, that's him all right. You think he's Mr. 'F'? It says here the name is Henrich Waldschmidt."

"Of course. He changed his name. Did you read why his picture's there?"

"He was wanted for murder," said Daisy. She looked up again, startled. "Oh, my! Our Mr. Pfrommer?"

"You remember, Mrs. Darling told us she thought he'd grown his beard to hide a scar. See the scar in this picture?"

Daisy looked down and nodded.

"And I bet he shaved his head to help conceal his identity, too," said Myrtle.

"But Yvette told her mother she was afraid of a Mr. 'F'."

"Yvette probably knew Mr. Pfrommer from his coming to the library to read the papers. And if she knew his name, she might have thought it began with an 'F', not a 'P,' since it sounds like an 'F.'"

"What now?"

"I had hoped to run into Henri so I could show this to him. I didn't want to knock on his door, since he's right across the hall from Mr. Pfrommer."

"Henri's not here," said Daisy. "He wasn't here for dinner. Mrs. Darling said he left to transport a prisoner to Marquette and wouldn't be back until morning."

"Darn!" said Myrtle.

"Besides," said Daisy, "just because he's wanted for those things in Quebec and we think he's Mr. 'F,' that doesn't mean he killed Yvette."

"You're right," said Myrtle, sinking down onto the bed. "We need proof."

"What do you mean?"

"We need to prove he killed Yvette."

"I mean, what do you mean 'we,' and what kind of proof can you get this many years later? Why don't you wait until morning and give this to Henri then?" Daisy looked at her watch. "It's almost eleven. I'm tired."

"That's it!" exclaimed Myrtle. "Yvette's watch. That's our proof!"

"I don't understand," said Daisy.

"I remember George telling me that Mr. Pfrommer collected watches. Yvette's watch was never found. And according to her mother, it was a very expensive watch. If Mr. Pfrommer killed her, he might have taken her watch. Okay," said Myrtle, pulling Daisy down onto the bed next to her. "Here's our plan."

"I still don't understand why I'm mixed up in this," protested Daisy.

"You're going to write a novel about this murder, aren't you?"

"Yes."

"Think how great it would be if you not only were the author, but helped to actually solve the crime, too."

Daisy's eyes lit up. "Okay. What's the plan?"

*****

The next morning, the two women watched from the parlor as Mr. Pfrommer strolled down the path to the road, turned and headed towards the college.

It was Thursday: his normal day for the trip to the library to read the out of town newspapers that had come in during the week.

Daisy was to follow him—without him knowing so, of course—to make sure he would be at the library. When he left to return to the boarding house, she would take another route and get back before him, allowing her to warn Myrtle he was on his way.

Meanwhile, Myrtle would search his room, looking especially for Yvette's watch, but for anything else that might implicate her fellow boarder in the young woman's death.

As soon as both Daisy and Mr. Pfrommer were out of sight, Myrtle scurried up the stairs and down the hall to the old man's room.

She grasped the door handle and turned it.

It was locked.

"Shoot!" said Myrtle.

She remembered the time she'd inadvertently left her room key at the library and Mrs. Darling showed her where she kept extra keys to all the rooms in the house.

Hurrying back down the stairs, she ran to the pantry, hoping she wouldn't encounter her landlady and have to explain why she was breaking into Mr. Pfrommer's room.

Myrtle snatched the ring of keys from the large hook on which they hung and rushed back up the stairs.

The third key she tried opened the door.

Myrtle froze. Did she really want to do this? Shouldn't she wait until Henri returned, as Daisy had suggested, and hand the whole affair over to him?

She shrugged, entered the room and turned on the light.

She wasn't sure what she had expected, but it wasn't this. Mr. Pfrommer kept an immaculate room, considerably neater than Daisy's, more so even than her own. The bed was made, everything seemed to be in its proper place. The violin lay resting in an open case on the chest at the foot of the bed.

On the dressing table were the old man's shaving instruments: a straight razor, neatly folded back inside its handle; a small piece of soap; a wide-mouthed glass with a little water in it; a shave brush; and a bottle of Dickinson's Witch Hazel. Next to a long comb was a jar of Prof. Barber's Goose-Grease.

Sitting on one corner, was a Pontarlier glass.

On the nightstand next to the bed lay an open copy of *Philosophy in the Tragic Age of the Greeks*. A pair of eyeglasses lay on the book.

George had said the watches were kept on top of the armoire. Myrtle looked up and spotted the cases. But how to get them? The ceilings were twelve feet high, the armoire eight. There was no way she could reach up there.

She looked around, searching for something to stand on: The easy chair wouldn't do. Flying from the room, she ran downstairs to the kitchen, grabbed a wooden chair from the table, and dashed back up to Mr. Pfrommer's room.

Placing the chair next to the armoire, she was just able to reach the bottom case. Carefully, she maneuvered it to the edge where she managed to get it down, along with the two cases resting on top of it.

Myrtle hopped down from the chair, carried the three cases to the chest, and set them down. Moving the violin to one side to afford more room, she opened the first case.

She looked at the fifteen watches, lined up in rows of five across and three deep. She could tell they were, indeed, excellent specimens.

But none were Yvette's.

The second case provided the same results.

When she opened the third case, her eyes were drawn instantly to the watch in the middle: a mother-of-pearl cover with the initials YMS—Yvette Marie Sinclair!

Myrtle picked up the watch—and felt something tight around her throat.

Dropping the watch, she reached with both hands, trying to dislodge whatever it was that was choking the life out of her.

But it was no use.

She spun around and staggered towards the dresser, feeling the pressure of a body pushing her from behind. The thing around her neck was getting tighter and tighter—she couldn't breathe.

The last thing she remembered before she lost consciousness was the sound of the Pontarlier glass shattering as it hit the floor.

CHAPTER FORTY-THREE

Myrtle opened her eyes to find Daisy hovering over her on one side and Mrs. Darling on the other.

"What happened?" she asked. Her voice was raspy.

"George saved you," said Daisy, as Mrs. Darling laid a cold washcloth across Myrtle's forehead.

"Saved me? Saved me from what?"

"Mr. Pfrommer," said Daisy. "He tried to strangle you—just like he did Yvette Sinclair."

Myrtle started to sit up.

"No, no, lay back," said Mrs. Darling. "No getting up."

"I don't remember," said Myrtle.

"You were searching Mr. Pfrommer's room and he must have come in and found you," said Daisy. "He tried to strangle you with his tie."

"His cravat," Mrs. Darling corrected her.

"His cravat," said Daisy. "That's when George appeared at Henri's door. Henri was going to take him for a ride in his automobile. George heard the commotion and rushed into Mr. Pfrommer's room. He saw Mr. Pfrommer choking you, so he whacked him on the head with his cane, and he fell down. Henri had just returned from Marquette and was on his way up the stairs. George told him what had happened, so Henri took Mr. Pfrommer down to the jail. That's when I got back here. Mrs. Darling and I helped you into your bedroom and George went for the doctor.

"He said you had a concussion, to let you rest. If you didn't come around in an hour or so we'd have to take you to the hospital over in Houghton. We were debating about going to get George to drive you."

"Wasn't Mr. Pfrommer supposed to be at the library?" asked Myrtle, beginning to remember.

"He started that way," said Daisy. "I followed him for a while, then I took another route so I would get there before he did. Plus, I didn't want him to think I was following him. But he never showed up—at the library, I mean. I waited and waited, and then decided I'd better get back here."

"Is she awake?"

The three women looked to the doorway, where Henri stood, a concerned look on his face.

"Yah, she is," said Mrs. Darling. "Come on in."

Henri walked over and took Myrtle's hand. "That was a pretty stupid thing to do," he said.

"I guess so," said Myrtle. "But he did it, didn't he? He killed Yvette."

Henri nodded. "He gave a full confession. Said he'd been carrying the burden too long, wanted to get rid of it. The story in the newspaper you found . . ."

"You saw it?" asked Myrtle.

"Yes," said Henri. "Before I took Mr. Pfrommer downtown Daisy showed it to me. According to Mr. Pfrommer, when that happened thirty years ago, he was a heavy user of absinthe. He had a woman friend who also used it with him. One night Mr. Pfrommer drank too much, or it was too strong—whatever, things got out of control, he went crazy and strangled her.

"He was afraid he'd go to jail, so he left Quebec, changed his name and came here to Booker Falls to work for George's uncle. Every Thursday he'd go to the library to check the newspapers from Quebec to see if there was any mention of what had happened.

"One day when he went in, Miss Sinclair approached him. She told him she'd seen his pictures in the paper and knew who he was and what he'd done. She demanded he pay her five thousand dollars to keep silent, and she'd turn the paper over to him."

"So Mr. Lawrence was right about Yvette blackmailing someone," said Myrtle.

"Yes," said Henri. "Mr. Pfrommer was to meet Yvette at the library the evening she was killed. But he'd already decided he wasn't going to let her blackmail him. He went there to kill her. When he arrived, he saw Yvette go into the library with Paul Momet, so he decided to wait. Sometime later, Paul came out, Mr. Pfrommer went in, and that's when he did it—that's when he killed her. He said he couldn't resist taking her watch for his collection, it was so beautiful."

"What's going to happen now?" asked Mrs. Darling.

"He'll have a trial, undoubtedly be found guilty," replied Henri.

"And what about Paul Momet?" asked Myrtle.

"I imagine eventually he'll be set free."

"I would never have guessed it was Mr. Pfrommer," said Daisy. "Every time we talked about the case at the dinner table he heard everything we said. He knew everything that was going on. And he was so nice."

"He admitted to poisoning Penrod, too," said Henri, "and leaving the note for you at the library. I asked him where he got the arsenic. He said he used it for his psoriasis. I guess that's the scales I saw on his arm the day I walked in on him in the bathroom."

Myrtle shook her head. "He must have been desperate for me to stop looking."

"I still don't know why he didn't show up at the library," said Daisy.

"Oh, he explained that, too," said Henri. "He set out for there, then realized he'd forgotten his eyeglasses, so he returned to the house to get them. That's when he found Myrtle in his room holding Yvette's watch, and he knew what she was up to.

"And Myrtle . . ."

"Yes?"

"Mr. Pfrommer wanted me to tell you he was sorry he hurt you. He was relieved to hear that you were alive."

No one spoke for a moment. A single tear ran down Myrtle's cheek. Then Mrs. Darling broke the silence.

"Now, den," said Mrs. Darling, "I tink it's time for tea. What kind shall it be? Dandelion or . . ."

"Thimbleberry," said the other three in unison.

EPILOGUE

TWO MONTHS LATER

Myrtle and Daisy sat on the porch, enjoying their tea—dandelion, of course, though greatly enriched by the ambrosia from Daisy's flask—and watched Penrod as he scampered around the yard chasing butterflies.

Adolf Pfrommer had been tried and found guilty in the same courtroom that had earlier witnessed Paul Momet's trial. Since he had confessed to killing Yvette Sinclair, he was sentenced to life in prison without the possibility of parole and was now serving his time at Marquette Branch Prison. Quebec officials had been informed of his arrest, but after learning the sentence imposed upon him by Michigan, had declined to initiate extradition proceedings.

Paul Momet had been released from the same prison that now held Mr. Pfrommer, and had returned to Booker Falls, only to find that during his incarceration his wife had filed for a divorce.

Myrtle leaned back and sipped her tea.

"What do you think of the new boarder?" she asked.

"He's certainly a step up from Mr. Pfrommer," said Daisy.

Pierre Longet, a fifty-two-year old widower from Massachusetts, had moved to Booker Falls two weeks after Mr. Pfrommer had been found guilty of the murder of Yvette Sinclair, to teach literature and French at Adelaide College.

Tall, handsome, with a physique that came from running marathons—including six times in the one held in Boston—Pierre traced his family's lineage back to the Renaissance era of France in the early 1500s. For over twenty years he had been a professor at Emerson College in Boston, but following the death of his wife from tuberculosis, had gone into grieving for an extended period of time.

Finally, his daughter, a senior at Adelaide, persuaded him to make a change in his life, to move to Booker Falls, and step into the void left by the retirement of one of the professors there.

"How long has his wife been gone?" asked Myrtle.

"Two years."

Myrtle arched her eyebrows. "That's long enough."

"Long enough for what?" asked Daisy.

"For you to start showing some interest in him."

"You mean . . ."

Myrtle nodded. "Yes, I do mean. I noticed you've begun wearing lipstick again."

Daisy's face grew pink.

"Uh, well, I thought since I had that one tube left..."

"...might as well use it," said Myrtle, smiling.

"Right."

The two sat in silence for a while before Myrtle spoke. "You know what yesterday was?"

Daisy thought for a moment. "Something special?"

"It was one year ago that I arrived in Booker Falls."

"Really?" exclaimed Daisy. "It seems like only yesterday."

"I know," said Myrtle. "So much has happened in that time. Have you started writing your novel?"

Daisy's face lit up. "I have. It's coming along pretty well. And how about you? I bet you're going to be bored to death now that there are no more murders to solve."

"Oh, I don't know," said Myrtle. "There are five rooms upstairs in the library that I have never been in yet. Who knows—"

Just then, Henri burst onto the porch from the house and flew down the front steps, taking them two at a time.

"Henri," Myrtle called out, "where are you going?"

Without slowing down, Henri turned his head and shouted, "Somebody just robbed the bank!"

THE END

ABOUT THE AUTHOR

Kenn Grimes is both an author and a screenwriter, with two published books to his credit prior to the Booker Falls Mystery Series—a collection of short stories: *Camptown: One Hundred and Fifty Years of Stories from Camptown, Kentucky,* published in 2005 by Arbutus Press (now out of print) and *The Other Side of Yesterday,* a time travel novel published in 2012 by Deer Lake Press.

A retired Lutheran minister who served congregations in Indiana, Kentucky and Missouri, Kenn at one time owned and operated *Simply Married*, the largest wedding service on Maui, Hawaii. During his ministry, he has officiated at over 4,200 ceremonies. He and his wife, Judy, also a retired minister, now split their time between their homes in Louisville, Kentucky, and Lower Northern Michigan, where they continue to officiate at weddings.

Strangled in the Stacks is the first in his Booker Falls Mystery series, and his first book with Cozy Cat Press.

COMING IN 2017

A New Booker Falls Mystery

A Trifecta of Murder

Here's a sample:

CHAPTER ONE

Rachel Steinmyer stared down the barrel of the biggest gun she had ever seen.

"Puh a mun n a bog," growled the man holding the gun, as he shoved a dirty, crumpled-up Eagle brand flour sack across the counter towards her.

Rachel looked at the man. The lower part of his face was covered with a bandana, even dirtier than the flour sack. A floppy hat was pulled down over his forehead.

"What?" she said, knitting her brow.

The man lifted up the bandana. "I said, put da money in da bag."

Even without the bandana, his words were slurred, and Rachel smelled the distinct odor of rye whiskey.

"What did he say?"

Rachel turned to her father, Isaiah, sitting at a desk in one corner of the room.

"He says he wants money, Father."

"Does he have an account with us?"

"No. I think he's robbing us. Are you sure you want to do this?" asked Rachel, turning back to the man on the other side of the cashier's window.

The man pulled up his bandana again and waved the gun at her. "Now! Put da money in da bag."

"You'll never get away with this, you know," said Rachel, as she began stuffing dollar bills into the flour sack.

"Did you say he's robbing us?" asked Isaiah. He didn't move from his desk.

"It's all right, Father. He won't hurt us."

"Beh bills—I wan beh bills." The bandana was down over his mouth again.

Rachel emptied the two teller drawers, about a thousand dollars in all.

"That's it," she said. "That's all I have."

"Geh a muny outa da safe."

"I don't have the combination," Rachel lied. "And my father's not here."

"Who's zat sitting there?" asked the man, waving his gun in Isaiah's direction.

"That's just the janitor," said Rachel.

The man frowned, then started to back away towards the door. "Don folla me," he said, as he stumbled out onto the sidewalk.

Rachel slipped out from behind the teller's cage and hurried to the door just in time to see the man duck into Alton Woodruff's barbershop—an establishment that provided more than just tonsorial services.

"What's he want?" asked Isaiah. "Is he going to kill us?"

"No, Father, it's all right. He's gone. I'm going to call the constable."

Rachel quickly made her way to the back office where she lifted the earpiece from the phone box and cranked the handle.

"Well, hello, Rachel," came the voice on the other end of the line.

"Hi, Maribel," said Rachel. "Don't really have time to talk right now. Can you put me through to Constable de la Cruz's office, please?"

"I could, Honey, but I know he's not there."

"How do you know that?"

"Because he just called Mayor Salmon a few minutes ago from da boarding house."

"Okay," said Rachel, "then put me through to Mrs. Darling's."

"Okay, then," said Maribel. "Will do."

A few minutes later Rachel heard, "Hello?"

"Mrs. Darling, this is Rachel Steinmyer at the bank. Is Henri there?"

"Hello, Rachel. Yah, Henri is here. I'll go get him."

"No, please, just tell him that the bank has just been robbed, and the thief is down at the barbershop right now, I'm sure celebrating by getting even drunker than he was when he was in here."

"Oh, my!" said Mrs. Darling. "I'll go tell him right now."

When Rachel returned to the front office she found her father slumped over his desk, the ink well he'd been using tipped over, black liquid spilling out onto the floor.